Jacob's Ladder

In memory of my mother and father

To my sisters, for their love and support

And to Julie, for the title and the unexpected plot twists

Jacob's Ladder

Joel Yanofsky

The Porcupine's Quill

CANADIAN CATALOGUING IN PUBLICATION DATA

Yanofsky, Joel, 1955-
Jacob's ladder

ISBN 0-88984-191-8

I. Title.

PS8597.A559J32 1997   C813'.54   C97-931482-8
PR9199.3.Y36J32 1997

Published by The Porcupine's Quill, 68 Main Street, Erin, Ontario
NOB 1TO. Readied for the press by John Metcalf. Copy edited by
Doris Cowan. Typeset in Galliard, printed on Zephyr Antique Laid,
and bound at The Porcupine's Quill Inc.

The cover is after a lithograph, *Ladders and the Ladder* (1954),
by Frederick Hagan. The author photo is courtesy of Julie Bruck.

Represented in Canada by the Literary Press Group. Trade orders
are available from General Distribution Services.

We acknowledge the support of the Canada Council for the Arts
for our publishing programme. The support of the Ontario Arts
Council and the Department of Canadian Heritage through the
Book and Periodical Industry Development Programme is also
gratefully acknowledged.

1 2 3 4 • 99 98 97

Acknowledgements

An excerpt from *Jacob's Ladder* first appeared in *Index* (May 1994). The author also gratefully acknowledges the support of The Canada Council's Explorations Program.

Additional and special thanks to Sheila Fischman, Mark Abley and Kenneth Radu for their encouragement and support at the very start. I am especially grateful to the members of my writing group: Pauline Clift, Joe Fiorito, Gordon Graham, Janice Hamilton, Janet Kask, Nancy Lyon and Denise Roig for their suggestions and for urging me to keep going when I would have rather not. Thanks also to other early readers: Douglas Glover, Bernice Mast and Lisa Lynch. And to Chris and Scott's dad for 'dome light'. Towards the end, I had the best readers anyone could ask for: Sheila and Denise again and Dawn Rae Downton. When the manuscript was done friends and colleagues Bryan Demchinsky, P. Scott Lawrence, Trevor Ferguson, David Homel, Carmine Starnino, Ray Beauchemin and Jim Boothroyd helped more than they probably realized. Thanks, too, to Elaine Shatenstein for the ad hoc editorial advice. Dinner's on me. Tim and Elke Inkster have been conscientious and concerned and a pleasure to work with. Finally, thanks to John Metcalf for telling me to stop worrying – again and again. And, most of all, for finding the whole thing funny.

At all times an old world is collapsing and a new world arising; we have better eyes for the collapse than the rise, for the old one is the world we know.

John Updike

One

Magical Thinking

Friday, June 20. This is what's happened so far: I'm expecting my best friend's wife to arrive any minute so we can begin our first official date. I'm also changing the linen on the queen-sized bed in what was once my parents' master bedroom. Optimism doesn't come naturally to me and never has, but I suppose I'm learning, a little more each day, that anything is possible. This is, by the way, the kind of revelation I've been waiting for all my life – the one I prayed for fifteen years ago when an oncologist at the Sacré Coeur Hospital said nothing more could be done for my mother and then, a year later, when another doctor at another hospital said the exact same thing about my father. So I stopped praying and eventually even stopped seeing it as an option. But when Angie parks her Toyota Corolla, red as a cherry Lifesaver, in what was once my parents' driveway, I realize that even here in the suburbs wishes come true.

And, yes, I admit the idea makes me dizzy with apprehension. Which is why I've started to keep this journal in the first place. To mitigate that familiar light-headedness – the chill down my spine, the hollow spot in my stomach, the perspiration on the top of my head – that always seems to come, for me, with anticipation. And, no, I'm not keeping this journal so I will have a record of what has already happened – my memory is good, sometimes too good, if you want to know the truth – but so I can keep track of what will happen next.

I was five years old when my parents moved to Court Séjour, a bedroom community a half-hour's drive north of Montreal. I wasn't consulted about their decision, but if I had been, and if I'd known then what I know now, I would have told them to go ahead without me. Not because I didn't like growing up in the suburbs, but because I liked it too much.

Thirty years later, the side effects linger and, frankly, they are embarrassing. I reread John Cheever's stories and, lately, his journals more often than is good for me and I mow the lawn more often than is good for it. And my predicament just gets worse. I can't, for example, watch reruns of the opening of 'The Dick Van Dyke Show' – with Rob Petrie returning each evening to his wife and child and home in New Rochelle, NY – without tears welling up in my eyes.

Sentimentality is a trap. Now that my parents are both gone and my brother and sister-in-law have moved down the 401 to Toronto, I spend a lot of time wondering about how I got here. And about how I am going to get out.

In his journals, published posthumously, John Cheever said that he longed for a world bigger than Shady Hill. Except he never found it. Or maybe he never tried hard enough. Either way, he stayed put, got drunker and hornier and convinced himself, a little more each day, that the choices he'd made were the right ones. 'We can live here through another winter,' he wrote to himself. 'But I wish my antici-pations were more cheerful. Perhaps I can make them so ...'

* * *

My mother never really convinced my father to move. She just wore him down until one day, when she knew he was watching, she filled out an unsigned cheque for one thousand dollars, the down pay-ment on this bungalow, and tucked it into the rotary dial of the tele-phone at his side of the bed. The cheque remained there for a month, like an overlooked RSVP, until my father endorsed it. He signed the cheque, even though he knew in his heart that he was making a ter-rible, probably irreversible mistake.

The men in my family have always been overly cautious, cautious to the point of inertia. We've never been the best judge of what is good for us. We've always been soft touches, too – easy marks for the women we love and the women who have, on occasion, loved us back. Diffidence is a male Glassman trait. Like light-headedness. Like our round faces and short legs. Or the bald spot, the size and shape of a small pear, which is spread, a little off centre, across the top of our skulls.

* * *

'What happened next?' Angie asks.

'We bought this house.'

'Would you have signed the cheque, Jacob?'

Angela Lokash (née Thomasis) is compact and built low to the ground. She has plump, round breasts that bounce when she talks and a habit, which I've just begun to notice, of standing with her hand on the curve of her hip, as if she were daring me to ask her anything, as if she had answers to all the questions – general and specific – that haunt me.

Another thing I've just begun to notice about Angie is that her eyes are different colours – the right one green, the left one brown. When she arrives at my door her usually frizzy black hair is pushed up on top of her head in a way that I haven't seen it before. I'm still not sure if it's that way as an afterthought or not. There are enough corkscrew wisps loose and down around the nape of her neck to make the case either way. She is wearing sandals and a faded blue-denim skirt that is short enough to show off her muscular, olive-skinned thighs. Her matching denim jacket is unbuttoned and reveals an emerald green halter top that almost matches her right eye and that had me short of breath the moment she turned into my driveway, stepped out of her Corolla, and waved in my direction.

There are people who say they care about me and who still want me to be different than I am; there are people who don't care about me – even one intent on doing me serious, lasting harm – who want the same thing. But the moment Angie arrived, I put all of them out of my mind. Her visit is not unanticipated, it only feels that way.

If I hadn't just started writing down my thoughts and emotions in this three-subject Hilroy navy blue notebook, I guess I mean if I'd always done this, it would reveal that things like this don't happen to me every day. Showing up at my parents' house like she has, with her green halter top and her discordant eyes, Angie is an unequivocally good omen – an indication that maybe I do know what is good for me after all.

'Hello? Jacob? Are you listening?' She lifts her fist in the air and shakes it as if she were knocking on an imaginary door. 'Would you have signed the cheque?' Angie asks again.

'Who me? Not in a million years.'

* * *

My mother's faith in the suburbs reached its peak in 1965 – a time that seems now like a million years ago, a time when suburban living had already been judged and found wanting, deemed a social cul-de-sac, an experiment that would never succeed. According to everyone who took on the task of analysing the phenomenon – psychologists, sociologists, urban planners, journalists – the suburbs, popular as they were with a certain type of person who wanted a certain kind of life, were undermining the culture, flattening personalities, reinforcing prejudices and turning us all into lawn-mowing, television-watching zombies. My mother either didn't pay attention to or, more likely, was unaware of these pronouncements. This made it easier for her to convince my father that it was worth risking the little bit of security he'd worked day and night to acquire for just a little bit more security.

My mother knew my father well enough not to make extravagant promises. If she'd said, for example, that our lives would be infinitely better in Court Séjour, he would have probably fainted, dizzy with expectation. My father contracted polio when he was thirteen and considered himself lucky to be alive. Lucky, too, to be making a modest living working at home as a sign painter. And especially lucky to have met and married my mother. So he worried about everything – in particular about leaving our cramped, roach-infested apartment in the centre of Montreal for a house outside the city, a house with a backyard, a garage and, most of all, a mortgage. He worried, too, that his handful of steady clients would not follow him to the suburbs – that they would find someone nearby to take their business to. But my mother convinced him that he had nothing to lose. Who could his clients find better? she said. Or quicker? Or cheaper? Or more conscientious? She was buttering him up, of course, building his confidence. He was the sort of man who needed reassurance.

Nothing is going to change, she said, even though what she meant was that everything was going to change. Still, her guarantee was enough for him. My father was a great believer in the status quo and I still haven't figured out why: whether it was because he learned, early in life when such lessons are likely to take hold, not to expect too much or because he was genuinely satisfied with what he had.

In this place where I live, at this time – the summer of 1995 – the term *status quo* is out of favour. Politicians, media pundits and constitutional experts, preparing for yet another referendum in the fall on whether or not Quebec will separate from the rest of Canada, use 'status quo' strategically, as a way of making their constituents, who are reluctant to vote for change, feel shortsighted and timid. The tone of the trial balloon questions that are floated is always the same: are you really satisfied with the way things are? Even politicians on the opposite side of the debate, those who want Quebec to remain in Canada, wouldn't be caught dead supporting the status quo. They have no intention of keeping things the same either. They're for change, too. What I don't understand, what I'd like explained to me, is how anyone who's watched someone they love die, let's say, or just walk out the door, wouldn't have figured out by now that, all things considered, the status quo isn't so bad.

* * *

Like my father, I am a man who needs reassurance, a passive man, though on a good day I can work my way up to passive-aggressive. That's Hope's joke anyway. She is the woman I am currently and unsuccessfully in love with, the woman I am doing my best to forget about by going out on a date with my best friend's wife.

I still haven't figured out how to talk to Angie, whether I should work harder at being glib or harder at being sincere. This is the first time I've seen her – and only the second time I've spoken to her – since she unexpectedly left my best friend Sandor 'Sandy' Lokash five months ago. Is it a good idea, for example, to be telling a woman who walked out on her husband because he didn't want children, stories about my family – my happy family – here in this house?

Strictly speaking, Angie and I are not inside the house. I am seated on the concrete top step of the front porch and she is sitting a step below me, leaning against the railing, vigorously chewing bubble gum. Every now and then, she tugs at the hem of her denim skirt. I am trying my best not to stare at her thighs. She is trying her best to be inconspicuous, but from where I'm sitting she appears to be losing more ground than she's gaining.

Being out here in the open like this is probably not wise. For one thing, Sandy lives only a few blocks away and even though he hasn't been leaving his condominium much lately, he could always pass by unexpectedly. (Angie has just come from seeing him, as a matter of fact. It was their first attempt at dividing the property they have accumulated during their thirteen years of marriage.) For another thing, I have just mowed the lawn and there are brown, uneven patches in the places where I lost control of the mower, places where my mind wandered anticipating Angie's visit. The more choices I have to make, the harder it is to concentrate on even the simplest task, even the most important questions.

'Are you going to ask me in, Jacob?'

'I don't know yet.'

When the connection to someone you've known for a long time changes dramatically, it's hard to know what to say or how to say it. I was best man at Sandy's wedding and I have played racquetball with him almost every Thursday for the last fifteen years – including yesterday – but we've rarely talked about anything other than baseball or the latest referendum and we've never felt the need to. I ask myself sometimes if I am using the term 'best friend' too loosely. Sandy and I are close, but in the way men often are – without displaying any real sign of closeness.

My experience with women is different. Take Angie, for instance, ever since she married my best friend, she and I have been able to discuss everything: from our most mundane hopes to our most unreasonable desires. Although now I do have the feeling that each word that passes between us is open to being interpreted in new ways.

'You think you're irresistible, is that it?'

'Yes, Angie, that's exactly it. But I also promised I'd take you to dinner, remember? So just give me a minute ... I'll find my keys.'

'We can always take my car.'

'No ... but maybe it would be a good idea if you left your car in my garage.'

'Why would that be a good idea? Hello? Jacob? We're not doing anything wrong here,' Angie says. She places her hand on her hip again and blows a small pink bubble at me.

'We're not?'

'Couldn't we discuss it inside, Jacob? Have you noticed it's awfully chilly for the first official day of summer?'

'You should have thought of that before you wore, well, what you wore.'

'Tell me, am I blushing?'

'You? In all the time I've known you I've only known you to blush once.'

'And in all the time you've known me have you ever heard me take no for an answer?'

'No, Angie, but you'll have to learn – even if it doesn't sound like I mean it … even if I don't.' I'm fine at flirting when it's just flirting, but when it carries with it the weight of promises I can't or, more to the point, don't know how to keep, I tend to lose my place in the banter, to mumble and lose my train of thought.

'You're really not going to ask me in?' Angie persists. 'I thought writers were supposed to be open to new experiences.' She winks her single brown eye at me and flashes me a half smile so I'll know, I suppose, that she is half joking.

'I've discovered I'm not that kind of writer. Besides the house is a mess.'

'Geez,' she says, her exasperation distilled into a pout so close to being irresistible I can feel, even on this unseasonably cool evening, the bald spot on the top of my head beginning to glow. 'Sometimes, Jacob, I don't get you. I just don't.'

'Welcome to the club.'

Incidentally, the house is not a mess. I never used to clean up after myself, but ever since my brother and sister-in-law moved out (they lived here for eighteen months after they were first married) I have become increasingly concerned about everything being in its proper place. Still, I come to housekeeping with no preconceived notions or standard of conduct, no hard and fast rules. Except to keep everything the way it once was. Otherwise, as my sister-in-law will attest, I tend to do everything backwards. It's not unusual, for instance, to find me breaking out the Lemon Pledge and polishing the furniture in the master bedroom well after midnight. Or vacuuming the wall-to-wall carpets first thing on a Monday morning when I should really be at work on my 'Up Next!' column or ghostwriting the 'Ask Your Therapist' column, which both appear weekly in the *Court Séjour News*. I try my best to keep the house immaculate, but even I am finding the way I go about doing it more and more disconcerting.

'Men!' Angie says as I abandon her out on the porch. I've heard that generalized complaint often enough to be tempted to take exception to it, but I don't. I am also tempted to let Angie in, after all, and show her exactly what this man is capable of.

But I don't do that either. Probably because I'm not sure myself. I do, instead, what I always do: try to make a joke out of the whole situation, closing the front door a little at a time, staring at Angie all the while, as if I am about to say, You will learn to love my idiosyncrasies. But just as my dumbshow is starting to take effect, just as Angie's mock frown seems to be reversing into a grin, the telephone rings and I slam the front door shut in one abrupt, one frantic and incriminating motion.

I have my reasons for keeping Angie out on the porch on what is officially our first date. The telephone is one. It would be too complicated to explain to her why I can't answer it – why I have avoided answering it for months. The other reason is that I've never had sex – intercourse, anyway – in this house and while I admit it may be jumping to conclusions to think that sex is what Angie wants, I am beginning to believe it's a possibility.

* * *

Let's make one thing clear right now: I am not keeping this journal to reveal secrets or explore areas in my life that are better left alone. So I've never had sex in this house, so what? What does that prove? Nothing. Except that the list of things I've never done seems to keep getting longer: never climbed a mountain, never been to Europe, ridden a horse, flown a kite, gone fishing, changed a baby....

'I can't even remember the last time I took a bus,' I told Dr Howie recently when we were discussing an upcoming 'Ask Your Therapist' column. 'I mean wouldn't you think a list like that would be finite?'

'Not at all,' he said. He is convinced that when men like me get to be a certain age – thirty-five, for the sake of argument – and start to look around for new adventures, their ability to take on those adventures will inevitably be compromised by all the things they haven't done yet.

'Think physics,' he explained. 'The laws of inertia say that "the tendency of matter is to remain at rest ... unless affected by some outside force." Yours is a classic case of inertia. The fact that you have, for all intents and purposes, lived in the same house all your life should not logically deter you from climbing a mountain or riding a horse – never flown a kite? really? – but of course it does. Adventure – or, more specifically, a man's desire for adventure – does not depend on what he does, it depends on the spirit with which he does it.'

He paused then, his usual pause, and I could hear him breathing heavily, through his mouth, into the receiver. When the idea for his column first came up two years ago, Ted Severs, the managing editor of the *Court Séjour News* or the *Snooze*, as some readers and most of the full-time and freelance staff call it, tried to discourage Dr Howie from running a photo of himself. My editor thought – and I agreed – that readers would be unlikely to trust an overweight psychotherapist. But Dr Howie insisted, adding that he was comfortable with his fat self.

'Actually, I like it. This "Never Happened" list,' Dr Howie finally said. 'It has potential. It could be a column.'

And no doubt it will be. This is the way Dr Howie and I collaborate. I mention a problem I am having, occasionally hypothetical, sometimes not, and we transform it into a question, attributed to an imaginary reader: *Dear Living in the Past* or *Dear Unrequited* or *Dear In Denial*. Then every week I transform the answer – from his accumulated notes and comments – into eight hundred words of copy. I receive no credit or by-line for the work. However, I do get paid reasonably well – better, in fact, than I do for my 'Up Next!' column. That's because Dr Howie's column is what is known in the community newspaper business as an advertorial. In other words, he pays for the space and a percentage of that money is, in turn, paid to me.

Dr Howie intended to write the column himself at first, but his spelling and grammar were so irredeemably bad that I was assigned the task of translating his prose into competent English. The only thing Dr Howie is responsible for writing now is his bio, which reads:

Dr Howard Weiskopf, BA, is a licensed psychotherapist.
For a personal or a group session
please call 686-6866 during regular office hours.
Comments and questions in reference to this column are always welcome.
Compassion is my business.

For the most part, Dr Howie and I have a good working relationship, though I do become irritated when he keeps spelling psychology wrong. How many ways are there to misspell it, after all? Meanwhile, he doesn't appreciate being called Dr Howie, which I don't do to antagonize him, not really. 'Classic passive-aggressive behaviour,' he says, unconvinced.

Twenty years ago, Dr Howard Weiskopf was Howie, the eight-year-old boy I used to baby-sit for. I did a lot of baby-sitting when I was a teenager – everyone in the neighbourhood seemed to have young children then – but of all my charges I remember him most vividly for eating the white cream and just the white cream from the middle of his Oreo cookies. This is one reason, though not the only one, I have trouble taking him seriously. Psychotherapist or not. Evidently, I am not alone. The compassion business is not booming. In uncertain economic or political times, people invariably cut back on psychological counselling, according to Dr Howie. Or as he puts it: 'Who has time for self-awareness?' The only steady income he earns these days is from a men's discussion group he leads called TLC or True Life Companions Inc. 'Women are disappointed by men and they are showing it. The result is that men are devastated. This is a constant,' Dr Howie once told me. His theory is that men have allowed their feelings about women to undermine their feelings of manhood and their relationships with each other. 'Outside of going bowling or drinking beer' – I said in the column I wrote on his behalf – 'men today are incapable of supporting or nurturing each other and are thus missing out on half of the opportunities available to women when women need a sympathetic ear or a shoulder to cry on.' Which accounts, we wrote, for the dramatic discrepancy between men and women in life expectancy, heart disease, suicide, sexual dysfunction, you name it.

'But what makes you think women can talk to men about their problems? Assuming what you say is true and they can't, then women are also down to fifty percent,' I asked. This was when the column and our collaboration was new and when I had more difficulty suppressing my doubts about some of Dr Howie's ad-libbed theories.

'You are overlooking a man's ability to feign interest in what a woman is saying. What's more, you are overlooking the value of feigned interest to the person, the woman, generally speaking, who is being listened to.'

'Do you really believe that?'

'I will. As soon as you've written it.'

* * *

Angie is also in the compassion business. A special education teacher, she deals exclusively with mentally ill and disabled teenagers. It was Angie who first defined magical thinking for me, right here in this house, six months ago, at a New Year's Eve party my brother threw for himself. He had moved out a few months earlier, but the party was his characteristically extroverted way of saying a final farewell to the suburbs, to his parents' house, to me.

He had asked me to throw the party for him, but I politely declined. It seemed redundant – the idea of coming back here just to go away again. His response to my objection was typical. 'Typical,' he said.

The real reason I was opposed to the party was because I was the one who would have to organize it and then spend the weekend cleaning up after it was over. It's not so much that I resented the task – which I did – but that I would do it anyway and do it without complaint. What really bothered me is that I would do it enthusiastically, as if I had nothing better to do.

There's a simple secret to keeping a house tidy: make sure there are never very many people in it at the same time. Which is why I hid in the garage, in the candy-apple red 1973 Malibu I inherited from my mother, trying not to think about all the extra housework being created for me. Meanwhile my brother's guests mingled upstairs in the kitchen, the living room and den, spilling cheap red wine on the hall carpet and stuffing paper plates under my mother's plastic-covered forest green sofa cushions.

Angie found me an hour before midnight. At the time, as far as we both knew, she was still happily married and I don't remember why or even if she'd come looking for me. I do recall being too embarrassed to tell her the truth – that I was hiding from a house full of sloppy friends and acquaintances. Instead, I rolled down the window on the driver's side and said the kind of thing I was always saying to Dr Howie during our brainstorming sessions, 'There's something about being at a party full of people that makes you feel more alone than actually being alone. You know?'

'I guess.'

'*Dear Alone in a Crowd.*'

'Tell me, are we talking about Hope?'

'Yes. Hope.'

* * *

Everyone who knows me knows about Hope Biehnstock. They know I've been in love with her for what will be three years in October. They know I have decided, unilaterally, that she is the right, the only woman for me. Hope and I see each other at least once a week and I tell her every other month how much I love her, need her and dream about her. It's become a habit, a running joke, something I can't not do. She tells me, in turn, that while she 'cherishes our friendship', these debates I insist on having with her about how she is wrong about me are pointless. Nevertheless, we have them everywhere: in restaurants, in our respective cars, in movie theatres, in airports. She is resolute, convinced that she is not in love with me in a way that she is not convinced about anything else. My luck. She can't return my feelings, she says. When I ask her why, she says she can't tell me. Her running joke.

'Can't or won't?'

'Is there a difference?'

'There is to me.'

I know Hope thinks that I won't be able to take the truth, but she's wrong. I am not really afraid of the hard, straight facts. It's unexpected things I worry about. The truth I can take. The truth I've had to learn to take. 'Yes,' Hope would say, 'take it or leave it.' (I am also not, as she has suggested more than once, in denial. I deny it, as a matter of fact.)

Hope and I first met four years ago when our jobs overlapped. She was a freelance radio researcher and producer then and considerably less well known than she is today as the host of the talk show 'Been There, Done That' on the specialty cable channel WTN or the Women's Television Network. She called me one day to inquire about an item on a man named Neil Topaz that had appeared in my 'Up Next!' column. Neil Topaz was a local entrepreneur who had just opened a Szechuan kosher restaurant called Chinese Shminese. The only extraordinary thing about Chinese Shminese – the thing that made its opening a story – was that it had its origins in a recent trip Topaz had made to Beijing and, in particular, an unscheduled detour he made to a remote village north of the city where he discovered a Chinese-Jewish community of nine people.

That's also where he met a young man who desperately wanted to emigrate to Canada to study the Torah and become what he couldn't become in his own country, a practising Jew. So Neil Topaz cut some corners, greased some palms, made some promises and, in effect, smuggled the young man out of mainland China. It turned out, as I wrote in my column, that the young Chinese man was not just an aspiring Jew, he was also an aspiring chef – there was some question about which came first – and Topaz set him up in business. Neil Topaz was the kind of man who welcomed a challenge and who knew enough to take advantage of a business opportunity when it landed in his lap.

Hope read about all this in my column, pitched the idea to the local CBC affiliate and ended up doing a live report from Chinese Shminese's grand opening. She interviewed Topaz, who described the entire incident as a mitzvah – Hebrew for good deed – and a miracle. That's when Hope did what she has since become known for, she followed her instincts instead of her script and made her interviewee break down and cry.

'Here you are, a man who has clearly climbed the ladder of

success: what made you take such a risk?' she asked him, turning away from the camera and looking him in the eye. The question seemed innocuous enough if you were around to hear it asked, but later, watching the moment repeated on television, there was something in the tone of Hope's voice, in the directness of her stare, that made you feel as if she had known you all your life and knew the one question to ask that would make you feel, for the first time in your life, that there was someone who really understood you. That must have been how Neil Topaz felt anyway.

'I read somewhere once that even after men have climbed – what did you call it? – the ladder of success, we sometimes wonder if we put the ladder up against the wrong wall,' Neil Topaz replied. 'I had to do what I did because I wasn't sure I could. I had to do it because I need to believe in miracles. My life leads me to no other conclusion.' Then he began to sob and tell Hope and her audience about how his parents had survived Buchenwald and how that miracle had just been the precursor for this one.

Later that evening, when Hope and I finally met face to face, she put her hand on my arm and thanked me for my help. Then she pulled a worn burgundy leather Filofax out of her purse and scribbled something onto a dog-eared page. 'This is a day for my diary,' she said. 'My first time on television, could you tell? That Neil guy is something. My therapist says you probably shouldn't trust people who cry so easily. Apparently, it means they want something from you and will go to any length to get it.

'See, I have this trust issue, according to my therapist. But then he's a jerk. Are you seeing someone?'

'Excuse me?'

'Oh no, a shrink, I mean. I'd guess no. I'm right, aren't I? You know that makes you a rarity these days? I'm thinking of changing shrinks. I have a restlessness issue, too. It's classic. I can't be happy with what I have and so I want what I can't have. Like being on television. I always wanted to do it, but now that I have I can see all the things that are wrong with it. Unsatisfactory, you know. All the pitfalls? See what I mean? No, I guess not. I'm sorry for rambling. Don't pay any attention to me.'

But I did pay attention. I studied her from that moment on, the way she worked the room, making everyone in it feel special just because she had stopped to ask them a question, making everyone she stopped to talk to feel as if they should tell her their most intimate, carefully guarded secrets.

Hope is tall, taller than me anyway, and slender, with big golden-brown eyes and a few freckles on the bridge of her nose that add a softness to her otherwise angular face. She isn't exactly pretty, but she has the capacity to be beautiful and often is, particularly in profile, where the expression on her face never seems set, always seems in transition. If you are trying to be a more optimistic person, as I sometimes am, then you will find Hope open to all kinds of interpretations. Her name suits her. In fact, I have always felt it would suit her even better if it had another syllable on the end – if it were Hopeful.

I drove her home that night after the party because she had misplaced her car keys – 'I'm always losing them,' she said, 'my last therapist was convinced it was no accident' – and she kissed me on the forehead by way of saying goodnight and thank-you. It took me another six months to realize that her openness and her interest in me were not fake – that the only reason these qualities had even seemed fake was because they were so unusually genuine. It took me the rest of the year to realize that I liked the idea of falling in love with a woman named Hope. But by then she knew me too well to think of me as anything other than a colleague and a friend. A good, good friend, she said when I finally admitted how I felt.

Hope has a theory: she thinks our relationship persists because I love her, because she loves me, just not in that way, and because we are both definite about this much, at least. Definite in a way we are not definite about anything else. It is a kind of compatibility, she says. A kind we both make the most of analysing. All things considered, the situation isn't nearly as crazy as it sounds.

* * *

'It sure sounds crazy,' Angie said, nudging me over into the passenger's seat of the Malibu, sliding in behind the wheel, and buckling her seat belt. My brother's New Year's Eve party was becoming noisier. Even holed up in the garage I could hear cherished plates and glasses, which my mother bought when we first moved into this house, toppling. I could also hear my brother calling to me from the top of the basement stairs, asking where the hell I'd hidden the dust buster. When there was no answer, I could hear him say, 'Typical,' over and over again.

'What is crazy, Angie, is that after all this time I still believe I can change Hope's mind; I believe there's something I can do or say or some way I can behave that will somehow make a difference, that it will...'

'Magical thinking,' Angie interrupted. 'The clinical term for your behaviour. It's textbook stuff. Kids do it all the time. The tendency to believe that thought can bring about changes in reality. That thinking makes it so.

'I have a student who sticks his index finger in his ear and stands that way for hours, days even. I've figured out he only does it when the 649 jackpot is more than five million dollars. You see, he's convinced that by putting his finger in his ear he'll win the money. My real concern is that one day he *will* win and then I'll never be able to reach him.'

Angie's job has given her a refreshing perspective on human behaviour. When it comes to craziness, what most people don't understand, according to Angie, is that there's an awfully wide margin for error.

As I listened to her talk about how her students were either falling in love with her all the time or putting elaborate five-part hexes on her, I came up with an elaborate hex of my own. Number one, if Angie were still here, in the car, beside me at midnight, then, number two, I'd kiss her on the mouth and, number three, I'd hold that kiss until, number four, both our lives had changed forever. (For example, she would have as many children as she wanted; I would never think about Hope again.)

'Rally caps,' I said, trying to take my mind off number five.
'Huh?'
'In baseball,' I said, my turn to explain a complex theory, 'when a team is behind, usually near the end of the game, players will turn their hats inside out or wear them backwards or sideways in order to help their side score runs. The thing is I've seen it work...'

'No, you haven't,' Angie said, gripping the steering wheel tightly, her knuckles going pale. Her hands were at ten and two o'clock on the wheel, which she turned absent-mindedly as if she were guiding us around a narrow corner. 'If my job, my life, has taught me anything, it's that you just can't expect more from people than they are capable of giving. You can't expect them to be something they are not.'

I didn't know at the time that she was talking about Sandy – her husband and my best friend – so I nodded. Then I glanced at my watch, but it was too dark in the car to make out the time. I assumed it was after midnight. It felt late anyway – felt like an opportunity had been missed. Besides I thought I could hear my brother singing 'My Way' upstairs, which is what he always sings at midnight on New Year's Eve. (He maintains that 'Auld Lang Syne' is too ambiguous: 'Is it about making new friends or dumping old ones?')

I opened my door and heard the lyrics 'for what is a man, what has he got?' and the Malibu's dome light flickered on like a brief, unexpected reprieve. Midnight was, by my digital watch, still a full minute away. In the same dim light I watched Angie's lips move. Her voice was steady and matter-of-fact, but I couldn't make out the meaning of what she was saying. Either I was preoccupied or, more likely, she was. I began my own secret countdown to the New Year while she kept talking about her job and how her patients – 'Sorry, students' – never changed, how no one really changes and you couldn't realistically expect them to, and how, being a professional – 'Sorry, caregiver' – she had to accept that and ...

And at zero, I leaned over to kiss her, not on the mouth, as I'd planned, but on the back of the neck. Her skin was downy and hot. The kiss startled her and we knocked heads as we both leaned into it a little more. I felt a familiar light-headedness, but I was determined to ignore it this time. I tried to pull her closer but she wouldn't budge because of her seat belt. Her hand slipped from the steering wheel onto the horn and the noise made both of us flinch, as if we were sharing an electric shock.

'Happy New Year,' I shouted as the car horn blared. Then she kissed me on the mouth. 'Happy, happy,' I mumbled, her mouth pressed against mine. The wet point of her tongue brushed against my teeth and, for an instant, against the roof of my mouth. She tasted like cherry bubble gum.

'Geez, that's right?' she said, gently pushing me aside, unbuckling her seat belt. She moved her frizzy hair away from her face. She was blushing now – from her earlobe to the hollow spot at the base of her throat. 'It's midnight, I mean. Sandy will be wondering where I am. Where am I? What are we doing here? In your garage?'

* * *

If what happened that night six months ago doesn't explain entirely to my satisfaction what Angie is doing on my front porch this evening, her hand on her hip, waiting for our first date to begin, it explains enough. Meanwhile, I am waiting for the telephone to stop ringing. I can usually tell who's calling by the number of rings. Hope or Dr Howie or Sandy or Ted Severs, my editor at the *Snooze*, or the university students for whom I've been ghostwriting English lit term papers on the selected prose – stories and journals – of John Cheever, know that they have to ring once, hang up and then call back immediately if they want me to answer.

If the phone rings six times and stops I know it's a casual acquaintance – someone like Russell Mintz, the real estate agent who's trying to sell my parents' house without my consent. If it rings ten times I know it's someone calling to try to get themselves or their organization in my 'Up Next!' column or to complain about a name I've misspelled or a date I got wrong.

If it rings twenty times or more I know who it is too – it's Joseph.

Joseph Alter is a rabbinical student who has lived in the house across the street from mine for as long as I can remember. Since there aren't any other rabbinical students living in the neighbourhood, there are a number of things about Joseph that stand out. Like the white socks he wears with his black suits and brown shoes. Or the laundry truck he has converted into a proselytizing vehicle called a Mitzvah Mobile, which is parked, on weekends, in front of his house.

Mitzvah Mobiles are rare in our neighbourhood these days, but some fifteen years ago, I remember a similar truck showing up early and regularly on Friday afternoons and parking in front of nearby schools and shopping centres. It was manned by three rabbinical students who would then fan out looking for fellow Jews, specifically males, who had not, at least not since their bar mitzvahs, put on *tephilim* – a traditional and daily form of prayer. The point of the prayer and the proselytizing was to change the world by changing one person at a time. How's that for magical thinking? Attempts were often made to entice me into the back of the truck, but they were never successful. Never for lack of trying, though. What always astonished me was how easily I was targeted, how assuredly I was picked out of the crowd.

But it is the way Joseph walks – even more than his white socks or the converted laundry truck parked in front of his house – that remains the most unmistakable thing about him. He was born severely pigeon-toed, a congenital condition that doctors corrected but not early enough. And while his posture, standing still, is fine, when he walks it's as if he were perpetually skipping, his right arm bouncing off his right hip like a metronome, his left arm hanging free. Every step he takes seems to defy gravity.

I knew Joseph well enough once to try to teach him how to catch a football, but that was more than fifteen years ago. Now, we are practically strangers. Incidentally, it is Joseph who intends to do me serious, lasting harm.

* * *

When the telephone finally stops ringing I can hear knocking at the front door and the muffled sound of Angie whispering my name through the letter slot. I'd forgotten all about her. Additional proof, if I needed it, that anything is possible.

Angie is holding up the brass flap of the letter slot with her tiny red thumbnail and through the slot I can see her matching red lipstick shimmer like a mirage as she repeats my name. Her voice is insistent, enticing. I kneel down, put my thumb on the brass flap so that she can let go. Then I smile apologetically, though I'm not sure she can make out my apology through the narrow opening.

'Your doorbell doesn't work.'

'I know. We disconnected it years ago. It's a long story.'

'You didn't answer the phone either? Don't you have a machine?'

'Disconnected too. Another long story.'

'Hello, Jacob, this explains a lot. Did you ever think the reason you don't date much is because no one can reach you?'

'Never occurred to me,' I say, shifting my weight from one knee to the other. 'But if I'm acting weird, it might have something to do with the fact that you insist on calling this a date.'

'Well, we could call it something else.'

'A fiasco?'

'A get-together.'

'Fate?'

'A friendly visit.'

'A mitzvah and a miracle?'

'I'll admit, Jacob, I didn't think I'd be down on my knees this early in the evening.'

'Excuse me?'

'Whoops.'

'Well, I could always propose while I'm down here.'

'So, tell me, what would you propose?'

* * *

I no longer take Joseph's calls so I can't say for sure if his desire for revenge has escalated or if he has had a change of heart. But when my answering machine was still connected he left a series of messages that I found impossible to interpret as anything other than threatening. I have transcribed and saved them and they all begin the same way, with Joseph clearing his throat and speaking in a slow, deliberate manner:

'I know you are there, Glassman, but never mind, I will leave my message, as you request. Here it is: betrayal is not such a terrible sin. Not when it is expected. Why do you feel you must hide from me? What are you afraid of? What are you ashamed of? I live across the street from you – do you not think I see how you avoid me? Do you not think I know you are there? Listening.

'So go ahead and listen: I do hold you responsible for everything that happened, certainly, but I do not hold a grudge. It is not in my nature or in the nature of my faith.

'So listen: I am only calling now because I want to understand why you did this. What did you think you could gain by causing such trouble, such suffering for me? Call it professional curiosity. I want to know what makes you do the things you do. When I become a rabbi next year, God willing, it will be my responsibility to deal with all types of people and I want to understand why you are the way you are.'

Even if Joseph isn't saying, in so many words, that he wants to harm me, I know him well enough to know what he's thinking. (I baby-sat for him, too: I watched him imprison caterpillars, torture them until they turned into butterflies.) It is, as far as I am concerned, a distinction without a difference.

Everyone – relatives, friends, colleagues, the police – tell me that even if these are threats, they are idle ones. He just wants someone to talk to, a friend, the police officer suggested after I played one of my tapes for him. Under normal circumstances, I would agree, except I know something no one else does. I know that Joseph has a good reason for wanting revenge.

* * *

'The mistake I made was the one that women always make,' Angie says. 'I believed I could change him.' We are in my mother's Malibu when Angie makes this confession, on our way to the Happy Garden Café in the Court Séjour Mall. Angie is on the passenger side this time, seat belt buckled, looking as vulnerable as she did six months ago on New Year's Eve. Her window is open and the unseasonably cool breeze is blowing in her face – shaking an occasional tear loose from her brimming brown eye.

'I thought when he said he knew what he wanted that, like most men, he didn't know at all, that he was just waiting to be told,' she continues. 'But then I guess you've heard all this before? I guess you two have discussed this in plenty of detail already.'

'No, Angie, we haven't.' Which is not true, strictly speaking. Sandy isn't talking about his separation any more, but up until a few weeks ago he talked about little else. Mostly, he wanted to make it clear to me that while the decision to separate was, for all practical purposes, a mutual one, what bothered him – really bothered him – was her absolute refusal to explain to him in any kind of logical way why she was leaving.

'Well, I don't care if you do know,' Angie says. 'It's not exactly a secret that I wanted a baby. When we were first married I guess we both thought it would just happen. You know, we'd slip up or something and that would be it. But it didn't ... happen. We even had tests done, but there was no problem anyone could pinpoint. So we did what people do: we put it off. Forgot about it.

'Except I never did and when I said I wanted to try again, to maybe have both of us checked out again, he said we'd agreed that we didn't want children. Hello? What agreement? I never made any agreement. He said this was just a phase I was going through. He wouldn't listen. It was like talking to a wall. It's not that he refused to listen, he was incapable of it.'

'I see.'

Considering the fact that it is my job to tape record, condense, summarize and then write down other people's stories, I am surprised at how often I find myself uninterested in those stories. That, in turn, makes it difficult for me to be as professional as I'd like. Take interviewing, for example: sometimes when I'm transcribing a tape I'm startled and a little embarrassed to hear myself ask questions that are completely off the topic. What was I thinking about? Hadn't I been ...

'Hello? Jacob ... Jacob? Are you listening?'

'Of course.'

'Was it so stupid to think that he'd see how important this was to me?' Angie asks. 'It wasn't even a question of him agreeing with me about having a baby or anything like that, I just wanted him to understand that we were at a turning point, a crossroads. That the status quo was no longer acceptable. But he couldn't see it. Or wouldn't see it.'

'I see.' I know that one of my shortcomings as a journalist and as an interviewer is that the more people go on about their problems, the more they sound invented to me, touched up, and the more my mind starts to wander.

'It happens just like that,' Angie says, snapping her fingers in front of my face like a magician lifting a spell. 'One moment you're happy or at least satisfied with your life and the next moment you can't understand how you ended up where you are. See what I mean?'

'Of course.'

'I'm sorry, Jacob. I didn't want this to come out all at once like this. If I'm – if it's making you uncomfortable, tell me, I'll stop.'

'Well…'

'But it got so bad in the last few months that whenever I saw an infant in a stroller or a pregnant woman in a restaurant or even in a TV commercial, I'd fall apart or lose my temper or start nagging and picking at Sandy. If it hadn't been for that, he would never have noticed anything was wrong. That and the fact that our sex life was, well, regressing,' Angie says, glancing at me, lowering her brown eye demurely and tugging at the hem of her skirt again.

'It's not what you think,' she goes on. 'Not less frequent, okay, not even less, well, you know, but less … less mutual somehow. We were just fucking, is all.'

Another thing I've learned from my job at the *Court Séjour News*: you can have too much information. I've been approached often enough by members of the community telling me, in great detail, how they survived the Holocaust or prostate cancer or an abusive marriage. Some of the stories are so intimate I cringe listening to them. But I always write down the person's name and number and assure them, usually more than once, that I'll get back to them. Usually, I don't. Not because what they have to say is not compelling – everyone has a story to tell and every story has value, I know this now, I've learned it the hard way – but because it's too compelling. Because I know that what they have to say will be too complicated for me to ever do justice to. The times I have tried – like the time I devoted a column to Joseph – I have only succeeded in betraying my subject's trust.

* * *

While I drive in narrower and narrower circles through the parking lot of the Court Séjour Mall, the story of Angie's sex life unravels in more and more intimate detail. It is Friday evening and on Fridays the parking lot is full. The only way to find a spot is to watch for someone leaving and follow them to their car. The procedure is embarrassing for both parties.

Fortunately, Angie is unaware of my predicament. She doesn't even seem interested in why I've brought her here. Or why I am trailing strangers to their cars, driving at a speed that barely registers on the speedometer.

'You know what? The sex actually got better the less we talked. There was this element of suspense. I know for Sandy the risk was wondering whether I was, well, taking precautions or not. I thought about lying to him, tricking him. I thought about it all the time, but I never did. Now I wonder if ... if that's all I had to do.... Sorry, I don't suppose this is the sort of thing you want to hear tonight. I can change the subject.'

'No, go on. If it ...'

'It does. Help.'

I have never really understood why people feel compelled to tell me their personal problems. I do not welcome it, even though I realize that there's an openness about my face, a literal roundness about it, that gives the impression that I'm a sympathetic listener, an easy touch, that I will not think the worse of you no matter what you tell me about yourself. I wish this were true. Writing a weekly column only perpetuates this misconception. Everyone who approaches me with their story thinks they are doing me a big favour.

That's what Joseph thought last fall when he first told me about a new organization called the Jewish Instructional Program (JIP) and the list of seminars and courses they were offering to the public – in particular, the course he would be teaching, 'The Art of Living Jewishly'.

'So listen, will you write a column about this? Will you help?' he asked. It was a chilly September morning and I was raking the leaves off the front lawn. Joseph was returning from synagogue. He crossed the street, reached out and wrapped his fist around the middle of my rake handle, halting my forward progress.

'Our community is disappearing, Glassman, do I have to tell you? You and I have lived here all our lives. I see it. You must as well. I believe it was Maimonides, blessed be his memory, who said, "that the times have no pity, that they erase and efface the old, the mouldy and the sacred." And that is what will happen here, to us, unless we do something. We do not want to throw away the baby and the bathwater as well.'

'Who's Maimonides?'

'Very funny. So you are a funny man. Fine. Tell me, can you also be a serious man?'

Of course, I'd noticed Joseph crossing the street – how could I not? – but I assumed this time wasn't any different from all the other times he'd crossed the street and walked past my house on his way to synagogue. I had no reason to think he'd stop. He never had before. If I'd thought he would, if I'd known then what I know now, I would have stayed in the backyard until he was out of sight.

The last time I had spoken to Joseph was fifteen years ago. He'd just celebrated his bar mitzvah and his mother complained to me about the way the other boys picked on him. 'He's different,' she told me. 'He takes everything to heart. But you he likes, he trusts. You were his favourite sitter.'

I promised to do what I could, which meant – in the absence of his father who had divorced his mother several years earlier and was an infrequent visitor – teaching him not to be afraid of a football. Practising in my backyard, I showed him how to catch the ball with his hands instead of letting it bounce off his chest. He was a surprisingly quick study, absorbing all my advice, at least until he got into a game and then all his bad habits returned. In pickup games on the street in front of our houses, he was hopeless. Still, I encouraged him to keep trying. (I admit this was for my own sake as much as his: I was trying to make a point, not a friend.) But no one bothered to throw him the ball; no one even bothered to cover him as he recreated the stop-and-go pattern I'd taught him. He ran, unguarded, one foot tangled up with the other, until just the fact that he stayed upright seemed like a miracle – one for the highlight package. That's when I told him to stop. To just stop. A dutiful boy, he did as he was told.

Over the last few years, there have been times when I have felt obliged to say hello to him or at least nod in his direction, but Joseph has always walked by as if he didn't recognize me. The irony is that he's the one who has become unrecognizable. I've monitored his transformation closely, but it still astonishes me. I remember him wearing a red, white and blue Expos baseball cap, back to front, one day; the next day he was wearing a crocheted blue and white skullcap, fastened in place with a large silver bobby pin; and then the day after that he was wearing a black fedora over the skullcap. One day he had sideburns, the next sidelocks; one day he neglected to shave; the next day his auburn beard was long enough to cover his shirt collar. The change couldn't have been any more dramatic if I'd been watching a werewolf movie.

'Glassman, are you listening?' he said, now his other fist wrapped around my rake. 'So the question is, will you help? You know you are in a position to.'

'If I can, of course, but my problem —'

'From problems, I know, Glassman,' he stared down at his scuffed, brown Oxfords and his severely turned-in feet. There was always something old about Joseph, even as a young boy. Now, as a grown man, he seemed like an artefact. 'For my sake, then, show some generosity. Soften your heart. You can be the way you are or you can be different; you can help or you can refuse to help. The choice is yours.'

He was right. The choice was mine. I try not to delude myself about my job at the *Snooze*: I'm not a columnist, not even a journalist or a reporter really. My main obligation is to publicize local activities and personalities, to get the dates straight and spell the names correctly. I know what I am: I am a community bulletin board.

But Joseph wanted more than publicity. He wanted me to sit in on his class so I could write about the experience firsthand and so I'd be able to understand how much his course meant to the people taking it. How much, I suppose, it might even mean to me. Suddenly, it was clear to me what Joseph saw in me: he saw what some people see in prime real estate. Or in an eligible bachelor. He saw just what he was looking for. An apathetic Jewish male who hadn't been in a synagogue since his bar mitzvah, who hadn't prayed since his parents died. In other words, a challenge worthy of his faith.

'This semester we are doing the Book of Job, so, you see, you must come. "Oh, that my words were now written! oh, that they were printed in a book!" Job, chapter 23, verse 17. Or maybe you would prefer a more literary quote. Fine. Good. "All sorrows can be borne if you put them into a story..." Isak Dinesen,' he added, winking at me.

But quoting famous writers back to me wasn't going to get him anywhere. Frankly, I don't think Isak Dinesen meant what she said. Which is a fact about professional writers that people like Joseph don't understand: they are not above writing things they know are not true. They are not above deception, even when their motives are not particularly sinister. I didn't intend for the column I wrote about Joseph to turn out the way it did. I didn't intend to call into question everything he believes in and has devoted his life to. But that's what happened.

What I don't understand is why people believe that talking about their problems, especially to me, will help somehow. Of course, the world is full of victims, when hasn't it been, but now those victims are becoming impossible to ignore.

Just turn on the television set any morning of the week, as I sometimes do when I'm in my office at home, working out on my StairMaster, climbing flight after flight, encountering more and more resistance, and I will inevitably catch Oprah or Ricki or Geraldo coaxing a heartbreaking tale out of guests who've been molested or abducted, who are bulimic, addicted to angel dust, left for dead after participating in a satanic ritual or who just love someone who will never, not in a million years, love them back. And the one thing they all have in common is that they've lived to tell about it. What astonishes me is how willing they are to reveal their most devastating and humiliating secrets.

There are secrets about me, for example, embarrassing ones that I could never even write in this journal or share with a solitary friend, let alone an audience full of strangers. There are days when I'm hardly willing to admit them to myself. So what are these people thinking? What in the world gets into them?

* * *

'Eventually, we stopped talking altogether,' Angie says, sidling away from the open window and moving closer to me on the Malibu's bench seat. 'Literally stopped. If there was something we had to tell each other we'd leave notes around the house or on the windshield of our cars. The only time we'd say anything to each other was when we were ... fucking.'

There is a catch in her voice when she says the word. This is the second time she's said it and though there are lots of other words she could use to make herself understood, it's as if she is forcing herself to use that one specifically.

'Then the words between us became ugly. Then it was more than words. Jacob, it was a side of him I'd never seen before. And, sure, a side of myself too. Not in thirteen years of … of fucking. It was as if each of us were trying to force the other to cry uncle.'

'You don't have to put yourself through this, Angie, I understand.' I place my hand gently on top of hers. I don't think she's going to break down, but when I glance at her I realize that it's a possibility. Then out of Angie's side mirror I see an elderly woman with a walker reaching into her purse for her keys and with my right hand still on Angie's hand and my left hand on the steering wheel I maneuver myself into position to follow her.

'I do, Jacob. I have to put myself through this.' Angie turns her hand over so that her palm is flat against mine. The gesture is encouraging. Except she looks as if she has just emerged from a trance. 'Why are you driving so slow?' she asks. 'Where are we? What are we doing here?'

* * *

I'm not surprised that Angie, despite having lived in Court Séjour all her married life, has never been to the Happy Garden Café. Everything about the place is unremarkable and, to be frank, a little cloying: from the rust-orange Naugahyde booths to the paper dragons clinging like large dead bugs to the stucco ceiling. I'm prepared, however, to overlook its shortcomings – at least until someone else points them out to me. Someone who probably doesn't have the kind of sentimental attachment to the place that I do.

The Happy Garden is the kind of place John Cheever would have loved. Or I used to think he would have loved it. A few years ago I was hired to write my first term paper for a chemical engineering student at McGill, a friend of a friend, who was stuck taking a compulsory make-up course in contemporary North American literature. He paid me five dollars a page to write a ten-thousand-word essay on Cheever's *Collected Stories*. My client received a B + for 'Shady Hill:

Paradise Lost and Found in John Cheever's Short Fiction'. So I know something about the man and his work. Of course, everything I thought I knew, I knew before I began to read his journals. Before I read what he wrote about being a captive in his own home, 'a prisoner ... trying to ... dig a tunnel with a teaspoon'. Now, I wonder why he didn't just hire a good realtor, pack up and leave – why he insisted on pretending to love the place in which he lived when all the time it was just a bad habit he couldn't break, when all along he would rather have been anywhere else.

I have been dining at the Happy Garden since I was six years old. Back then, the clientele consisted mainly of young Jewish couples – now all the young families in Court Séjour are Greek or East Indian or Portuguese – second-generation men and women with small children for whom a night out every weekend at the nearby Chinese restaurant was their only enduring ritual. They honoured it the same way their parents went to synagogue on the high holidays or their grandparents refused to switch on an electric light on the Sabbath.

The Happy Garden was the first restaurant I remember my parents taking me to. Mr Ho, the proprietor, always greets me by saying, 'Comme ou stad?' He's a slightly stooped, good-natured man who allows himself to sound foolish for sentimental reasons, who never forgets that the first time he waited on my family he thought we were Italian. My parents played along. They didn't have the heart to tell him the truth – that we were Jewish and anyway he was speaking Spanish. Mr Ho also remembers the time I drank the hot water in the finger bowl, mistaking it for soup. He teases me about this whenever he escorts me to my booth in the back. He's a sweet man, whose concern for my welfare goes beyond professional courtesy. Still, I'm relieved that when Angie and I arrive he isn't around to greet me, to talk endlessly, sentimentally, about the past.

'This is interesting,' Angie says. But I can hear a squeak as she frees her bare thighs from the Naugahyde seat. I flinch watching her flinch.

'The food is good,' I say apologetically. This is true, but I also know that the menu, which Mr Ho refuses to complicate with newfangled Szechuan dishes, is hopelessly out of date.

'Do you come here often?'

'Not often, I …'

'Can I ask you something?' Angie says, taking my hand this time, then letting it go when Mr Ho steps out of the kitchen, spots me and comes over to our booth.

'Order usual, Mr Jacob?' he asks, picking up our menus.

'I think we'll need more time,' I say, trying to snatch my menu back, but he holds on to it tightly for a moment, grinning as if this little tug-of-war is an inside joke. It takes him a while to figure out that I am serious, that I want him to let go of the menu. Once he does figure it out he backs away from the booth, looking confused and disappointed.

Mr Ho is no good at being inscrutable. I remember the first time I picked up a take-out order after my mother died, he wouldn't accept money from me. He also made the point of putting a fortune cookie in my hand and making sure I opened it in front of him. 'You see,' he said, pointing to the tiny slip of paper. 'Rife goes on.' It was an elaborately corny joke and he'd gone to considerable trouble to pull it off: removing the original message from the cookie with a pair of needle-nose pliers, whiting out the L, typing in an R, then reinserting the message in the cookie.

'What I wanted to ask you – and then I won't bring it up again – is how Sandy is doing? I mean how is he doing now? Does he mention me?' Angie says as soon as Mr Ho retreats to the kitchen.

'I thought you two saw each other … this afternoon?'

'Sure, with that horrible little real estate agent, Mintz, there between us. Yammering about missed opportunities and the buyer's market and how we'd better sell before the referendum. Didn't Sandy tell you?'

'Tell me what?'

'We're selling the condo. Sandy's not happy about it. There's an understatement. He signed on the dotted line and then practically locked himself in the bathroom. Selling was my idea. Buying was also my idea. You remember all the trouble I had to go through to get him to commit to the place. But now, all of a sudden, he loves it. Wouldn't think of leaving. He's even fixed it up, which is funny because he never took much interest in it before. I don't know what's going on inside his head any more. That's why I'm asking you, Jacob. I realize this is awkward for you and I don't want to put you in the middle or make you have to choose sides ...'

'I'm on your side, Angie.'

'But you can't be married to someone for thirteen years and then pretend you're not even curious about how he is, about what he's doing, about his welfare. You can't just erase someone from your life, someone whose whereabouts you knew every day. Whose bowel movements, for heaven's sake, were part of your schedule. You see what I mean. And since you played racquetball with him yesterday, I thought ...'

'I cancelled the game. I thought it would be, well, like you said, awkward.'

Sandy and I did play racquetball yesterday afternoon, as always, mainly because it would have been awkward not to. In fact, I had to pester him to show up. Lately, he's been harder and harder to pry loose from his condo. I don't know if Angie knows this or not, but he's even started operating his travel agency out of his apartment. Like the rest of us who have stumbled into freelance careers for lack of anything better or more permanent to do, Sandy is lowering his overhead, cutting his losses.

That aside, he is all right. If I decide not to tell Angie so, it's because I'm still not convinced the truth is what she wants to hear when it comes to her soon-to-be ex-husband, especially not if the truth is that he appears to be getting along fine without her.

* * *

That wasn't always the case. The day last February when he called to tell me that Angie had walked out on him wasn't a Thursday but we decided to meet at the racquet club anyway. We changed into our sweat pants and T-shirts, put on our knee pads, laced up our sneakers, all in silence, and went out on the court just as if we were going to play a game. Except neither of us brought a ball.

'Ultimatums,' he said. 'How come ultimatums? This is not like her. Angie always made sense before. She was logical, almost to a fault.' He pointed his racquet at me as if it were an open hand, like in those old movie musicals where rival tap dancers are trading routines and one, having wowed the audience, holds out his hand to the other, as if to say top that.

'Did she mention – is there someone else?'

'No, of course not,' he said, and then he slumped to his knees right at the centre of the court. I knelt beside him and placed my racquet on his broad shoulder. I don't think he was crying, but it was hard for me to tell. He had covered his face with his hands and he wasn't making any sound at all. The club's pro, an eager young man who never seemed to have enough to do, opened the door to ask if Sandy had been hit in the eye. I said that he had and the pro rushed off and returned moments later with his first aid kit and an ice pack.

'I'm studying sports medicine and I see a lot of this. You guys should really be wearing safety goggles.' I nodded and then wrestled the ice pack out of the pro's eager hands and applied it to the side of Sandy's unbruised face.

* * *

'It came as a big surprise to me, too. I didn't stop missing her. I just stopped feeling tense, anxious, waiting for her to come back. I also realized that everything I needed was right there at home. You know, I hardly ever have to leave the place,' Sandy told me yesterday, as he stepped around my serve, his new goggles perched on top of his head, his racquet resting loosely in his left hand.

'One zip,' I said, catching the ball as it ricocheted around him, off the side wall, the back wall and then back to me.

'That serve was long.'

'You couldn't have seen it. You haven't stopped talking since we got here.' Actually, he hadn't stopped talking since I picked him up at his condo. He was being propelled by a kind of nervous energy that would have seemed comical if it wasn't also so unsettling.

'I saw it. It was long.'

Sandy has never beaten me at racquetball, but it's not a statistic either of us keeps track of. He is taller, quicker and fitter than me and he hits the ball harder. But his temper has always been the flaw in his game. Whenever he makes a mistake, particularly in a close contest, he'll begin to talk to himself, throw his racquet across the court and brood for the next few points. Then I can pretty much make any shot I want – the easiest lob or the laziest return – and count on him to strike the ball with all his force, swinging his racquet like a sledge-hammer, smashing the ball into the floor or hard off the back wall, setting me up with an easy chance. It's a game of inches, he always says later in the shower, as if bad luck were the solitary reason he keeps losing to me.

'My serve was good. One zip.'

'Okay, Jake, fine. Forget the score for a second? I have something serious to ask you.'

He moved in closer to me until we were both standing between the narrow red lines that marked out the server's box and I remember thinking, at that moment, that he knew everything there was to know about Angie and me. I'd suspected we couldn't keep our date a secret forever, that it was just a matter of time before Sandy found out the truth, but I never expected he would find out before Angie and I had even gone out. Sandy is thirty-five, my age, but he looks older, more mature than me, a sturdy man with broad shoulders and a broad East European face. His parents came to Canada from Yugoslavia after the Second World War and in their effort to leave the past behind refused to tell him whether he's Serbian or Croatian. They still refuse. Which is fine with Sandy because it's just one more thing he doesn't really need or want to know. His features are more nondescript than Slavic anyway – regular eyes, nose, ears, mouth. His eyebrows, alone, betray his roots: thick and black, they curve in towards the bridge of his nose and meet there in a V, his V for victory, he calls it. Standing face to face with him yesterday, I wasn't able to see his right hand, but I was trying to remember what it felt like to be punched when I realized that being punched was something else I had to add to my ever-expanding 'Never Happened' list.

'Do you know anything about being a Real Friend, Jake?'

'What's that supposed to mean?' I'd never actually punched any-one either but I could feel, almost against my will, my right hand clenching into a fist behind my back. No one sets out to lead a shel-tered life. You just fall into it, the way you fall into most things because there are questions you never answered, because there is a protocol you never understood. For example, was I supposed to hit him first?

'Real Guys. True Pals. I can't remember what it's called.'

'I have no idea what you're talking about.'

'True Companions, that's it. True Life Companions. It's a workshop. A support group. That therapist from your newspaper runs it. It's for guys like me, separated guys, guys trying to make friends with themselves, as Dr Weiskopf puts it, without the influence of women. The idea is that you and you alone are your only true companion. We meet every other week.'

'I thought you'd decided to stay home more.'

'Yeah, sure, but we've been meeting at my place. Neil Topaz told me about it, remember, the Chinese Shminese guy. How'd he know I was divorced? Anyhow, I'm telling you about it because we were all talking and we thought there would be a column in this for you.'

* * *

When Mr Ho comes over to our booth with the bill and a plate of fortune cookies, it's already past midnight. The waiters are putting the chairs on top of the tables, a bus boy has begun to mop the floor, the chef has changed into a jogging outfit. Mr Ho pushes the cookies in my direction, winks, and then vanishes before I can thank him. The fact is he could have stayed and talked for a moment since Angie is away from the table using the telephone, calling the sister she moved in with after she left Sandy.

'My sister worries about me. She thinks I'm still at a vulnerable stage, you know, the you're-so-mixed-up-you're-capable-of-doing-any-crazy-thing stage,' Angie explained, smiling shyly as I directed her to the telephone booth at the back of the restaurant. 'She says that if I'm going to be late I have to call and tell her, so she won't imagine the worst. This is the first time I've had to call.'

'I'm flattered.'

'You better be.'

When Angie returns to the table her smile is less reluctant, wider. Maybe I'm imagining it, but she looks as if she has just stopped giggling. 'Shouldn't we be going?' she says, either because she's in a hurry to leave or because she doesn't want to have to slide back into the booth. Then she says, 'Don't you want to know how late I told her I would be?'

'Okay, how late?'

'Very.'

I pay the cheque and Angie picks up a fortune cookie, opening it before I can choose one for her, which is a habit with me whenever I bring a date to the Happy Garden. Angie hesitates for a moment and hands me the tiny message.

ELIMINATE DUBIOUS ACQUAINTANCES FROM YOUR LIST

'Whoops,' Angie says, her shy smile returning.

'I wish you'd stop saying that.'

* * *

I always get lost trying to find my way out of shopping malls, even ones I've been coming to all my life. I used to wonder if my sense of direction was fatally flawed, but now I realize shopping malls are designed so that leaving is not just difficult, it is pointless. Why would you want to? Everything you will ever need or want is right here: Chinese buffets, bookstores, camping supplies, movie theatres, shoe stores, hair salons, gyms, passport photo booths, dental clinics, day care centres ...

'I think we came in that way,' Angie says, pointing to a Toys 'R' Us sign.

'I don't remember passing a toy store.'

'I do.'

I'm almost out the electronic front door before I realize that Angie is no longer beside me. Instead, she's dawdling in front of a window display of strollers, adventure castles, Barbie dolls, and high-powered water pistols.

'Why has it been so easy for him to walk away, Jacob? You know that he actually went down on his knees and begged me to stay just one more night when I told him I was leaving. He kissed my fingertips, each and every one.'

I turn away from Angie when she says the word 'fingertips' because I know what the look on my face is saying: it is saying a person can have too much information.

'I did stay. I shouldn't have, I knew that right away. So you know what he said? He said, "How can you go after last night?" It was a good question, so good I almost stayed the next night too. And now, after all that, why has it been so easy for him? Why does he want to buy out my share of our place? Why has he moved his office there? Why does he want to fight over who gets the dishwasher? I don't understand.'

'Some of us are good at adjusting to new situations, Angie, and some of us aren't. Take me, for example.'

'Right, take you,' she says, trying hard to smile until she's doing it, smiling – and bumping into me with the sharp angle of her hip. As I watch her reflection through the darkened glass of the toy store window, I can hardly believe my luck. Here it is: what I wished for.

* * *

I will admit it in this journal and nowhere else: I'm not accustomed to things going right, which is why I can't help wondering if somehow, in some way, I'm also responsible for what happened next. Laugh too much and you'll cry later, my mother used to say.

When Angie and I return to my house we discover the windshield of her Corolla has been smashed. Before we left she had backed her car into the driveway at my request and as we pull up she is the first to notice that something is wrong. I just notice Joseph's Mitzvah Mobile parked, as usual, in front of his house. It is covered with bumper stickers, proclaiming the arrival of a new Jewish messiah, the authentic one this time: *The Moshiach Is Coming, Bienvenue le Moshiach, Next Year in Jerusalem*. I also notice a curtain move in the bedroom window directly across from my parents' bedroom and a head disappear from view. But it's Angie who sees the tiny shards of green tinted glass gleaming like emeralds on the asphalt driveway.

The glass is everywhere: scattered on Angie's dash, on her front and back seat, and all over the driveway, the freshly mowed lawn and the front walk, halfway to the front stairs. Neither of us is prepared to say so, but we both know, as we assess the damage, that the windshield has been broken with thoroughness and premeditation. Attached to one of the windshield wipers hanging limply over the car's dash, there's a large index card, held in place by an oversized silver bobby pin. The card is composed like a ransom note, the letters in the message cut out of magazines and pasted together. It says: WHY HAVE YOU BETRAYED ME?

Angie won't let me call the police. She tries instead to gather up all the broken glass, thinking perhaps if she puts it all into a neat pile, it will reassemble itself.

'But you have to have a police report. For the insurance.'

'I don't care about that.'

I notice then that the palm of her hand is bleeding and I take hold of her shoulders and pull her back from the hood of the car. I turn her around to face me and though I intend to hug her, she steps back – more distracted than upset. Again, I expect her to break down; again she surprises me and doesn't. She just glares down at her car, shaking slightly, muttering to herself, 'Fuck him. Fuck him.' The glass on the ground snaps conclusively beneath her sandal.

'Come inside,' I say, guiding her up the front steps. I unlock the door and lead the way to what was once my parents' bedroom. The furniture still smells of Lemon Pledge from earlier in the afternoon; the room is impeccably tidy. Everything in its proper place.

* * *

Saturday, June 21. When I was twelve years old I came home from school one day to find myself locked out of the house. Although I was old enough by then to have my own house key as all my friends did, I never needed one. My father worked at home; my mother shopped, ran errands and delivered my father's signs in the morning and was always home in the afternoon, waiting for me. Back then if anyone had told me that one day I'd be locked out of my house I wouldn't have believed them. My response would have been, 'It won't happen.' Even after it happened, I never took precautions. I didn't get my own house key until after my mother died.

I know from talking to Dr Howie that this is the kind of incident that can leave an indelible mark; in my case, it hasn't. It would never have occurred to me then that something bad had happened. (I learned later that evening that my father fell down the last two basement stairs and fractured his left wrist. My mother had intended to leave a key with a neighbour and a note on the front door for me, but in her rush to get to the hospital, she'd neglected to make either arrangement.) It also would never have occurred to me then to be frightened. I suppose I was surprised more than anything else: surprised that something this unexpected was happening to me.

I did think, initially, that I'd made a wrong turn – that I'd entered a parallel universe like in an episode of 'The Twilight Zone' where everything in your life is the same, except all the people you know and care about – your parents, let's say – have vanished.

As I sat on the front step, I remember glancing at the address above the screen door, thinking maybe I'd transposed the numbers. I even walked down to the corner to make sure I was on the right street. There was a precedent for this sort of thing in Court Séjour; there were stories, probably apocryphal, I realize now, maybe I even read them somewhere, about children coming home from school to a duplex or split-level cottage or bungalow identical to their own and not realizing that they weren't where they were supposed to be until they were seated at the dinner table.

The point I tried to make in that term paper I was hired to write about John Cheever's *Collected Stories* was that his characters were always getting stuck somewhere they didn't want to be – in elevators or airports or dental offices or commuter trains or the suburbs – and then discovering that being stuck wasn't so bad after all. They routinely, instinctively, confined themselves inside quiet neighbourhoods that all looked the same, that were only distinguishable by the things no one could possibly see from the outside.

In my experience, the suburbs are designed to look alike, not, as most people assume, because of a lack of imagination on the part of its inhabitants, but because of too much imagination. The suburbs are meant to shut out anything dispiriting. What's remarkable is how well they succeeded. Of course, this success, like any success, came at a cost. After seeing *Dr Zhivago*, John Cheever returned to his suburban home and wrote in his journal, 'Will I never be caught up helplessly in the storms of history and love?'

I suppose I could have knocked on a neighbour's door and I suppose I would have been taken in. (Not any more: aside from Joseph Alter and his mother, I no longer know any of my neighbours well enough to impose upon them.) I suppose I could have forced or broken the basement window and let myself in. But I didn't. I stayed outside for the remainder of the evening and realized that feeling safe is the kind of thing you can start to take for granted. Eventually, it can become a habit – in the long run, a dangerous one.

* * *

'Every habit is a bad habit, Jacob. So if this is about me smoking, well then, bugging me about it won't help,' Hope says, extricating herself from the same booth Angie and I were sitting in the night before. 'Don't you think that the more people bother me about it the harder they make it for me to stop? Do I ever ask you why we keep coming back here all the time?'

Hope lights her own cigarette, pays her half of the check, as always, turns her back on me and then walks briskly out of the Happy Garden. I hurry after her, stopping just long enough to grab two fortune cookies from the tray Mr Ho is holding out for me. When I say goodnight to him, he winks at me. His way of congratulating me on what he thinks is my very active social life. His way too of letting me know I am forgiven for last night.

I don't have to go far to catch up to Hope. I just follow the trail of smoke from the front of the restaurant to where she is inhaling in front of Toys 'R' Us. Hope has stopped to watch a clown with a bright orange wig, a red rubber nose and huge, floppy slippers entice children into the store. The store has stayed open later than usual Saturday night because of a special promotional tie-in with a new Disney movie playing at the other end of the mall. But the promotion is backfiring. The clown is only succeeding in frightening children and unnerving their parents.

Hope's bad temper can probably be attributed to the fact that she is trying, without much success, to stop smoking. And although it's true that I have been one of the people pestering her to quit, now that she has decided to I can't help wondering why she is doing it and, like everything else that happens in her life, what difference it will make between us.

She has been cranky ever since I picked her up at the airport earlier this afternoon. She was in Toronto for a week of meetings with the executives in charge of 'Been There, Done That' and she snapped at me when I told her she looked pale. 'You'd look like a ghost too if you were stuck in an office all week with bad air and a bunch of sanctimonious women debating your hairstyle. Pros and cons.'

Usually, I enjoy nothing more than meeting Hope at the airport. Because of her job she travels frequently, doing the show from various locations around the country. I have a photocopy of the schedule she keeps in her Filofax and I always show up to meet her flights. We don't arrange anything beforehand and she has complained more than once about taking advantage of me, but I know that she expects me nevertheless. That's one of the reasons I do it – so she will come to depend on me. There is also something about arriving at the gate just before she does, checking the monitor to see if her flight is on time, watching other separated couples greet each other with a lingering embrace, that brings to this simple act of being the one she will look for when she arrives home an intimacy we don't share at any other time. Even if it is a one-sided intimacy. Even if it ends as soon as she sees me, smiles and gives me a companionable hug.

The difference between defending the status quo and being stuck in a rut is a subtle one, I acknowledge that. I even acknowledge that there are times when it is indistinguishable. Sometimes I think even I would do anything to shatter the complacency that is at the core of my relationship with Hope, including something completely out of character. Which is why it was my intention to tell her about Angie even before Angie and I had our first date last night. The backup plan was to tell her at the airport tonight, then in the car on the way to the restaurant, then during dinner. But all of that was planned when I'd still assumed that what I had to tell her would be more straightforward and less open to interpretation than it is. I've hardly ever lied to Hope or invented stories to impress her or make her jealous – largely because I was afraid if I started I wouldn't be able to stop – but, frankly, it's becoming more and more of a temptation. It may be the only way I can expect a reaction from her.

The orange-haired clown, tired of making children cry, tries to entertain us instead. He hops up to us, squeezes a bicycle horn in our faces, and then turns and wraps his arms around himself, his white-gloved hands caressing his neck.

'What a clown,' I say and Hope laughs, despite herself.

'It's been a long day,' she says, walking with me toward the exit to the mall, looking contrite, extinguishing her cigarette in an ashtray on the way out. 'I do have to quit. Soon. It is a dangerous habit.'

It's not in Hope's nature to stay mad at me for long, although there are times I wish she would. Times when I wish she'd tell me to fuck off and leave her alone. Instead she shrugs. This is a familiar gesture by now. Her narrow shoulders lift and with them the upper half of her long-waisted body rises slightly. Then her thin top lip curls upward into a rueful smile which she holds in place with the concentrated effort a child expends holding its breath. Her pale gold eyes, her pretty brow are next to ascend, raised like a question.

I shrug back and, as always, stare into her golden eyes too long, so long that she is, as always, the first to look away. Sometimes, we will spend a whole evening together this way – with me staring at her sympathetic, regretful face and with her looking resolutely away.

'Take one,' I say, forcing her to glance in my direction again, offering her first choice of the two fortune cookies.

'Let's not and say we did,' she says, dropping both cookies into her purse like spare change.

Every so often her message or mine will be enough to change the course of our evening. The last three times we've been at the Happy Garden, for example, she drew the same prediction: BE ALERT TO POSSIBILITY RIGHT BEFORE YOUR EYES.

While she shrugged it off the first and second time, calling it a coincidence, the third time it took her until two o'clock in the morning to explain to me that we couldn't sleep together on the basis of what was revealed in a fortune cookie.

Hope may be resolute, but she's not unfeeling. I know it's hard for her to have to reject me every other month, but the truth is it has become a habit for her. She tried, at first, to be diplomatic, to provide excuses which would make it easier for me to accept the situation. But, as she has correctly pointed out, 'Who expected this to go on so long?'

I know what she means. How can you calculate persistence? How do you gauge it? How much is too much? Is there a line between perseverance and self-delusion and how do you know when you've crossed it?

Take Joseph Alter, for example: while I expected him to be angry at me, I never expected him to hate me as much as he has for as long as he has. I never expected his anger to escalate to the point where he would be capable of anything. I remember from my days teaching him to play football that he was nearsighted and refused to wear glasses because he thought he looked enough like a nerd already. Now, he probably doesn't wear glasses because he believes God will make sure he sees whatever he needs to see. My guess is that he thought Angie's red car was my red car. What I can't guess is what he is likely to do once he realizes his mistake.

* * *

'It's been a long, hot day,' Hope says, rubbing her eyes and yawning.

In fact, it's still early. The sun hasn't set yet; it's as bright and orange as the clown's wig. The cool temperatures of the night before have been replaced by the kind of stifling humidity that is an inevitable part of summer in Montreal. Days change dramatically here, without warning. Hope has been complaining about the heat and yawning ever since I came up with an excuse for stopping off at my house before driving her back into the city. I said that I had to make sure I'd locked the swimming pool ladder to the back fence. I explained that there had been a rash of break-ins and vandalism in the neighbourhood.

'Swimming without permission?' Hope asked.

'It could happen. I'm responsible if someone drowns.'

Hope has heard my excuses before. All of them transparent, all of them designed so I can extend my time alone with her; all of them so preposterous that Hope can persuade me to abandon them just by yawning. Normally, I take the hint and make it easy for her to go home early, except I don't intend for this to be a normal evening.

'Come in for a little while,' I say, pulling into the driveway and punching the remote control gadget that opens the garage door.

'It's too hot and I'm too tired. Do I really have to?'

'You're not tired. You're just saying you are.'

'You know that, do you?' She sighs and smiles wearily.

'You always say it.'

48

'You're exaggerating?'

'Just come in for a little while. Besides, this is the suburbs, there's air conditioning.' What always surprises me is how easy it is to be in love with Hope, even though there is no possibility she will return my feelings. I know it should be hard to keep this one-sided relationship up, I even like to tell Hope how hard it is, but, honestly, it isn't. Honestly, I don't know what I would do if I had to stop loving her, cold turkey.

'A little while?' She shrugs at me and gives me an exasperated look, the one that says, *Please, not this again, not the same thing over and over again.* But tonight I feel immune to her frustration. I'm too busy trying to decide how much I can tell her about last night: how much will be to my advantage. Tonight, I am a man with a plan.

'Too late, you're in,' I say as I roll into the garage and punch the remote control again to close the door behind us. The Mitzvah Mobile, which is parked in front of Joseph's house, disappears from my rear view mirror. I'm not taking any chances; I won't risk leaving my car outside in plain view.

I decide to tell Hope everything about last night, up to a point, and then just not tell her any more. Which is not lying, really; it's more like revising, editing. I'll leave out the part about Angie's windshield ... about the note ... about ...

Betrayal is not the right word anyway. Not for what I did to Joseph. It was a misunderstanding. I made choices about which part of his story I'd tell and which part I'd omit. Editorial choices – it wasn't anything more sinister than that.

And it's not as if I planned any of it. If anything I put off attending Joseph's 'The Art of Living Jewishly'course for as long as I could. I avoided him for months, which wasn't easy, since he lives across the street. As an excuse, I used the fact that I couldn't get an okay for the column from Ted Severs, managing editor at the *Snooze*. I explained to Joseph, during one of his daily telephone calls, that Ted was in and out of the hospital and was unable to take care of anything except the most urgent matters. That was true, too, up to a point. Ted Severs had been hospitalized, but he wasn't exactly ill. Instead, he was in the process of becoming Trish Severs.

'I was one of those women you read about or see on talk shows who go through life trapped in a man's body,' Ted, now Trish more or less, explained when I visited him in the hospital last December. At the time, the trouble over the column I'd written about Joseph had just surfaced and Ted wanted to see me so she could apologize for not being more diligent in proofreading and editing my copy. She wanted to explain why she'd let it go through practically unchanged.

'I was preoccupied,' Ted said. Sitting in an armchair beside her unmade hospital bed, she would frequently shift in her seat – an expression more of surprise than pain on her face.

'I understand,' I said, sitting on a cushionless visitor's chair on the opposite side of the bed.

As a man, Ted was tall and extremely thin. As a woman, Ted is less wraithlike, more substantial. Even so, she was hard to locate in her chair, surrounded by a dozen or so pillows, propped up against her like sandbags against the deluge. Wearing a blue tartan bathrobe and matching men's slippers, she was, she told me, taking things slow at first. Which explains why she had very little make-up on, except for a trace of blue eye shadow and some lavender lipstick on the corners of her mouth. Her short, chewed fingernails were painted, a little erratically, to match her lips. As haphazard as her appearance was, she still looked as if she'd spent a lot of time preparing for my visit. My guess was she didn't have many visitors.

'You see, even then the Teddy side of me was still very confused about what the Trish side had in store for him – about the operation. You know something, Jacob, it's not what most people, most men, think. Nothing's cut off exactly –'

'You don't have to …'

'Just redesigned, pushed in, kind of,' she continued, laughing self-consciously, clapping her long, narrow hands to the sides of her face in a familiar Jack Benny-like gesture, the kind Ted Severs would use when he was amused by something in one of my 'Up Next!' or 'Ask Your Therapist' columns, usually something I hadn't meant to be amusing.

Look, I'm not that unsophisticated, not that easily shocked. It's not just that drastic changes make me light-headed, it's that I don't understand them – the point of them. And I don't understand what is required of me when other people decide, unilaterally, to change the way everything has been up until now.

So what was I supposed to do – kiss Ted on both cheeks when I saw her? And what, for instance, was I supposed to bring somebody in the hospital for that particular operation? The one where nothing is cut off, just pushed in. Flowers? Cigars? Chocolates? Magazines? Which magazine: *GQ*? *Ms.*? *Cosmopolitan*? *Chatelaine*? I decided on *Vanity Fair*; I also bought a tiny white stuffed bear named Tuffy in the hospital gift shop and placed it on the edge of Ted's unmade bed. Then I shook just the fingers of her hand as she cautiously raised herself up to greet me.

'Jacob, whatever my personal problems were at the time, I should never have let them interfere with my work. My mind wasn't on my job and now you're the one suffering because of it. That's not fair and that's not the way I want to begin my new life.'

'Forget it.'

'How can I? I felt I had to talk to you before you made any decisions about your future with the paper,' she said, cradling the bear in her redesigned lap.

'I'm not sure I ever had a future with the paper.'

'Life is not a dress rehearsal, Jacob.'

'I'll try to keep that in mind, Ted.'

'I know this is hard for you to get used to,' Ted said, after a long pause, 'but my name is Trish now.'

You know what's hard for me? Believing people when they say they've changed their lives, when they tell me everything is different now from the way it used to be. How is that possible? How can they say it and mean it?

* * *

Last November Joseph became frustrated with my stalling tactics and went over my head and Ted Severs's head, too, and spoke directly to the chairman of the *Snooze's* board of directors. The chairman, a retired orthodontist, was still adjusting to the fact that the man he'd hired to be his managing editor was becoming a woman. He left a message on my answering machine informing me that if I had, in fact, promised this Alter guy a column then I should go ahead and do it already.

Which is why I showed up at the Court Séjour Community Centre on a damp evening in November with my note pad and tape recorder and a plan to write a flattering piece about how a young, determined rabbinical student was helping his own generation rediscover their faith and find their way back to Judaism. The working title for the column was 'Joseph's Dream'.

The Community Centre is walking distance from my house. It was, before the demographics of Court Séjour changed irrevocably, an elementary school, my elementary school. Now, the two-story building serves a steadily aging population: offering Israeli folk dancing, self-improvement courses, and an annual adult education lecture series on the future of the Jewish community in Quebec. Predictably, attendance drops every year.

'You are late, Glassman. I was beginning to doubt your existence,' Joseph said, meeting me at the entrance, taking hold of my elbow and hurrying me through the narrow, familiar hallway.

'This place hasn't changed much.'

'I would not know,' Joseph said. 'I attended Hebrew school.'

'You did? I always thought you went to school here like the rest of us.'

'Of course not,' Joseph said abruptly, ushering me into a classroom that might have been my classroom twenty-five years ago. 'I am afraid you have missed a great deal over the last twelve weeks,' he went on reproachfully. 'You have, for one example, missed my commentary on the Book of Job. The gist of my argument being that the story of Job is truly a document for our time. Have you read *When Good Things Happen to Bad People*? By Rabbi Harold S. Kushner? No? You should.'

'Joseph, this is no big deal: I'm going to put you in my column so you don't have to worry about it and you don't have to sell me, all right?'

'You are approaching this with the wrong attitude, Jacob, as always.'

'What's that supposed to mean?'

'It means what it means. As you should already know, it is the fifty-sixth anniversary of Kristallnacht tonight and I will be putting this horrific event into context. So you see, despite your procrastination, despite your attitude, you have chosen to be here on a truly consequential evening.'

A fact that was not immediately apparent by the attendance. There were just eight students sitting behind miniature desks in a classroom meant for forty third-graders. They were all in their late twenties, Joseph's age, with one exception. Joseph gave me a challenging look, as if to say, *That's right. There are just the nine of us, ten with you, enough for a minyan, so make something out of it.*

I recognized the one older student as Neil Topaz, the owner of the Chinese Shminese restaurant. He was sitting in the last row, wearing, like the others, a crocheted skullcap held in place by a large silver bobby pin. The similarity ended there. While his classmates looked nondescript, dressed in black suits and white shirts with yellowing collars and ties as wide as a fist, Neil Topaz looked sharp. Sharpened, in fact. He was a sleek figure, his hair just long and just grey enough to look as if he never stopped fussing with it. He was wearing a tan suit, a powder blue button-down shirt with cuff links shaped like the Hebrew letter *chai* and a blue silk tie that was decorated with a Marc Chagall print – a levitating violinist. He was also talking into a cellular phone. I nodded to him and as soon as he recognized me he folded up his cellular, tucked it inside his jacket pocket and got up from behind his tiny desk to shake my hand vigorously.

'Well, well, well, it's been a long time. Alter's been talking about you showing up one of these days. It's good to see you,' he said, tightening his grip, his thick gold wedding band digging into my palm. 'I never thanked you properly for that write-up you gave the restaurant. And me. You really started the old matzoh ball rolling.'

'It was nothing. Don't mention it.'

Behind me, I could hear Joseph clearing his throat, so I pulled free of Neil Topaz's grip. But as I looked for a seat at the back of the classroom, he continued his side of the conversation:

'Another thing I never thanked you for was putting that TV producer on my trail. She's doing pretty good for herself these days. A real ... dynamo. But then I don't have to tell you, do I? I've seen that show of hers a couple of times, too. I feel kind of responsible, being her first interview and all. It's good to see good things happen to good people, isn't it?'

I tried to smile nonchalantly, but it probably came out looking more like a squint. Neil Topaz was a confident man and confident men play havoc with my posture. I can feel my shoulders slouching, the muscles in my back tightening. As much as I want to believe they have a side of themselves, a concealed side, that is timid and full of insecurities, frankly, I never manage to remain in their company long enough to see it. Trying to make small talk with them can be especially painful, so I was grateful that before I had to come up with a reply about Hope and her success, Joseph began coughing again, even more conspicuously.

'I'll catch you later,' Neil Topaz said, winking.

But he didn't. I left immediately after Joseph's three-hour seminar on suffering and misery, which was, as it turned out, full of his own suffering and misery. I didn't stay to talk to Topaz or anyone else afterwards because I couldn't think of a single thing to say. Later that night when Joseph called to find out where I had disappeared to, I tried to let him down easy. I told him I didn't think the column would work out after all. It was, I said, a little too religious for a community newspaper like the *Court Séjour News*. 'I'd be happy to put in a couple of paragraphs about the program and about your course, in particular, but that's the best I can do. You know as well as I that we don't have as many Jewish readers as we used to.' Thankfully, Joseph hung up before I was forced to come up with any more excuses.

Early the next morning, Ted Severs called to relay a message from the newspaper's chairman of the board. 'The message is: 'Just write it. Get this guy off our back,' Ted said, his voice becoming noticeably higher each day.

So I wrote it. I could have concentrated on the history lesson Joseph began the lecture with. How Kristallnacht wasn't just another pogrom – like the ones that had convinced my grandparents and his that it was time to leave Russia and come to Canada at the turn of the century – how it was really the dress rehearsal for the Holocaust. But I didn't. This is what I wrote instead:

Joseph's Dream
By Jacob Glassman

Rabbinical student Joseph Alter believes it's high time other Jews his age learned just what it means to be Jewish.

Alter, 27, is practising what he preaches. In addition to his own studies of the Talmud and a Master's thesis on the Book of Job which he hopes to complete some time next year, he is teaching a course called 'The Art of Living Jewishly' at the Court Séjour Community Centre (CSCC).

Alter's course is part of a larger Jewish Instructional Program (JIP) held at the CSCC which offers weekly classes in keeping kosher and observing the Sabbath. According to Russell Mintz, the 43-year-old JIP administrator, the program is filling a real need in a community that has seen its Jewish population dwindle dramatically in the last two decades.

For Alter, teaching one of the JIP courses affords him an opportunity to make people understand fully what it was like to be a Jew at the worst of times.

'I know what suffering is and I want the people who take my course to know too. *Mensch tracht und Gott lacht.* That means, Man plans and God laughs,' Alter explained, referring to his pronounced limp, caused by 'a congenital orthopedic problem.'

The evening I sat in on Alter's course was also the anniversary of Kristallnacht (the Night of Broken Glass) and I watched as Alter demonstrated his unorthodox lecturing methods. He began by draping a prayer shawl over his head and, despite his disability, climbing on top of a stepladder and shouting and sobbing, 'Oh my God, we are betrayed. They are going to kill us all. We are all going to die.'

Alter's shouts and sobs succeeded in attracting the attention of administrator Mintz who came into the classroom and requested that Alter 'get down from that ladder, and return it to the janitor, for God's sake, before you hurt yourself.' As Mintz explained later, 'Mr Alter sometimes gets carried way. This program is not about suffering per se. It's meant to demonstrate how practical being Jewish is for young people today.'

According to Mintz, all you need to know about living a successful life is available to you in the Talmud. Mintz, a Court Séjour realtor, added that he once passed an examination for which he was unprepared by drawing on his knowledge of Talmudic land law. 'So go figure,' Mintz said. 'What I want to impress on the young Jews who have remained in this community is that being Jewish flat out makes sense.'

Mintz also suggested that 'Mr Alter may not be as far along in his thesis on the Book of Job as he sometimes says he is. I promise I'll talk to him about what went on the other night.'

Although Alter declined to comment on the progress of his thesis, he did say that we cannot continue to deny that life is suffering. 'If I have a plan, it is to make the people who take my course realize this.... If I was carried away in my class, it is because I see people around me deceiving themselves all the time and deception is not the way of the Lord.'

Of course, the question then becomes: Is Joseph Alter deceiving himself as well? Like so many people who feel betrayed by life, who feel damaged or somehow left out, Alter clings to the odd promise of religious salvation as if it were some kind of magic formula. Asked if this was true in his case, Alter had no comment.

–30–

Do I even have to add that I never expected the column to run, especially the way it was written, especially the final paragraph? But it struck a chord with Ted Severs who had spent his entire adult life deceiving himself, and was, as a result, growing breasts. He proofread my copy for spelling errors, okayed it and entered it into the computer. He came up with the headline himself: RABBINICAL STUDENT ONLY FOOLS HIMSELF.

* * *

It's possible that the reason none of my plans to get Hope interested in me have worked yet is because I haven't come up with the right one. Before I blurt out that I spent last night with my best friend's wife, Hope is, in fact, on her way out the door to wait for me to back the Malibu out of the garage. When I finally do blurt it out it sounds like a terrible secret I've been guarding. Which is perhaps why Hope steps back inside the house, frees a brochure from the mail slot where it has been stuck all day, walks past me to the kitchen, takes a diet Sprite out of the refrigerator, sits down at the kitchen table and drums her fingers expectantly.

'Selling?' she says, handing me the brochure which has a smiling photo of Russell 'Rusty' Mintz on the cover. Below his picture a question is printed in big block letters in French and English: FAITES COMME VOS VOISINS? DO YOU LIKE YOUR NEIGH- BOURS? Inside, the brochure there is a list of the thirty-three houses Rusty has sold in the area since 1991. Six of the addresses listed and underlined in red ink are on my block. Rusty's business card is stapled to the brochure and his home phone number is scribbled on it in red ink. He is covering all his bases.

Ever since I interviewed him last November at the Court Séjour Community Centre, Mintz has been trying to sell my house. If he was ever upset about my column on Joseph or the JIP, he never let on. I keep telling him I'm not interested in moving, but he doesn't seem to be able to take no for an answer. He phones every weekend to make sure I haven't changed my mind.

'All right, so out with it. What happened?' Hope asks.

'Nothing... I'm not selling the house. This guy just doesn't believe me when I tell him so. When I say no, when I repeat it, he says my no sounds like a yes. He calls Saturday mornings. Sundays. I think he's got one of those deals where if he makes one more sale he wins a free trip to Bali or Tahiti or some place. It's hard to imagine anyone being that persistent and at the same time that obtuse –'

'I'm not talking about the house, Jacob. I know you're not selling the house. I'm talking about last night. How did it go? With Angie?'

'Oh, that. That went okay.'

'That's all. That's all you're saying. Dear Diary: It went okay. Men!' It's difficult to describe how irresistible Hope looks when she is genuinely interested in what I am saying. I guess that's why I'm always trying to think of things to surprise her with. I'm not deceiving myself; I know I can't make her jealous, but I can at least make her curious.

'To tell you the truth, I don't feel right talking about this.'

'Then why did you bring it up?'

'Sandy is my best friend, after all.'

'It never sounded to me like you even like him.'

'That's beside the point. I mean I was his best man and we've been

57

friends for as long as I can remember. He's an okay guy, really. And this is wrong. But it also feels out of my control somehow – you know?'

'I do.'

'And it's not a feeling I like. Or at least one I'm used to.'

'I know,' Hope says and then becomes quiet.

I take the fact that she isn't giving me advice, or telling me what her latest shrink would say about all this, as a hopeful sign. I'm also grateful she isn't asking for details because I'm still trying to decide which ones to leave out.

* * *

Should I tell her, for example, that once Angie and I were in the master bedroom last night, the telephone began to ring again and this time when I wouldn't answer it, Angie stared at me as if she knew the reason why? And that when it kept on ringing, she shook her head, convinced she knew who was calling?

'How long has this been going on?' Angie asked.

'What?'

'How long has he known about us?'

'Who?'

'You know who.'

'No, Angie, I don't know and neither do you. You just think you know, but that's not the same as knowing, not in this case, believe me.'

'What does that mean?'

'That's not Sandy calling. Sandy didn't break your windshield. Or leave that note. He doesn't know anything about us.'

'Stop that. Why do men feel obliged to protect each other?'

'Maybe I should just disconnect the phone.'

'No, let it ring.'

'Are you going to be able to ignore it?'

'I'm going to try,' she said, pushing me backward onto the bed.

'Me too,' I said, clasping my hands around her wrists and pulling her down on top of me, her body falling onto mine like a wide, warm comforter.

Should I tell Hope, for example, that we couldn't ignore the telephone's persistent ring after all? Should I describe how Angie sprang back up a moment after she lay down, like an image rewinding on videotape?

'Maybe I'll just answer it,' she said, pacing in a semicircle around the bed, occasionally glancing down at me. 'Maybe I'll just do that. If he has something to get off his chest, then let him just go ahead and do it.'

'I don't think that's a good idea,' I said. Then I surprised myself by laughing out loud.

'This is not funny.'

Angie was right. It wasn't funny, not from her point of view anyway. She couldn't have understood that what I was laughing at was the thought of her telling Joseph Alter – before he had a chance to interrupt with an appropriate quote from Exodus or the Book of Job – that she'd fuck whomever she pleased whenever she pleased and that if he didn't like it, he could just go fuck himself. Oh yeah, one more thing, he was paying for the fucking windshield.

Finally, should I tell Hope that while the telephone kept ringing nothing happened between Angie and me? Or that when Angie did stop pacing, she sat down again on the edge of my parents' bed – so close to the edge I worried she might fall off – and spoke in a voice so hushed, I thought for a moment there might be someone eavesdropping in the next room?

In profile, Angie looked different: not exactly less appealing, but less substantial. Her most impressive features are three-dimensional ones. She's at her best when she's coming at you. Or walking away.

'This is so – embarrassing. Here I am – thirty-four years old – and I feel like a teenager breaking curfew – You know I've only been with one man – which, I guess, makes you the second – Or it will – Oh fuck!' Angie said, breaking up her speech so that it would fit between the pauses when the phone stopped ringing and when it was about to ring again.

'It's like I'm starting over again … sexually?' Angie continued, hurrying. 'It's as if suddenly everything is possible? – So yes, sure, I know what I want one particular moment – But then the next moment what if I want something else – you know? – I mean what happened tonight could mean that he still cares about me – in a completely unhealthy sort of way, all right – but still. And what's happening here – between us? – What happens next? – Are you going to be number two? – Geez, I'm sorry Jacob, that came out wrong – At least, you're not laughing any more.'

The telephone stopped ringing eventually. After eleven minutes. Par for the course for Joseph, though it was unusual for him to be calling on a Friday night (an orthodox Jew, Joseph is not permitted to use a telephone on the Sabbath, let alone a sledgehammer). Then again, as Joseph could attest, there are precedents for this sort of thing in the Old Testament – for piety taking a back seat to vindictiveness. Even God puts a premium on revenge.

The silence was welcome, liberating. But I also felt as if I was back at square one – as if I should be holding my breath, crossing my fingers, so I could return Angie and me to where we were before the interruption, before all the evening's interruptions, before I started feeling queasy and light-headed.

'Tell me what you want right now, right this moment, Angie?' I said, struggling to my knees on the bed, propping myself up against her to keep my balance and combat my dizziness, my hand stroking the back of her neck.

'I want a station wagon. A Volvo station wagon with an integrated child seat in the back,' she said, leaning across me to switch off the reading lamp on the night table beside the bed. Then she also got up on her knees, slipped off her emerald halter top and kissed me. This was our first kiss since my brother's party and since I was never convinced that that one counted, coming, as it did, on New Year's Eve, this was our first kiss with genuine possibility attached to it – possibility acting like ... like what? A cold shower. The kiss was, in other words, a disaster.

* * *

'I have something to tell you, Jacob and I don't know how,' Hope says. 'I don't even think I should tell you. No, that's not true. I know I shouldn't tell you.'

Hope is convinced she knows me better than I know myself and that's part of the problem between us. She's convinced there's nothing I can say or do that will surprise her. And so far nothing has. I told her, for example, that I was ghostwriting Dr Howie's column and she nodded as if she had suspected it all along. I told her I was writing terms papers for lazy or illiterate university students and she frowned, but still took the news in stride. I told her once that I had punched a woman in the face and broken her nose and she didn't even blink. 'It's not something I'm proud of,' I said, 'but it happened, you know.'

It never happened. I told Hope this to transform my image in her eyes. I was tired of being viewed as harmless and safe. I wanted to surprise her, startle her – to have her think I was the kind of man who was capable of anything, including striking a woman. What I was, in actuality, was the kind of man who was capable of pretending to be the kind of man who would strike a woman. When I eventually told Hope the truth – that I'd made the whole thing up for her sake – she just smiled and said she'd figured as much.

And that's the real reason I'm keeping quiet about what happened or didn't happen between Angie and me. Because if I do tell her, I know that Hope will just smile or nod. I know what she will think – she will think, Typical.

Of course, I also know her well enough to know that she's not going to be able to keep her secret for long. So I'm patient. I wait as she gets up and stretches, lifting her arms over her head, then swiveling her hips back and forth. A former aerobics instructor, still a dedicated jogger, Hope stretches the way other people pace or perspire. As a way of killing time until you finally have to deal with the things you'd rather not deal with.

'Give me a hint,' I say.

'This isn't twenty questions. This is serious,' Hope says, leaning over to touch her toes.

'Is it animal? vegetable? or mineral? Is it bigger than a breadbox? Is it your job? Are you leaving town? Are you in love?'

'I'm sorry I brought this up.'

'That's it. You're in love. Is it me? Because if it is, tell me, I'll want to make a note of it in my agenda.'

'I'm pregnant,' Hope says, jogging in place.

I guess I love everything about Hope except this – this uncanny knack she has for topping me, for somehow knowing when I have something important to say and revealing her own, more important information first.

'Preg – Nant?' I say, splitting the word in half, as if it were too difficult to pronounce whole.

Hope stands still and nods. Her expression is so doleful, so beseeching that it occurs to me that the reason she's finding it so hard to tell me this is because I am responsible. Technically speaking, that's impossible. Still, once it's in my head, the thought won't budge.

'How did this happen? How could this happen?'

'Nothing is foolproof,' Hope says, shrugging.

'All right, who is it? Who's the guy?'

Hope stares at me. She begins to speak, but stops. Begins, then stops again. Each time I'm more convinced it is my name she's about to say. 'It's you, Jacob,' she'll say. 'Don't ask me how it happened? It just did.' And I'll say, 'Nothing's impossible.'

While Hope struggles with how to break this extraordinary news to me, I'm already thinking about how I will, in turn, explain it to Angie. She's Catholic, so I'm hoping she'll understand miracles. She'll understand that you can't plan them and that when they come along you can't ignore them. It's not as if anything actually happened between Angie and ...

'Neil,' Hope says finally and lights a cigarette, another first here in this house. I have asked her not to smoke in my house or car and she's always been careful to obey my wishes. She thinks it's because the smoke makes my eyes water. That's not it, not exactly. What I don't want is the odour lingering, reminding me of her after she's gone – reminding me of all the times she's not here. When she realizes she's lit the cigarette she holds it up apologetically and steps out onto the back porch.

This is the problem with keeping a journal – it makes you look foolish. Especially in retrospect. It's designed to. For example, do I have to put everything down, not just everything that happens to me, but everything I feel? John Cheever did and it didn't just make him look foolish, it made him look unworthy of his reputation: petty and sad and, to use his own description, wayward.

The long summer twilight has finally slipped into darkness; the lawn in the backyard looks greener and lusher at night. Hope is sitting cross-legged on an old, pillowless redwood deck chair on the patio, streams of blue smoke drifting above her head like a caption in a cartoon, a caption that reads, 'Didn't see that one coming, did you?'

My parents used to sit out in the backyard on summer mornings and talk. They were always waking me up and I was always banging on the window to make them stop. They would, but only temporarily. Then they would begin to whisper again and inevitably their voices would rise and I'd be unable to sleep, staying awake, straining to hear what they were talking about. I couldn't imagine then or now – especially now – what they had to say to each other day after day.

'Neil who?' I ask Hope. But the question is ridiculous. I know the answer, but all I can think of is that she's done it again, topped me. 'Not that Neil. Not the one I introduced you to. Tell me it's not him. Tell me it's Neil Armstrong? or Neil Young? or Neil Sedaka?'

'I knew you were going to react like this ... Neil Sedaka?'

'Never mind.'

'And I knew I shouldn't have told you.'

'You're right about that.'

'But there's something I can't explain between us, a sort of wham pow,' she says, clapping her hands. 'It's been going on for more than a year. I was in love with him. I think I might still be.'

'How can you say that? This guy is despicable. I hate everything he stands for.' I can still hear the words 'wham pow' as clearly as if she were repeating them over and over again. I suspect I will keep hearing them for a long time.

'What are you talking about, Jacob? You don't even know what he stands for. He doesn't stand for anything. Who stands for things? Besides you don't hate him, you admire him, you said so yourself.'

'I do not. Maybe I wrote in my column that I admire him, that what he did on that trip to China was admirable, in an obvious sort of way, but I didn't mean any of it. I never mean what I write. If you had told me this about anyone else I would have –'

'What? Rejoiced?'

'All right, I would have acted the same way. But this I hate. Really. Hate.'

'Don't do this to me, okay?' Hope says, lying flat on the redwood chair, covering her face with her hands. In the dark, the flaws I always search for – the sharpness of her chin, a bit of fuzz above her lip – at the worst times, times like this when I want to give up this ridiculous relationship, vanish and I am left with just my idea of Hope. That and the news that she is pregnant by another man.

I wait for her to sit up again before I say, 'He's married too. Of course, he is. We met his wife, both of us, that night at the restaurant opening. She's a wonderful woman, don't you remember? You interviewed her.'

'Don't point your finger at me, okay?'

'They have children.'

'They don't have children.'

'All right, but she is wonderful. She took in that Chinese-Jewish-refugee-chef-kid and treated him like he was part of the family. He stayed with them for some ridiculous amount of time – eight months or eighteen months – remember? I could look it up. It's in my files.'

'Don't you think I know all of this?'

'She taught him how to make matzo balls, for God's sake.'

'Okay then, I know she's wonderful. Wives are wonderful. Every last one of them.'

Hope has what she calls a track record with married men. She had just broken up with one when we first met. She told me then that she'd been involved with this guy for almost a year when she realized that they'd never eaten a meal together. When she mentioned this to him, he ordered a pizza on his car phone and had it delivered to the motel where they were planning to spend the evening. She made him stop the car and let her out. She took a taxi home.

That first night we met, at the opening of Chinese Shminese, Hope also shared her shrink's 'magic cunt theory' with me. I remember I choked on the miniature egg roll I was eating and she had to run into the kitchen to get me a glass of water.

'My trouble,' she continued, patting me on the back, 'is not that I'm attracted to unattainable men, though it's true I am. It's that I think I can make them attainable by sleeping with them. It never works, of course, but I can't stop believing it will. It's crazy, so you don't have to tell me.'

Hope's capacity for openness inspires openness in others. Although this quality makes her a natural to host a television talk show and accounts for her success in her career, it's also a burden – this ability to make people say things they are certain to regret later. That night we met, for example, I told her that if it was any consolation, I believed in her 'magic cunt theory'; I have regretted telling her so ever since.

'Matzo balls!' I say again, shouting it out into the humid night air like a curse. 'Remember his wife told me that story about the matzo balls for my column? I didn't use it, but it was a wonderful, poignant moment. Remember? She said that the Chinese-Jewish-refugee-chef-kid cried when he saw her matzo balls floating in her soup and she asked him why he was crying and he said that they were just like dumplings. And she said, "You know, young man, people are a lot like dumplings. We're all the same, we're just called by different names." I'm paraphrasing. But I could look it up.'

'I told you not to point your finger at me,' Hope says, rising from the redwood chair and slapping at my hand. Then she goes back into the house, slams the back door and locks it.

'I'm only telling you this for your own good, Hope. It won't work,' I shout at the closed door.

'I know that. Do you really think I don't?' she says, shouting down at me from the kitchen window. 'Only you have no business talking to me that way. Every night I write here ... here,' she holds up her battered, burgundy Filofax and waves it in the window, 'that this is another day I continued to do what I promised myself I wouldn't. So I don't have to hear it from you. Not from someone who is supposed to be my friend.

'Some friend you are. You don't have time to be my friend. You're too busy being in love with me. A fat lot of good that does me. I don't need someone else to be in love with me. You think I'm not worried – about what I'm supposed to do now, about what happens next? You think it's not keeping me up nights? Only that's not your problem, is it? Because you love me. How nice for you. How nice and safe, just like living here in this house. Living here like an orphan, like some thirtysomething Oliver Twist. Well, I'm sorry, but to hell with you.'

I can see her stretching in front of the kitchen window now. Pushing her arms up above her head, her hands locked. Doing jumping jacks. She stops and takes a cigarette out of her purse, but she doesn't light it. Instead she opens the window screen and throws a fortune cookie at me.

'There, Jacob, go ahead and read it to me. Wait, let me guess, it says: BE ALERT TO POSSIBILITY RIGHT BEFORE ... and so on and ecetera. Did you really think I didn't know you were behind that? Forcing that poor man to put that message inside. Who did you think you were fooling?

'And this big date of yours yesterday. Well, did something happen or not? Not is my guess. What's the real story? You know the truth, the facts. Did you sleep with your best friend's wife? Or did you stay up all night watching old movies? Don't tell me, let me guess: *The Apartment*. Shirley MacLaine. Jack Lemmon.'

Do you know what I'd like to know? I'd like to know whose journal this is anyway? The fortune cookie at my feet breaks in two and for the second time in as many nights Mr Ho has fouled up. The message reads: ADVERSITY SOMETIMES COMES IN DOUBLE DOSES.

'You know what you are, Jacob? No? No answer? Okay, I'll tell you. You are a mama's boy and the dumb part, the really dumb part is you don't even have a mother. So don't talk to me about matzo balls and wonderful wives and don't you ever point your finger at me again,' she says and she throws the second fortune cookie at me. This time I catch it before it hits the ground and I tuck it, unopened, into my back pocket.

* * *

Maybe disaster is not the best word to describe what happened after I kissed Angie. Because now that I am locked out of my house and in possession of new information about Hope and Neil Topaz, tonight feels a lot more like a disaster. That, I'm discovering, is another problem with keeping a journal. You write things down and when you go back to them later, you wonder what you could have been thinking. You wonder how you could have thought things were so bad or good or just so different from the way they actually turned out to be.

Our kiss was too brief, that's all, too caught up with short-term considerations to make a difference. Angie's mouth was slippery, so was the side of her face and the hollow of her neck and her breasts. I found myself sliding down her body, less by design than by an absence of it. And what I didn't know is that I was heading for disappointment.

Disappointment is the better word, the right one.

'It's been a while, Angie, since … between …' I muttered, raising myself up on my elbows.

'It's okay, Jacob. We can go slow. There's lots of time.' But just as she finished reassuring me the telephone, as if on cue, began to ring again.

'I'm answering this time,' Angie blurted out. I watched as she stretched her bare right arm in the direction of the night table. She lifted the phone and I couldn't even say stop, couldn't even speak, because my teeth were, at that instant, attached to a small nub of flesh that extended from her belly button. I reached up to stop her, but I never made it. Instead, I stumbled face first into the hard space between her breasts.

'Ouch.'

'Sorry.'

She waved away my apology and lifted the phone to her ear. She didn't speak, she just listened, concentrated. She looked tentative suddenly, placing her palm over the receiver and handing the phone to me as I struggled back up onto my elbows. I was still off balance when I took it from her and I toppled over again. This time, Angie slipped out of the way.

'It's him. I can't believe it. It really is. He's asking for you,' she whispered. Then she lifted her halter top off the floor and, facing away from me, slipped back into it as quickly, as astonishingly, as she had slipped out of it. Gazing at the narrow band of emerald material across Angie's naked back, I couldn't help thinking that this too is a game of inches.

'Who is it?' I asked, still disoriented.

'You can tell him for me he has nothing to say about what I do or who I see any more. He didn't care when we were married, why should he care now?'

'But who is it?'

'Who do you think?'

I had assumed it was Joseph, but it wasn't. It was Sandy. I tightened my hand over the receiver until I realized what Angie would have if she'd just taken another moment to listen. That he didn't know she was with me. He was calling, at two o'clock, Saturday morning, to cancel our Thursday afternoon racquetball game.

'And tell him for me...'

'Angie, please, I can't talk to both of you at the same time,' I said, my hand still clasped over the receiver.

'Then don't,' she said and left the bedroom, slamming the door behind her.

'Jake, hey. Hey, is anyone there? Am I interrupting something?' Sandy said.

'No... Nothing.'

'And tell him he's paying for my fucking windshield,' Angie whispered from the other side of the door.

'If someone's there, I can call back,' Sandy said.

'It's the television. Go ahead. Is anything wrong?'

'No. I was saying I won't be able to make racquetball and I wanted to let you know.'

'Now? Do you know what time it is?'

I can't say I listened to Sandy explaining why he couldn't keep our usual appointment or why he was calling so late at night and so far in advance to tell me about it. For one thing, he was talking fast again, too fast for me to keep up with what he was saying. For another, I was preoccupied with Angie, pacing and whispering behind my door. I remember regretting that she didn't smoke. At least that would have been quieter.

'I can't seem to step outside the condo, Jake.'

'Fine.'

'What do you know about agoraphobia?'

'Okay, Sandy, we'll make it the following Thursday then.'

'Agoraphobia. That's what it's called when you're stuck in one place, right? What can you tell me about it?' Sandy asked, his words sounding like one prolonged buzz. 'I think I might have come down with a slight case and I only seem to be able to get as far as the elevator and then my heart starts pounding and I can't move and I can't seem to take a step forward. I called Howie Weiskopf but he kept asking me if I knew what time it was, though he did say it was probably just an anxiety attack. Post-traumatic stress from the breakup.'

'Post-traumatic stress?'

'Right. I don't think it's serious either. I've just been staying in too much, over-cocooning, you could say.' He laughed nervously. 'Anyway I wanted to let you know about Thursday.' Sandy remained on the line, saying nothing for a long time. His silence proved to be more disconcerting than his chatter.

'Do you want me to come over, Sandy, is that it?' I held my breath, waiting for his answer.

'No, I'll be fine,' he said as I exhaled. 'Dr Weiskopf said it was probably a panic attack. "Small potatoes," he said. Nothing to worry about.'

'Howie is not a doctor, you know that, Sandy, don't you? He just has a BA in psychology and a column in a community newspaper.'

'That's right. You're right. That's why I called him because I can trust him. He's a good man. And a true friend. Like you.'

When I said goodbye I said it loudly. I also made a lot of noise hanging up the receiver. I waited in the bed for ten minutes or so, giving Angie enough time to be sure I was off the phone so she could come back in. But she didn't. Instead, I found her down the hall, in my office. She was working out on the StairMaster, dressed only in her halter top and panties, watching my tape of *The Apartment*.

'He doesn't know about us,' I said, lying down on the couch.

'Then who broke my windshield?'

'That's a long story.'

'Tell me, why is it that everything with you is such a long story?'

On the TV screen Jack Lemmon was waiting in the rain outside a Broadway theatre for Shirley MacLaine. What he didn't know was that she was standing him up to resume her affair with Lemmon's married boss. What she didn't know was that Lemmon's boss was taking her to Lemmon's apartment. Lemmon had swapped the key to his place for tickets to *The Music Man*. Bad timing and missed

69

connections are built into Billy Wilder's plot like a trap door. Both characters lack a crucial piece of information, a solitary fact, that would, if they possessed it, force them to re-evaluate their situation. The irony is that if they had this information, it would make the movie's happy ending virtually impossible.

'If he doesn't know about us, Jacob, then why did he call?' Angie said, as she climbed down from the StairMaster and lay down beside me on the couch. 'What does he want?'

'I'm not sure,' I said. I unfolded a blanket over both of us and Angie tucked her head into the narrow space between my neck and shoulder. She fell asleep before the movie ended happily. I listened to her breathing and I knew exactly what Sandy wanted: he wanted his wife back.

* * *

'I forgot that I wasn't supposed to answer the phone. I'm sorry Jacob.' Hope is holding the back door open with her hip. 'He wants to talk to you. He says it's important.'

The light is on above the back door so that even in the darkness I can make out that Hope's eyes are puffy. Even if Joseph Alter hadn't called, even if she'd remembered not to answer my telephone, she wouldn't have stayed mad at me. She is a pushover – up to a point, of course. Adoring Hope the way I do isn't easy, but being the object of adoration is no picnic either. And while I know she can't return my feelings, she has nevertheless become accustomed to them.

'Tell him I'm not here.'

'He knows you're here, Jacob. He probably saw us drive up.' Hope is bouncing the aluminum screen door off her bottom nervously as if she's developed a twitch.

'Then just hang up.'

'All right.... Jacob, I'm sorry.'

'My crazy neighbours are not your fault.'

'Not about that. About what I said before. I didn't mean it. I shouldn't have told you about Neil, but I couldn't help it. In case you haven't noticed, I tell you everything. I know I shouldn't under the circumstances; I know it was a shitty thing to do under the circumstances. That's what I'm sorry for.' She takes a step towards me and then realizes the door is closing and lunges backwards to stop it.

'Be careful, Hope, or you know what will happen – we will both be on the outside looking in.'

'Oh, Jacob, how come we can make each other so miserable? Don't look like that. Like I'm complimenting you.'

But it was a compliment in a way. I couldn't make her love me, no matter what I did or said, but at least I could make her miserable. I'd have to take that into consideration in any new plan I came up with.

'Jacob, what are we supposed to do with our two broken hearts?' she says in a sputtering voice, somewhere between laughing and crying. If Hope were interviewing me on television this would probably be the moment where I would break down and cry too. Sentimentality is a trap all right.

'Are those hormones talking? I've heard stories about pregnant women losing their minds. I've also heard stories about pregnant women going wild with uncontrollable lust. Just my luck, you go mushy on me.'

'We are best friends, Jacob, real best friends, whether you like it or not, okay? With all the other stuff, we both forget that sometimes. You're the only person I can trust. I need someone I can trust.'

'I know, you have a trust issue.'

'Seriously, I sometimes think I need that more than anything else. Someone who won't let me down or deceive me and, like it or not, that's you. You're the only thing in my life that's consistent, that's dependable.'

'Please, not dependable. Shoot me first,' I say, sighing and sinking to my knees in the wet grass as Hope smiles down at me. There are moments like this when I want to do nothing more or less than put my arms around her. I suppose there are best friends who can do that sort of thing, but it is gradually becoming clear to me that we do not fall into that category.

'You want to know my gut feeling, Jacob: we're stuck with each other. Come in and I'll explain it to you. It won't get us anywhere, but I'll explain it to you anyway. I'll tell you all the reasons why I can't do what I know I should be doing.'

'I'll drive you home soon. It's late... For us. But there's something I have to do first.'

'That's all right, I can wait, only where are you going?'
'There's something I have to take care of.'
'Now?'
'No time like the present.'
As I pass Hope in the doorway she pats me on the back and says,
'Is that really you saying that?'
'The new me. How do you like it?'

* * *

When I woke up on the couch this morning Angie was already waiting for the police to arrive. She was wearing one of my T-shirts over
her halter top – it was already too muggy for her jean jacket – and I
could still see the green fabric through the thin white cotton. She
said that I should go back to sleep, but I didn't. Instead I made coffee
and we waited together, saying nothing to each other.

The officer who filled out the report glanced at Angie's broken
windshield and informed us that there had been a lot of similar
incidents in the area. 'Kids for sure,' Constable Roberge said. 'But
me I never see some things like I see now. Not like when your people
they live here. They were quiet. No trouble like now.'

Constable Roberge then went on to catalogue all the crimes,
minor and major, he had recently witnessed on his beat. He had seen
everything – from shoplifting to extortion.

'It change sure,' he said, turning to Angie.

'I don't live here any more,' she said quickly.

'That's good news for you,' he said, shaking his head and laughing at his own joke.

I shook my head in response, but I'm not convinced he's right
about the neighbourhood. I've heard the stories, of course, and
noticed that they seem to be originating closer and closer to what has
always been my quiet, eventless community. Closer to me. Now, I
am approached for money by dazed kids in oversized trousers at the
dépanneur around the corner. The homeless and the derelict have
also made it to the suburbs. So has prostitution. And sexual assault.
And kidnapping. And murder. Now, I receive flyers in the mail that
offer a ten-thousand-dollar reward for information leading to the
arrest and conviction of the person or persons responsible for fatally

shooting a woman in a nearby parking garage. And it only gets worse: a car bomb exploded near the park at the end of the street the other day. In an adjacent suburb, three teenage boys broke into the house of a retired minister and bludgeoned the minister and his wife to death with a beer bottle and a baseball bat. There are reasons to be concerned, more and more reasons, so why is it that anything unsavoury that happens here still feels like an aberration to me?

Two summers ago we had a break-in at our house. The burglars came in through the kitchen window, using the ladder from our above-ground swimming pool in the backyard. (That's why we have locked the ladder to the back fence ever since.) I remember I got home before my brother, who was still living with me at the time, and somehow I didn't realize what had happened. I didn't notice the footprint in the kitchen sink or the breeze blowing through the open window or the ladder propped up beneath it.

Instead, I blamed the untidiness in my room – open dresser drawers, clothes on the floor and bed – on my brother. I waited for him to come home, rehearsing the argument we were going to have, the one about how if he had to go through my things when I wasn't around he could at least have the courtesy to straighten up afterwards.

'What were you looking for?' I planned to ask him. 'What do you think goes on in here?' I suspected him of trying to find a clue to explain what I did all day, at home, alone. Or, equally puzzling to him, an explanation for why I persisted in seeing a woman who was obviously not attracted to me.

My brother returned home an hour after me. He knew immediately what had happened and called the police. To this day, he still can't figure out how I didn't know we'd been robbed.

In the John Cheever story 'The Housebreaker of Shady Hill', the title character wanders through his neighbours' open screen doors and lifts the cash from their pockets as easily as he would pick weeds from the front lawn. Why? Because he needs the money and because it's just that simple. Because in the suburb of Shady Hill there is no precedent for this sort of action, for stealing from your neighbours. While John Cheever's hero recognizes the advantage of being the one to set the precedent – unlocked entrances, soundly sleeping victims – by the end of the story he also recognizes the danger. Twitching with remorse, he breaks back into his neighbours' houses, this time to replace the stolen money. Our actions, the worst of them, push a hole through the world, Cheever is saying; our actions, the best of them, are meant to stitch up the hole. That's what I believed until I read his journals and understood that the hole is always a gaping one.

Angie left as soon as Constable Roberge completed his insurance report. She said that she was going to try to find a garage where she could have her car repaired.

'Can we try this again?' I said, kissing her through the space where the windshield used to be.

'I guess,' she said, slipping my T-shirt up over her head and handing it back to me. The gesture – the way she crossed her arms at her waist and tugged the shirt over her breasts and then up over her head, uncrossing her arms at the end – made my head spin.

'Don't guess.'

'I don't know.'

'What is it, Angie?'

'We didn't get off to a very auspicious start. I'm not sure.... I mean it's not just this,' she said, pointing to the place where her windshield used to be. 'But you seemed so unsure last night. So reluctant. I had the feeling you didn't want –'

'Of course, I wanted to. Of course, I wanted you.'

'Was it Sandy calling like that? Was that it?'

'No.'

'Is it Hope? Is that the problem.'

'No.'

'Then what, Jacob?'

'I told you it has been a long time between ...'

'I know. For me too.'

'I mean I don't have a lot of experience.... I mean the truth is...'

'We were both nervous. You're right. We'll do this again.'

Angie started the Corolla and I could have let her drive away. I still believe that's what I should have done. But as she shifted her car into reverse I realized that I wanted her to know the truth. I didn't want her to think that the reason nothing happened between us was

Sandy or Hope or the way she looks in profile or anything else she might imagine and blame on herself. I still believed I'd wished her here, wished her right into my bed, after all, so I said, 'The truth is I don't have any experience.'

'What do you mean?' Angie shifted the car back into park with a jolt.

'I mean none at all.'

* * *

I'm keeping my head down as I walk briskly – run really – across the street, catch my breath and take cover for a moment behind the Mitzvah Mobile, then hurry around the side of Joseph Alter's house to his backyard. There's a fence, but the gate opens easily, with only the slightest, gentlest push. A dim light is still on in Joseph's bedroom.

(That's right, as of today, as of this moment, I am a virgin. I never planned to mention it here, in this journal, but maybe I am being too sensitive. Approaching this the wrong way. It does, after all, make me unique. If I wanted to, I could be on Oprah or Rickie Lake or Geraldo tomorrow. They would fly me into Chicago or New York or L.A., put me up at a downtown hotel, and then when I appeared on their show the first question they would ask me is how does a thing like that happen? The audience would jeer and hoot and I would have no explanation, except to say it happens the way everything happens to me, incrementally. First you're eighteen and you know you're going to have sex someday soon, you have to, everyone else has. Then you're twenty-one and you're overdue. You keep asking yourself the same question: what ever happened to the law of averages? Then you're twenty-five, thirty, thirty-five, and sex no longer seems like an option. All your experience centres around the people who were once in your life and no longer are, instead of the people who aren't yet and someday will be. And you get light-headed and queasy the couple of times you have an opportunity, and you find yourself becoming anxious, so anxious you sort of black out. Faint, I guess. Some kind of Virgin Vertigo. So you don't come close any more. Never, in fact, reach the stage where going through with it is even a possibility. And then the whole business becomes a metaphor and you realize you hate metaphors, but that's still what it is – a metaphor for everything you haven't done. Everything you will never do – from flying a kite to getting laid.)

Joseph has a swimming pool in his backyard, an above-ground one like ours with a free-standing ladder. The ladder is just five feet high so I only have to crouch a little to stand under it. Then I lift it out of the water and walk with it balanced on my head right up to Joseph's window.

(*You're an incredibly passive person, is that it?* Geraldo will ask cynically. *On a good day, passive-aggressive,* I'll say. *More like passive-passive,* he'll fire back, inducing a cheer from the bewildered, suspicious crowd, who are all prepared to hoot again but no longer know what point hooting at me would make.)

Water drips on the back of my neck and I can almost taste the chlorine; it's as strong as it used to be when every house on the block had a swimming pool and young children to go along with it. Four rungs up the ladder and I'm eye level with Joseph's ledge. His room is identical to my own. His single bed, like mine, is pushed up against the wall beneath the window. There is a writing desk perpendicular to the bed and a standing lamp on the other side of the desk. The closet is next to the door.

But Joseph's room is more spartan than mine – no television, no stereo, not even a transistor radio I can see. There are books, all hard cover, all unshelved, piled on top of one another on the uncarpeted floor. The walls are bare except for a bright yellow bumper sticker – the kind he has on the Mitzvah Mobile – over Joseph's bed that reads: *Moshiach: Be Part of It!* Beneath the message, in small print, there's a telephone and a fax number to call for additional information on Judgement Day.

(Dr Howie will devote a series of columns to 'Virgin Vertigo.' I'll be a case study in the book he's always planned to write or planned for me to write. Hope will run a segment on 'Been There, Done That', called 'Haven't Been There, Haven't Done That.' Like Kato Kaelin, I will be famous for doing nothing. Strange women will be calling me up and volunteering to be first. But I will insist on maintaining my amateur status. It doesn't count unless it's someone you know. Someone you love.)

Joseph is seated at his desk in a folding chair with his back to the window. The light in the room isn't coming from a lamp. Instead, he's holding a pocket flashlight in one hand; in the other hand he has the telephone receiver pressed up against his ear so tight that it almost looks as if it is a part of him, a natural appendage

The back of his head is shaved and two auburn locks of hair are curled around his ears. He is wearing a black skullcap, white jockey shorts and a fraying white singlet that is damp with sweat. His shoulders and arms are broader, more muscular than I would have expected. As if he had lifted weights once. What hasn't he done to try to find a place for himself? To fit in? (Some of us are better at retreating than others. Some of us take to it naturally.) His black suit and fedora are hanging over the back of another folding chair beside his bed. An aluminum window screen, resting flimsily in its track, is all that separates us from each other.

If I climb up on the top rung of the ladder I know I can force the screen open and I know I can do it without making much noise. It's unlikely Joseph would even hear me over his persistent mumbling. 'Answer,' he is saying, over and over again. He is saying this, I realize, to my disconnected telephone.

I am up at the top of the ladder when Joseph puts down his phone and flashlight, stands, turns and faces me. I raise my arms as if I've been caught committing a crime and latch on to the aluminum rain gutter at the edge of the roof of the house to keep my balance. The fall will be a short one. I'll survive. But how will I explain?

(Which will be one more thing in a long list of things I'm unable to explain. Like how do I tell Hope she has to have her baby? Or Sandy that I didn't have sex with his wife this particular time, but next time I probably will? Or Angie that next time I may become dizzy, may even faint, but that it's no reflection on her? And how do I tell Joseph I am sorry?)

He is staring directly at me now, but he still doesn't notice me. One more thing I can't explain until I realize his eyes are closed, his bare knees are turned in on each other and buckling, his head is rocking back and forth. He has stood and turned to face the West and pray.

He is singing rapidly in Hebrew and speaking intermittently in

English. His fingers are moving constantly, as if he were counting. Even in the dim light I can see a tinge of grey creeping prematurely into his unkempt beard. He looks much older than me as he sinks to his knees, holds his hand over his heart and speaks in a singsong voice:

'For, behold, the Lord will come in fire and harm will be done to His enemies. And His chariots shall be like the whirlwind; to render His anger with fury, and His rebuke with flames of fire.'

Then Joseph whispers an amen and crawls into his single bed, making sure his skullcap is secure. He is restless, still humming like a top, when he realizes he's left the flashlight on. When he rises to switch it off, he finally sees me.

'Glassman,' he says nonchalantly, almost as if he's always been expecting some vision or other at his window, 'do you want to come in?'

'Joseph, I want you to stop doing what you're doing. Calling me. Leaving those messages … and, well, worse. So just stop it. You're acting like a lunatic. Don't you realize that? Don't you see how you're ruining my life?'

'Glassman, I would be remiss if I did not point out to you that at this moment it is you who stands outside my window at – what is it? well past midnight surely – quite uninvited, on a ladder. I presume you are on a ladder. But never mind that, please come in. We can discuss this. You may not realize it, but I am determined to help you.' He continues to totter back and forth as he speaks.

'You're the one who needs help.'

'You are.'

'NO, YOU!'

Joseph shines the flashlight in my eyes and removes a navy blue velvet bag with gold lettering from beneath his pillow. Then he walks towards the window, holding his left hand out, palm flat. 'Come in,' he says again. 'You want to. Why else are you here?'

Why am I here? For a confrontation? Not really. To scare Joseph? I thought so, but no, that's not it. I am here for the sake of my journal, that navy blue three-subject notebook. That's the problem with writing down what happens to you every day, it makes your life look ineffectual. So you write down all the bold things you might do and eventually do them: to prove to yourself you can. In his journals, John Cheever was always boasting about dancing naked on his front lawn. What kind of juvenile thing is that to boast about? Why else would he do it, except to impress himself? To make his journal worth reading? For, God help him, material.

The window screen still divides Joseph and me, but it seems even less sturdy now than before, as if all either of us has to do is blow on it and it will fall away. He puts his flashlight down on the inside ledge and opens the window. It squeaks. Loud enough to wake the neighbours.

'Like me, you are a stranger in a strange land. We were friends once, we can be friends again. Here, come, put on the *tephilim* with me. I will show you how,' he says. From out of the velvet pouch he removes the traditional leather straps and holds them out to me like a parent offering a child a toy. 'You have never done this before, is that it? I understand. I will show you. It is easy. Come. Pray with me. You are lonely, I know. I was lonely too. You have suffered. I have too. I know how hard it is when bad things happen to good people. Like your mother and father. How hard it is to accept.'

'I accept that bad things happen to good people. That good things happen to bad people. That good and bad things happen to people, who are both good and bad. I accept all that. You're the one who doesn't. You're the one who can't leave well enough ... who can't leave me alone.'

'Do not speak so harshly.'

'We're not friends. We never were. I felt sorry for you. I still do.'

'Do not say this, Glassman. It is not true.'

'Besides, I'd be a lot less lonely if you just stopped terrorizing my dates.'

'I am sorry. I thought the car was your car. The colour –'

'And that makes it all right?'

'She is a married woman.'

'How would you know?'

'Adultery is a sin, Glassman. So is fornication.'

'How the fuck would you know?'

'Please, come in, please. If I cannot help you find your way, who can I help? And if I cannot help you now, then when? I had a dream about you. In the dream you came to me, just like this. You were searching, you were yearning,' he says, extending his hand – not to be shaken, it occurs to me, but to be grasped. I forget where I am for an instant and instead of stepping down, I step back ...

I hate slow-motion scenes in movies. Nothing happens in slow motion. I am falling, swearing – Holy shit! – and landing in real time: before I know it, in other words, with barely a moment to figure out how any of this happened. How I got here? How I will get out? I am perilously close to the patio, but I land on my behind on the lawn. The thud is followed by a tiny snap that worries me until I remember the fortune cookie in my back pocket. The grass needs mowing; it is high and it absorbs my fall. I'm okay, fine, I think, until my right heel, the last part of my body to come down, hits the corner of the patio and an old hibachi – who has hibachis any more? – which has probably been placed outside in anticipation of the first summer barbecue. There is a sensation of heat radiating up from my instep to my ankle and then to the back of my leg and I wonder, for a moment, if the hibachi is still lit.

But I can't smell charcoal; I can't smell anything except the grass right under my nose. I am lying face down now, which is all right except I don't remember having had the time or presence of mind to roll over. Then just before all my attention is concentrated on the pain, I look up and see Joseph standing over me, nodding.

'And so prayers are answered,' he says, kneeling down to take my fallen head in his hands.

Two

Answered Prayers

Sunday, September 20. My mother used to say, 'Laugh too much and you'll cry later.' This was a family joke in the Glassman household, also an admonition. It came out of a steadfast belief that you should never take anything for granted. But after my mother died, I couldn't help feeling that, once again, I hadn't been listening. I wasn't a kid fifteen years ago, but I was still young enough to think everything would stop, hold still once she was gone. Of course, nothing did. Me, least of all.

'You think you had a choice? Is that it?' Dr Howie said to me earlier this week when we were discussing an overdue 'Ask Your Therapist' column. We'd been planning a five-part series on the stages of loss – denial, anger, fear, bargaining and acceptance. I already had our question from an imaginary reader written: *Dear Dr Weiskopf: Can you skip a few of the stages? Signed, Looking for a Shortcut* – when we became sidetracked, as usual, talking about me. Something that's been happening more and more often since my accident. My guess is that Dr Howie doesn't have enough clients, which explains why he always seems so interested in what I am experiencing and how I am feeling.

After my accident I decided to give up my 'Up Next!' column at the *Snooze* – as it turns out, the editorial board had been trying to get my byline out of the paper ever since the story I wrote about Joseph appeared – but I couldn't afford to give up the 'Ask Your Therapist' column. The newspaper didn't want to lose his column either and, to his credit, Dr Howie refused to write or pay for it without me.

'Besides, take a look at yourself for a second,' Dr Howie continued, 'look at the way you live. Can you honestly say that everything didn't hold still? Look at it in retrospect. Look at the way you dwell on the past. I've done a lot of thinking about this. Do you want me to fax you my notes?'

'Don't fax me,' I said. I could already tell by the way he was pronouncing retrospect that he would misspell it. 'My problems are not for publication.'

I could hear him shuffling papers in what was probably a large, expanding file folder, breathing heavily through his mouth, practically saying the words, 'Since when?' Instead he said: 'You should get this off your chest. For your own sake.'

'Fine, I'll fax you *my* notes.' This was intended to be a joke, but that's exactly what I did. I faxed Dr Howie my notes.

* Fax Transmission: Dr H. – 09/95 *

You're the licensed therapist, what does this mean?

I remember sitting on the edge of my mother's hospital bed a few days before she died and saying, 'I love you' again and again. In fact, saying nothing else. But it was more a question than a declaration. And each 'I love you' required a response and my mother, who was too weak to sit up or even speak, would glance at me and smile.

Why did I do that?

By then she had lost most of her hair; there were just a few strawlike wisps at the back of her head. Her green eyes were round as quarters and getting rounder and more luminous the weaker she became.

I remember I looked into her eyes and said it again – I love you' – waiting for her to acknowledge me. The tone of my voice was relentlessly upbeat. My brother as well as my father and I had convinced ourselves she didn't know she was dying. It was a crazy rationalization, of course, but one that we clung to for dear life.

It was crazy, wasn't it?

In my mother's presence we were always cheerful. We even insisted that anyone who came to visit her behave the same way. We quizzed them before they entered her hospital room, asking what they were going to say and how they were going to behave. We suggested they plan it all beforehand the way we did. We went so far as to tell my mother's brother, who'd just arrived from Vancouver, to invent a cover story for his visit to Montreal so that my mother wouldn't think he'd come to see her one last time. When he wouldn't agree to our demand, we barred him from the room.

What do you think?

I know, we weren't just in denial, denial was our home. We owned the place. We'd moved in and settled down.

That's why when I said 'I love you' one more time, in a cheerful voice, I assumed I was doing what we had been doing all along – putting a good face on the worst possible situation. At least that's what I assumed – until I realized that both my brother and father were fidgeting, clearing their throats, tapping their toes loudly on the hospital's tile floor. Finally, my brother came up behind me and whispered, 'Cut it out, will you. What are you trying to prove?'

What was I trying to prove?

I swear I don't know. I do know I ignored my brother and said 'I love you' again and then repeated it like it was some kind of tune you can't get out of your head.

I kept saying it even though I knew she didn't have a moment to spare, even though I knew she needed all her strength to leave us. But I wouldn't let her go. I prayed for her to stay, even if it meant staying the way she was, even that.

My prayers were answered. I remember she lingered a long time – six days.

* End of transmission *

The fax I received in return from Dr Howie said: 'That's small potatoes, believe me.' I didn't, not for a moment. Because what he calls 'small potatoes' was, at least until recently, the most inexcusable thing I've ever done.

* * *

The consensus so far is that I need therapy. Faxes to Dr Howie won't cut it. This is not the conclusion I would have reached. However, I seem to be outvoted.

'Not therapy exactly, Jacob, just someone you can talk to about, I don't know, about all your issues, your unfinished business,' Hope says, as she parallel-parks my mother's Malibu. I stare out the back window to make sure she's not too close to the curb or to the car behind her. Our destination this morning is a garage sale a few blocks from my house. Our goal is to try to find some of the things Hope will need once her baby arrives. Or so I thought. I didn't know we would also be discussing my emotional well-being.

'Once you're done with the physiotherapy, of course,' Angie adds, holding my crutches for me as I pull myself out of the back seat. 'We mean once you're back on your feet, both of them. It's something to think about at least.'

'What did I say? All I said is that I don't trust Joseph, that I think he may be up to something again. What does he have to do? Push me off another ladder?'

'He didn't push you. You were the one who –'

'Maybe we should drop this for now. Angie?' Hope interrupts.

But Angie persists. 'Geez, Jacob, you fell. You missed a step and fell,' she says, folding her arms across her substantial chest and frowning. Stooped over my crutches, I am exactly the same height as Angie and sometimes when we are standing, face to face, eye to eye, I feel as if I were being measured – as if she were adding to, more likely, subtracting from her estimation. We never had that second date. My accident was one explanation, though I'm sure it wasn't the only one.

'I can't believe it. You've both been discussing this. Me. What else have you discussed?' I glare at Angie, who looks away.

'Now, don't get cranky, Jacob,' Hope says. 'We just think you could use someone to help you work things out. Someone neutral?'

'And, what, you two aren't neutral enough?'

'That's not fair,' Hope says. She and Angie walk ahead of me, just barely resisting, I'm sure of it, the urge to link arms and whisper to each other. For once, at least, I don't have to guess at what they could possibly find to talk about. This time I have a pretty good idea; they're talking about me and my unfinished business.

* * *

Hope and Angie met three months ago, when they were visiting me in the hospital the day after my accident. I'd just undergone an operation to place three screws in my right ankle and I awoke from the anaesthetic feeling light-headed and queasy. With good reason, for once. I don't remember whether or not I threw up, but I do remember having two separate hands, both cool, both tender, stroking my brow. I remember I raised my head gingerly and saw Hope and Angie standing on either side of my hospital bed.

This is a dream, I thought, and waited patiently for it to get interesting. Except it never did. Instead, there was a buzz of hospital noises: clattering trays and gasping machinery, the rustle of back issues of magazines, intercoms sputtering, nurses and doctors repeating inane questions, visitors whispering to each other. I can still remember what Hope and Angie were talking about – the Martha Stewart phenomenon. They were both giggling, discussing a recent program in which Martha made a three-layer chocolate cake in the shape of the Taj Mahal for a child down the street. 'What gets me is that he wasn't even a relative or the child of a friend,' Hope said, 'he was a neighbour kid.' 'The woman is all-knowing and all-seeing,' Angie added.

This is a strange dream, I thought, just before I realized I wasn't dreaming.

Hope and Angie have each, in their own way, decided that it is their job to take care of me. Hope has even gone so far as to move in with me on weekends. The night I was pushed – or fell – off Joseph Alter's swimming pool ladder she drove me to the Sacré Coeur Hospital just across the Court Séjour Bridge. She had misplaced her own house keys again, which is also why after she took me to the hospital she returned to Court Séjour to spend the weekend.

She has kept returning since then, and though she is reluctant to admit it, it is as much for her own sake as mine. Since learning she was pregnant she has tried her best to avoid Neil Topaz and has discovered that if you want to disappear without a trace there is no better place than Court Séjour. So far Topaz, who she often finds staked out in front of her apartment on week nights when she comes home late from taping 'Been There, Done That', has not thought of looking for her here. For her part, Angie put me in touch with Lisette, my physiotherapist. Angie is also dropping by more and more often on her way to or from visiting Sandy, who is continuing to find it difficult to leave his condominium.

Although Hope and Angie have become friends in the last three months, it has been a gradual process. They were suspicious of each other at first, but they have discovered they've a lot in common, even though I am still trying to figure out what, aside from Martha Stewart, that might be.

There is me, of course. Hope is starting to wonder if all the attention I've received from her and Angie is proving to be counterproductive. An obstacle to my recovery. She hasn't actually shared this theory of hers with me yet, but I know about it from an entry I read in her Filofax. According to Hope's combination day-planner and diary, Angie, who is described as 'someone who knows about these kinds of things' concurs. Angie is quoted, referring to my situation as 'Typical.'

They are right, but not in the way they think. The truth came to me three months ago, the day they both signed my cast: 'From now on, start climbing mountains and avoid ladders. Get well soon. Love Hope & Angie.' Reading that playful, good-natured note, I realized that instead of being involved in one impossibly platonic relationship, I was now involved in two. I would be lying if I said this revelation has not had a demoralizing effect on me.

* * *

My cast was buzz-sawed off a month ago so I shouldn't still need crutches, but as my physiotherapist keeps telling me, everyone heals at their own rate. Here's a scoop for this journal: I am a slow healer. Remarkably slow. In the meantime, I've become good at handling crutches and can walk without hobbling or limping much. From a distance, it looks as if I'm not using them at all. So if I lag behind Hope and Angie it's because I've purposely slowed my pace – because when I do catch up to them I know that I'm the one who will have to apologize … once again. And there will be plenty of time for that.

Hope, Angie and I are doing what we've been doing bright and early most Sunday mornings for the last two months – making a tour of the neighbourhood garage sales, which are abundant in Court Séjour. On any fall weekend, you'll find handmade posters taped to every other stoplight, street sign and telephone pole, indicating the address of the nearest sale.

Garage sales were my idea. I read in my copy of *The Pregnancy Handbook for Today's Woman* that they are 'a maternity gold mine,' an ideal place to buy reasonably priced second-hand items for infants. Our first stop this morning is a split-level a few blocks from my house.

Angie hands Hope a bassinet as I limp up beside them. They are standing side by side, studying it as if it were an ancient relic. Both women are dressed for summer – in T-shirts and sandals and shorts. Everything about the last three months seems to have held still – including the hot, humid weather, which has never dipped much below thirty degrees Celsius since June. In addition to the political uncertainty and apprehension about the provincial referendum next month, the weather is making everyone short-tempered and cranky. That's one reason I've been so lax in keeping my journal, but there are others.

'Sorry. I guess didn't sleep much last night.'

'Never mind,' Hope replies quickly. Angie is less forgiving, her arms across her chest as if she never doubted an apology was coming. Never doubted I would give in first.

Angie passes on the bassinet and puts it down on a bridge table next to a pile of *World Book Yearbooks* from the 1950s and 1960s, a swizzle stick collection, a martini shaker, Tupperware, a fondue set, horseshoes, ping pong paddles, a dart board, a game of Twister and a silver-plated menorah. Angie's approach to garage sales is practical. She arrives early with three lists: the items that Hope needs now, the items she will need later and the items she will need much later. Every now and then when Hope passes on something in the final category – like a tricycle – Angie will buy it and say, 'You never know.'

For her part, Hope goes along with most of Angie's advice. But she doesn't do much more than go along. This is, she says, part of her garage sale strategy. She read somewhere that enthusiasm drives up the price. She didn't read it somewhere, she heard it from me. I was the one who did the preliminary research on garage sales and infants. Anyway, Hope's lack of enthusiasm has more to do with the feeling she hasn't been able to shake that she shouldn't be pregnant. That the incremental changes in her body – from her widening belly to her swelling ankles – shouldn't be happening. As a broadcast journalist she is an expert at making snap decisions – about people and issues – an expert at trusting her instincts. But when I watch her pricing second-hand strollers on Sunday mornings I know what she is thinking: she is thinking that she is making a terrible, irreversible mistake. She is thinking, *Instincts? What instincts?*

A bassinet and a stroller are at the top of the list of items Hope needs now and Angie arrives prepared to haggle on her behalf. The problem, this morning, is that there is no one to haggle with. The only person in the vicinity who is not shopping is a thin elderly man wearing a Toronto Blue Jays cap that looks two sizes too big for him and a Blue Jays T-shirt that looks two sizes too small. He is also wearing powder blue bermuda shorts and golf cleats. While this is clearly his garage sale, he seems indifferent to the potential customers who have stopped to look over the array of knickknacks, old clothes, books, furniture and household appliances scattered up and down his driveway like treasured possessions rescued, at random, from a fire.

Instead, the man in the Blue Jays cap is playing golf on his front lawn. Not golf exactly, but a solitary version of the game. He has leaned his golf bag up against a sign: VENDU, REAL ESTATE AGENT, RUSSELL MINTZ, and he's swinging at a yellow Top Flite attached to a long, thick elastic band. The ball, after it's been struck and has reached its highest point, stops and returns to him. He then tees it up and does the same thing again. Occasionally, a shopper interrupts his lonely game to ask the price of an item. 'Can't you see I'm busy?' he says abruptly, swinging away.

When I smile at him, it is, I confess, as sincere as it is involuntary. I've discovered these last couple of months that my attitude towards garage sales is increasingly sentimental, even for me. I've developed a surprising affection for my neighbours – for people who sit outside all weekend long, guarding the bits and pieces of the past they no longer have room for in their more and more complicated or more and more simplified lives. But when the man hidden under the Blue Jays cap grins back at me – recognizing, perhaps, that I have no interest in buying any of his old stuff – I know I've made a mistake.

'This was the wife's idea,' he says, leaning on his driver. 'I didn't want anything to do with it. I told her as much, but they never listen, do they? Women! They always get their way too. If they didn't, would you even be here on a Sunday morning? Tell the truth now.'

'I'll take the fifth on that.'

'Hah! So which one of these lovely ladies dragged you out here?'

'Over there,' I point to Hope and then Angie who are taking

turns holding up a Snow White and the Seven Dwarfs mobile.

'Two? Well, well, well.'

'It's a long story.'

'You'll have to tell me all about it some time. So what do you think: am I ready for the links?' he says, glancing down at his golf cleats and at the ball teed up at his feet.

'You look ready to me.'

'Hah! Never played a game in my life.'

Up close, he's older than I thought. In his early seventies probably. He takes off his cap to wipe his forehead and I notice that his thick hair is more white than grey; his face is narrow, the skin stretched and loose, freckled with large brown spots. There is a deliberate, breathless quality in his voice that makes me want to ask him if he'd like to sit down for a moment. I sometimes wonder how my parents would have aged. My mother was fifty-five when she died, my father fifty-eight. What would they have looked like? How would they have behaved? Would they have arranged all their collectibles, old board games and sporting goods on a table and set them outside for strangers to handle? Would they have done these things to embarrass me?

'So how did that happen?' he asks, pointing to my crutches with his club.

'Missed my step. Fell off a ladder.'

'Where were you headed?' He winks and then glances over at Hope and Angie.

'Nowhere in particular.'

'If you say so. It's Glassman, right? Jacob? I'm Sol Rosenstein. I knew I recognized you. Used to be everyone around here knew everyone else. You went to school with my boy Ronnie. Remember. Everyone called him Rosie.'

'Sure.' I shake Mr Rosenstein's hand even though I have no recollection of his son.

'He's living in Toronto now. Doing beautifully. He's a corporate lawyer. Did you know that? He has a fifteen-year-old daughter, Tiffany, and a son, Aubrey, who just had his bar mitzvah. Tiffany and Aubrey. Can you believe that? All this baby stuff is his. We've been storing it forever.

'So yeah, we're joining him there in Toronto. There's nothing left for us here. No friends to speak of. No family. None we still talk to anyway. No, my kids are there and the grandkids, so what I say to myself is why stay?'

'I'm sorry.'

'What's to be sorry? This community is a goner. Finished. Kaput-ville. I'm not even going to wait for that *meshuggeneh* referendum. No point in voting. No matter what the result is it's all the same. I can't wait to leave – to pack up and hit the highway. My wife is taking it hard, but Ronnie promised that he and I would go golfing the moment I arrive, so I'm preparing. I don't want to make too big a fool of myself.'

'Well, give him ... give Ronnie ... Rosie my best.'

'Can I ask you a personal question? You don't mind? This is none of my business, but what are you still doing here? A young fellow like you. You should get out while the getting is good.'

Would my parents have taken up hobbies? Would they have used words like 'kaputville'? Or moved to Toronto by now? Or asked strangers intimate, embarrassing questions?

Or would they have had to make up stories for the neighbours to explain why I was still living with them? Would I still be living with them? (Sometimes I think the reason I remain in Court Séjour is because my parents left me before I had the chance to leave them; other times, I think that just sounds like a convenient excuse.) I can't imagine being much of a source of *naches* for my mother and father. Here I still am: no wife, no children, an inconspicuous career as a ghostwriter. *Naches*, the Yiddish word for parental pride, is a burden every Jewish child feels. Maybe, every child. Would my parents have been proud of me? Would I have lived up to their expectations? Would I have been different than I am?

Hope wheels a stroller over to Mr Rosenstein, but before she can ask him for a price, he turns his back on both of us. He adjusts his grip, addresses the ball and swings, shouting, 'Fore!' At the same moment, a woman wanders onto his imaginary fairway and lifts a toaster oven over her head for cover.

'What is with that man?' Hope whispers.

'He's in denial and moving to Toronto. I advised him to see a shrink, you know, for all his unfinished business.'

'Geez, Jacob, we're sorry. Just forget the whole thing,' Angie says. She has followed Hope over to find out the price of a pink rattle she's holding in her hand. She shakes it at me briefly and then drops her head in what I think is an unnecessarily dramatic gesture.

'You have to understand, Jacob, it wasn't easy for us to bring this up,' Hope adds. 'I knew … we knew it would upset you. But you've only broken your ankle. It was an accident. Not a curse.'

'How can you be so sure?'

* * *

Joseph has yet to apologize, though he did send me a get-well-soon card after I came home from the hospital. The personal message on the card sounded more ominous than contrite: 'Now, Glassman, we can start again,' he wrote. 'I dreamed we would have a fresh start. This is a sign that our fates are intertwined after all. I do not doubt it; I never did. For your own edification, I recommend you read Genesis: 32:26.' The card was signed, 'With new respect and admiration, Joseph Alter.'

I've also reconnected my answering machine, a fact that Joseph is taking advantage of. He has been leaving messages that are no longer threatening but that are just as disconcerting as ever, updating me on everything from the progress he is making on his master's thesis on the Book of Job to his new job as a co-host of a Sunday evening radio program called 'The Jewish Variety Hour'.

'I would very much like for you to be a guest. We will be having discussions all next month on the political situation in Quebec, the upcoming referendum, and what impact it will have on our community. As someone who has lived here all his life, your perspective would be greatly appreciated. Please call me back, Glassman, and let me know which Sunday is convenient for you.'

Which only goes to show you that some people never learn. A fact that continues to worry me. But, according to Hope, none of this is worth being concerned about. If anything, she thinks I am the one exaggerating the situation, blowing it out of proportion. She hasn't said this to me directly, but I know what she thinks: she thinks some people never learn.

The last time I spoke to Joseph was at the hospital, a few days after the operation on my ankle. He dropped by at the end of visiting hours. Trish Severs, my editor, was also visiting at the same time and she kept him out, at my request. Trish had come to the hospital to bring me flowers and to tell me I could take some time off if I needed it.

'But I want you to know you are my "Up Next!" columnist. No one else. I want you to know that. Whenever you are ready,' Trish said, her voice full of emotion. After two years of slow and steady progress, of hormone treatments and psychological counselling, Ted's transformation into Trish was finally complete. An unqualified success, the doctors said.

Unqualified is not the word I would use. Not all of the preparations Ted has undergone on his way to becoming a woman have taken and sometimes she tries too hard, overcompensates for medication that still needs to be adjusted or therapy that falls short of the mark. Which accounts for the floral pantsuit she was wearing. My guess is that Trish still doesn't have a genuine image of what it means to be a woman and, as a consequence, she always seems to be on the verge of hysteria.

'I'm not sure about the column, but I'll do some freelancing for you, if you want me to. I'll stay in touch,' I said.

'People are always saying that,' she said, her lip quivering.

Over Trish's shoulder, I noticed Joseph peeking in past my hospital door. I noticed his scruffy, auburn beard first. 'My God, look at what I have done,' he said, but the words came out sounding more like a boast than an apology. When he saw my cast, he took a ballpoint pen out of his pocket.

'Get him out of here,' I said to no one in particular. But Trish, still confused enough to have a chivalrous side, took this as her cue to take action. She gulped back some tears and started shoving Joseph through the swinging hospital door. If Joseph had resisted it would have been a mismatch, but he didn't. Instead, he seemed pleased to have a woman in a floral pantsuit roughing him up.

'Do not worry, I will be back. There are many issues to discuss,' Joseph said, waving his pen over Trish's head. Then he disappeared out of my room and my sight.

* * *

Issues. Do you want to know about issues? Let me tell you about unfinished business.

Last night, Neil Topaz drove up to the door and honked his car horn twice – a prearranged signal. Meanwhile, Hope grabbed her purse, shrugged that shrug of hers and asked if she could borrow my house key because she'd misplaced the spare one I'd made for her. She said that she probably wouldn't be late, but that I shouldn't wait up.

'Jacob, this is not a date,' she said, rushing out like a teenager off on a date. With no warning. No explanation. Of course, I didn't need one. I knew Neil Topaz was coming – I read about it in Hope's Filofax. I also knew why he was coming. *He and I have things to settle,* Hope wrote to herself, *but I could never tell Jacob about any of this, he would never understand. I've arranged it so that Neil will just show up and I'll just leave.*

I leave Mr Rosenstein's garage sale the same way – without warning or explanation. Hope offers to drive me back to the house, but I decline, reminding her that they have at least three more garage sales to get to. Angie just frowns, the rattle shaking in her hand with adult frustration.

'I'm sorry about last night,' Hope whispers.

'There's nothing to be sorry about,' I say, pretending to be a good sport, but still unable to resist adding, 'is there?'

'No. I mean I'm sorry I didn't tell you about it before.' Hope isn't a good liar, I wanted to believe her, but I had to be sure. I also knew a way I could be sure.

'Apology accepted. But this isn't going to become a regular thing, is it? You two aren't going steady again, are you? Because if you are –'

'No, but maybe I shouldn't be staying with you any more. It's becoming complicated.' Hope lowers her golden eyes and stares at me sympathetically. I look away. This is a game of chicken I don't want to be playing. When Hope did start staying in Court Séjour on weekends, neither of us mentioned it except in the most cursory way. Mostly, it just happened and we just let it happen. Almost as if I had wished her here. Besides, we probably both knew if we discussed it, it would seem so preposterous we wouldn't be able to go on pretending it wasn't. Which is why the idea of her packing her things and leaving now is unthinkable and unbearable. A little more unbearable, as it turns out, than the idea of her staying. I have to get home now more than ever. The fact that Hope and Angie think I'm leaving because I'm angry at them is an unexpected advantage.

'FORE ! Hey, look out!' A yellow object whizzes by my head and I let go of my crutches and drop to the ground, holding out my right hand to break my fall. Mr Rosenstein's Top Flite just misses me. It flies by like a line-drive and keeps rising, a short tail of elastic trailing behind. When the ball finally lands it is two hundred feet up the street. Then it hits the pavement and bounces for another fifty, just missing a parked car and coming to rest on a lawn on a cross street. Taking into account the fact that Mr Rosenstein has never played golf before in his life, it is a miraculous drive.

'Sorry about that,' Mr Rosenstein says, rushing off to find out what kind of lie he has.

'What are you using?' I shout to him.

'A three-iron. Can you believe it? That kind of thing is not supposed to happen,' he shouts back.

'The man is a natural. It gives a person hope,' I say to Hope as she helps me up and hands me my crutches.

'Are you all right?' she asks.

'A close call, that's all. You know what they say about luck: it's when the arrow hits the other guy.'

'Maybe your luck is changing?'

'Are you asking me, Hope, or are you telling me?'

* * *

I proposed to Hope two months ago in her gynecologist's waiting room. It was a sticky July afternoon. I wasn't used to my cast yet and sweat was pooling up in an unreachable spot near my heel. I was itchy and irritable and wondering why I wasn't at home in my air-conditioned office.

Then I remembered why. A few days earlier when I was helping her look for her lost keys I'd noticed Hope's Filofax, concealed behind a framed wedding photograph of my parents, on top of a seven-foot-high oak armoire in the master bedroom.

I had no intention of reading her private thoughts then – I wasn't even sure she kept a record of them in that businesslike book – but after she found her keys and went out to run an errand something drew me back to the armoire. Maybe I just wanted a clue to explain why she was staying with me. Or maybe it was the fact that the Filofax had been hidden from me in my own house. Whatever the reason I returned with the stepladder from the kitchen pantry, climbed it gingerly, still leaning on my crutches and opened the book to the previous night. There, along with the entries of expenses, appointments and messages to be returned were Hope's concerns about going through 'all this' by herself.

I am so dreading the appointment next week. I know no one can make this decision for me, she wrote to herself, *and I've never needed or wanted anyone to tell me what to do, only this time I wish someone would. I've always trusted my own instincts, only I don't know how I can any more. If I could, would I even be in this position? Would I have to go through all this alone?*

Hope's doctor was running late. The receptionist apologized for that as well as for the fact that the air conditioner in the office wasn't working.

'Just my luck,' Hope said, consulting her Filofax, then putting it back in her purse. 'I have a production meeting in an hour.'

At the time, Hope still hadn't told anyone at the television station she was pregnant. She was keeping it a secret because even though the talk show she co-hosts deals routinely with personal, provocative, even kinky topics (if you ask me) she wasn't sure how her producers would feel about a pregnant, unmarried host. She was equally worried that they might love the idea and decide to make the most of whatever gossip and prurient interest Hope's situation might attract. Neither prospect appealed to her.

Even then, it was clear to me that the one thing Hope didn't have to worry about was her job. Her program had already expanded to an hour and it was being rerun once at night and once in the morning on WTN. She was also being courted by agents and there was talk of the show moving to the CBC. Hope's ratings were growing steadily and people routinely recognized her in public. That included the

JOEL YANOFSKY

unambiguously pregnant woman sitting across from us in the waiting room.

'Could you make it out to Nicole and Nicole, Jr?' she said, holding out a glossy magazine called *Lesbian Life* for Hope to autograph. 'I'm naming my baby after me. If you ever want to do a show on artificial insemination … well, there you are.' Nicole, Sr, pointed proudly at her enormous belly.

'That's great. I'll keep it in mind,' Hope said, trying to sound enthusiastic. She still wasn't used to being a celebrity. Like extroverted people who are always insisting that they are shy, Hope is a public figure who doesn't like to be noticed in public. *People see enough of me already,* she wrote in her Filofax, *there has to be some place where I can just be alone and private and not worry about what anyone else thinks. Like Court Séjour. Ha ha.*

Unlike Nicole, Sr, Hope was hardly showing. One month into her second trimester, she still didn't know what to do. Time was becoming a factor – at least according to my copy of *The Pregnancy Handbook for Modern Women* – but Hope still wanted to discuss all her options with her gynecologist first. We both knew that all her options consisted of precisely two: she could decide to have the baby or she could decide not to have it.

As we waited in the waiting room, we both knew that one way or another a decision couldn't be postponed any longer. I had asked to come along to offer moral support because that's what Hope needed from me, what I'd read she secretly wanted, but I was proving to be no help at all. I knew it. Hope knew it. Even Nicole, Sr, seemed to know it.

Hope had called me 'squeamish about these kinds of things' in her Filofax and I wasn't sure whether she meant I was squeamish about her pregnancy or about making decisions. I suppose either one would have been right. I couldn't bring myself to ask Hope if she was leaning in one direction or the other. (In her Filofax, she had divided a page in half, listing pros on one side and cons on the other. There were exactly the same number of reasons on both sides of the page.) Sitting beside her in that stifling office, the back of my legs sticking to the vinyl waiting-room chair, I couldn't even make small talk. I was too overwhelmed by where we were – by the ads for breast pumps and the cervical centimetre chart – to speak. So I just stared at Hope's profile. For once, it was fixed in an involuntary frown. Her eyes were redder and sleepier than usual, her lips pursed and tight. At first, I thought she was scared, but that wasn't it. She was disappointed with herself, so much so that I had to sit on my hands to keep from reaching out and taking her in my arms.

Forget that. It's not true. I couldn't have touched her even if I thought she wanted me to. I felt too much like a voyeur. Like I was watching her think. Watching her aim her considerable enthusiasm and instincts at a problem she would never be able to resolve satisfactorily no matter how many lists she made. Occasionally, she would move her lips but she wouldn't say anything. The silence between us wasn't so much uncomfortable as it was fragile, as if a single wrong word could do the kind of damage that could never be undone. And so, for the first time since my parents had died, I prayed – prayed hard. God, I said to myself, let me be able to help her.

'I should do a program on why doctors always keep you waiting and always get away with it,' Hope said, talking to Nicole to pass the time. 'My theory is that they do it so you won't forget who the boss is.'

'How about their hands, eh? Why are they always so cold? I think they put them in ice before you come in,' Nicole added. A woman well into her forties, she was as giggly as a girl. She was embarked on a big adventure and everything about her – from her military style flattop to her overalls – seemed to be saying she was not only prepared for the future, she knew what it held.

'Or stirrups? How about stirrups? Whose twisted idea was that?' Hope said.

As Hope and Nicole's chat about gynecological procedures became more graphic, I tuned out and rehearsed my speech, the one I'd been working on ever since I found out Hope was pregnant. The one I'd started memorizing the day she began to stay with me in Court Séjour.

The speech begins with me reminding her how happy my parents were. How if there is a relationship gene, I've inherited it. You know, Hope, I would say, I never once heard them fight or even raise their voices to each other. I know what you think, Hope: you think in the fifteen years since they've died, I've idealized my parents' marriage. (I read that in her Filofax, too.) You think because I was still young and impressionable when they died I never had the chance to see their relationship from a mature perspective. I never saw the weaknesses, the problems, you'd say. All right, I'll grant you that. But you have to grant me – grant them – something too: fidelity, companionship, kindness, affection, respect, trust. These aren't just words. Or they didn't use to be just words. They count for something. You know that as well as I do.

(Actually, what Hope wrote was: *Why am I always falling for the wrong guy? Why isn't it ever anyone I can depend on and trust. Someone who loves me unconditionally. Remember that first time with N., remember he left my apartment and I watched him walk down the hall and the first thing he did, before he reached the elevator, was take out his cellular phone. He couldn't even wait till I wasn't looking before he called his wife to tell her he was on his way home. Why didn't I know then? What's wrong with me? Do I have a stupid sign on my forehead?*)

Hope, I would say, taking her hand in mine, you need someone who loves you unconditionally. Me, for instance. I know that you think the only reason I keep chasing you is because I think I'll never catch you. I used to think that too, but that's not the reason. It can't be.

Look, Hope, I've learned to let go of everything. I'm great at it. An expert. The world champion at throwing in the towel, cashing in my chips. 'Giving Up' should be my middle name. But I haven't given up on you and that must mean something. You don't have to tell me this all sounds crazy. It is crazy. But what if I'm right – what if my instincts are right for once and yours are wrong? What then?

I could feel the pool of sweat inside my cast rising from my heel slowly, like a tiny, inexorable wave, rising until it reached the top of my head. I was drenched by the time I completed the daydream – as groggy as someone who'd just woken up from a long nap in the sun. I picked up a back issue of *Expecting* magazine and started to fan myself with it. Hope turned to ask if everything was okay, but before I could answer, the receptionist called her name.

'The doctor will see you now,' she said.

Hope walked towards the examining room. There wasn't time for a long speech and so I stood without my crutches, hopped towards her, placed my hand on hers and said, 'Keep the baby, Hope. Keep it and marry me.'

I wobbled, propping one hand up against the wall. And when she turned away, there it was, that familiar shrug: part genuine concern, part exasperation. The door to the examining room closed and I turned to see Nicole holding my crutches. I thanked her and she just nodded and returned to *Lesbian Life*, thinking, no doubt with good reason, that she had been right about men all along.

'Artificial insemination?' I imagined myself saying to Nicole, Sr, and Nicole, Jr. 'That's small potatoes. We've never even had sex.'

* * *

There are two messages on my answering machine when I return home from the garage sale. The first is from Rusty Mintz.

'All right, all right,' he says impatiently. 'I'm waiting for the beep. Jakie, you there? I'm at Rosenstein's. Your girlfriend – girlfriends? – here said that you went home, so where are you? What I need to know is when can I start showing your place? Playing hard to get is fine, Jakie, but I have three serious offers and you're not going to do better. Not now. Not here. Not with the goddamn referendum around the corner. One hundred and fifty thou. Ask Rosenstein what I finagled for his place. Remember he who hesitates gets screwed, so call me, will you?'

I was right about Rusty; one more sale in this neighbourhood makes him eligible for a trip to Bali or Bora Bora and he seems determined to take it this winter. I asked him once why he was so convinced I wanted to sell when I kept saying I didn't.

'Because,' he said, improvising his pitch, 'you don't belong here. We both know that. What are you? Thirty-five? Forty? Single. Unattached. You're not supposed to be living in Court Séjour. Court Séjour wasn't meant for you. You're just here by luck. Bad luck, okay, but luck. A fluke. It's only a matter of time before you realize it and when you do, I'll be ready with a dotted line upon which you can gratefully sign.'

But Rusty has been putting less pressure on me lately – particularly since Hope has been spending most of her weekends in Court

Séjour. ('You won't even know I'm here,' she said. Then we both laughed for a long time and didn't discuss it, except for the practical details. She didn't want to stay in the master bedroom at first, but I insisted. I'd already converted my brother's bedroom into my office and the basement was too cold and damp for an expectant mother. She keeps a toothbrush, here, her orthopedic pillow, some T-shirts and underwear, a sweat shirt, leggings, a kimono-style bathrobe, one flannel nightgown and, of course, her Filofax.)

The second message on my answering machine is from Neil Topaz. Prior to last night, Hope's final meeting with Topaz – or what she had promised herself would be her final meeting – took place the day last July when she told him their affair was over, once and for all. That was a few days after she decided to keep the baby and a few days after she refused my marriage proposal. It goes without saying that I shouldn't know about any of this. Hope told Topaz she was having an abortion; she told him their affair was over. In both cases, he refused to believe her.

They were parked in front of Hope's apartment building down-town and he wouldn't let her out of his car. He held on to the buckle of her seat belt. He scared her, she wrote at the time. *July 4th. A Thursday.* Even when he finally did let her go he remained outside her apartment until three o'clock in the morning. Her entry for that day says:

I was wrong about N. and J. was right. If N.'s wife couldn't trust him, J. said, what makes you think you can? J. seems to be right about a lot of things lately. It's like he has some kind of sixth sense. Why did I think I could trust N? I'm a dope, that's why. I thought I loved him and, okay, probably I still do, only that's not good enough any more. Especially now. Now, he is starting to frighten me...

I listen to Topaz's message one more time, then I retrieve the stepladder from the kitchen pantry and carry it into the master bed-room and find Hope's Filofax in the usual place, atop the armoire, behind my parents' wedding photograph. Like a kid with a smutty magazine, I close the blinds, shut out the September sunlight, sit down on the bed and begin to read. As always, I skim at first, looking for my name. Then I read backwards to discover in what context my name is mentioned. The Filofax opens automatically to yesterday's date: *September 19th. A Saturday.* My hands tremble, even though I decided weeks ago that, under the circumstances, I am doing the only thing I can do.

Hope needs me, even if she hasn't realized it yet. Betrayal is the wrong word: this is not a breach of trust, this is a necessity. I need more information. For once, I welcome it.

'So much of one's vitality goes into false alarms,' John Cheever said in his journals and I want to believe he was right. Maybe the same is true of Hope's date last night – not even date, meeting is more like it – with Neil Topaz. But just as I convince myself that I am jumping to conclusions, I read the close of Hope's entry for yester-day. The words are not reassuring: *Whatever else you do, do not tell J. any of the details.* Does that sound like a false alarm? Reluctantly, I flip back a few pages and I find everything Hope has vowed not to tell me.

* * *

Men cannot be trusted. I should do a program on it or a whole series. Why did I show up anyway? He asked and kept asking. Okay, even when he's a prick, he's a forceful prick. He wore me down, that's why. It wouldn't be the first time. Ask any one of my shrinks.

All right, I really believed I could set him straight. Tell him he had to stop camping out in front of my apartment building every night. Tell him my work was suffering. He'd understand that. I could say that I can't sleep, knowing he's out there. It's funny, but he could never stay out with me this late when we were seeing each other. Then, he always had to get back to his wife.

Anyway, my eyes have dark circles under them almost every morning. Trudy, the make-up artist at WTN, thinks I'm having too much fun. Right. Fun. I want to tell her that you don't know what fun is till you've spent the weekend in Court Séjour.

Besides, staying in Court Séjour is hardly fair to J... A. is right about that. I wish I knew what happened between them because it looked promis-ing, so hopeful. That would have got me off the hook too. Okay, that sounds terrible, I know, only there you are. Now, A. spends all her time trying to coax her ex into the elevator.

All J. does is buy baby books. They are piling up in his office like some kind of monument to human reproduction, to prenatal and postnatal care. He's turning my pregnancy into one of those term papers he writes for lazy pre-law students.

And what about the garage sales? Every Sunday morning … right, that means tomorrow morning, too. Why did I ever agree to that? I can't even remember whose idea it was. I know it wasn't mine. Then just last week J. asks me when will we, get this, we, be starting childbirth classes?

* * *

In my own defence, I thought that's what she wanted – someone to attend Lamaze classes with. I read it right here, in her Filofax: *August 27th. A Sunday.* Sometimes, I wonder how I could be so in love with someone so fickle. It also makes me wonder what point there is in continuing to try to help her. If, from one day to the next, she's not going to know what she wants, then how can I? I suppose it's obvious by now that I don't understand her restlessness. It's more than that – I am incapable of understanding it. I read about how she can't decide who she should be with or what she should be doing almost every day now and I am beginning to realize we don't complement each other at all. We couldn't be more unlike each other if we tried. I am always looking for the same thing in different places; she is always looking for different things in the same places.

So there N. is, waiting for me, outside J.'s house. It all sounds like one of those dopey old movies J. is always forcing me to watch. Anyway, I get into N.'s car and he doesn't say anything. There is just this look of enormous relief on his face. And he drives me to the restaurant in complete silence, and he puts his hand on the back of my elbow and guides me to a table for two in the corner. There is no waiter and no menu and no one around.

He tells me what he's going to order and, for an instant, this whole setup – the single white rose in a crystal vase, his dark blue suit, the Star of David cuff links, the way he takes out his cellular telephone, switches it off and tucks it away in his breast pocket – all make me see red. As if he thinks things can ever be the way they were. As if I would even want them to be.

I tell him I don't want anything to eat. That I'm not here for that and that I feel like puking all the time anyhow and that the thought of sweet and sour anything makes me retch. Only he looks hurt and so I say maybe I'll have some soup. He cheers up instantly – men are such babies.

Then he says, 'You look more beautiful than ever, Hope.' Good thing for him he doesn't say 'radiant' because if he had I would have been out the door or I would have decked him. Instead he says my name, he says 'Hope' and I remember the way I used to feel when I heard him say it, the way you always feel when the person you love says your name as opposed to the way you feel when someone you used to love says it. And then he goes off to the kitchen, turning around a couple of times to make sure I'm still there. I mean, come on, where would I be?

This is not a date, this is not a date, I keep telling myself. But all the while I'm sniffing the white rose on the table and sipping my wine glass filled with ice water – 'No alcohol for you,' he says – and I know I'm not fooling anyone, not even myself.

Because I feel it, despite myself. The wham pow. N. looks good. Prosperous. Like a success. He always looks that way, even when he looks lousy. He's wearing a three-piece suit, though that seems a little much. And then there's those Star of David cuff links, for God's sake, the ones he was wearing the first night we met. He's wearing a lot of cologne, too, as usual. As usual, Calvin Klein's Obsession. I'd always tell him he didn't need it, only he'd never listen. Dope that I am, it took me forever to figure out that the thicker his cologne the less likely his wife would be to smell my perfume, smell me on him. This is not a date, I tell myself again. Only he does look good. Forceful. He looks like a man who knows what he wants and has no doubts about his reasons for wanting it.

N. is a salesman, first, last, always, and he can convince anyone of anything. Even himself. Especially himself. I've heard him talk himself into this affair as if it were the most logical thing in the world – good for him, good for me, good for his wife, good for his unborn children, good for Quebec, good for Canadian unity, good for the Western Hemisphere. And he comes back to the table and he's doing it again. Selling. Selling me.

'I know when you stopped seeing me, Hope, it was the right thing to do. I understood. I did, truly. We needed time apart,' he says.

'If we needed time apart,' I say, 'then why do you keep turning up everywhere I go? Did you really think I wouldn't notice you in front of my apartment at three o'clock in the morning?'

'You didn't let me finish, Hope.'

He used to say that – 'You didn't let me finish' – all the time and it would drive me up the wall. It does again and I'm glad. I know at that moment that there will never be anything between us again. Good, I think, keep talking. Keep getting yourself in deeper because J. will be expecting me at home. If I get back early maybe I won't have to put up with his inevitable sulking. Maybe, I won't have to explain. We'll watch The Apartment. *That'll make him happy. We watch it all the time, like it was some kind of morality play. I mean, I got the message the first time: I'm Shirley MacLaine, he's Jack Lemmon. He's a mensch; I'm a fool not to see it.*

I resent this. I don't sulk and I didn't know I was such a chore to be around. And who considers himself a mensch anyway? Not me. Would a mensch be reading this diary? I know how Hope feels about her privacy. I accidentally picked up the phone once when she was on it and I stayed on the line until I knew for sure that the man she was talking to was her producer. She made a joke about it later, but she wasn't joking. 'If you ever do that again,' she said, 'I'll have to kill you. Not literally, of course.' No, I never set out to be a mensch and, if I am, it's only in Hope's eyes and only in comparison to some people whose name I won't mention but whose initial is N.

'You didn't let me finish,' N. repeats. 'What I was going to say is that you were right about us taking a break from each other. And it's true, I didn't accept it at first. But I do now. I want to now. I never wanted to hurt you. I want to help you in any way I can with the baby. This is my responsibility too. I want us to be friends, Hope.'

(Right, friends.)

So I applaud. I shouldn't, but I do. (Good for you, Hope.) *He looks devastated.* (Tough luck.) *But just then, as if on cue, the chef, the Chinese-Jewish kid he smuggled out of China, comes over to say hello.* (Of course.) *It didn't occur to me then, but it does now, writing all of this down, that this is a business presentation. A sales pitch. The chef shows up to demonstrate to me that N. is the kind of man who takes his responsibilities seriously and has done so at extraordinary risk to himself. He nods at N. and says, 'How are you, Mrs?' before he disappears into the kitchen.*

The whole thing feels more and more like a setup. (No kidding.) *But I guess I fell for it anyhow because the next thing I know we're in his office and he's showing me a shelf full of videotapes of me – all carefully numbered and dated. Every program I've done. 'Remember this one, Hope,' he says, 'about Day Care. Here's Budgets. Alcoholism. In-vitro Fertilization.*

Phone Sex. Panic Attacks. Surprise Makeovers. Surprise Makeovers, Part II.?

'I notice the episode on Adultery is missing from your shelf,' I say. (Good for you.) *Which only succeeds in making him look sheepish and me feel guilty.* (Guilty about what?)

Then he's weeping and saying the usual stuff about how he can't live without me, how his life is excrement – he refuses to swear in front of the baby – since I left, how he prays every night for me, for our baby, for himself, for all of us.

I swear I don't understand women who complain about the men in their lives not being able to cry. Every man I've ever known cries at the drop of a hat and I can tell you, right here, right now, it's not all that it is cracked up to be.

But, sure, all right, my maternal instincts are right out on the surface anyway and so the next thing I know I'm comforting him, shushing him, rocking him in my arms, telling him that everything will be okay. (No.) *Only his Obsession for Men is so strong I back away from him. Then he pulls me back and kisses me. According to one of those books J. keeps reading, my hormones are all out of whack which probably explains why I'm feeling so angry and ... so horny suddenly and so, all right, I kiss him back.* (Please, no.) *And then the next thing I know he has his clothes off and he's sliding my tights off and I'm pulling him down on top of me on his leather couch which, incidentally, smells like a big smelly egg roll.*

And he's apologizing. He's inside me and he's still apologizing. And still talking and selling, nonstop. Asking me questions like why am I hiding from him? And where am I hiding? And why can't we still see each other? And, okay, like a dope, I tell him it wasn't just a coincidence he picked me up in Court Séjour this evening, that I've been there all along. Yes, hiding from him. And I tell him the reason I'm there is because I was afraid of this exact thing happening. And so he wants to know about J. Is there anything between us? How do I feel about him? And again like a dope, I tell him the truth – that J. and I are just friends, good friends.

Then there is this dopey smile on N.'s face – almost a smirk – and when he comes he shouts out my name so loud I think everyone in the restaurant will hear. Only I don't care. Not really. There, I said it: I don't care. That's what I kept saying to myself the whole time and then I come too...

Now, get this: we've just done it on his leather couch, in his office, in the back of his restaurant, a picture of his wife staring at me from the wall behind him and do you know what he says? He says: 'You don't realize this about me, but I am a deeply religious man and every day, every single, solitary day, I pray, God forgive me, for my wife to find out about us.'

That's what he says. You know at that moment, with this married man who is the father of my unborn baby lying on top of me, his four-hundred dollar pair of pants down around his ankles, his cuff link leaving, I'm sure, a Star-of-David-shaped indentation on my backside, I can't think of a single thing to say except, 'Don't worry, everything will be all right.' I even pat him on the shoulder.

Now, when it's too late, I know exactly what I should have said. I should have said, 'Excuse me, do you see a STUPID sign anywhere on my forehead?'

I went to see him with a plan, okay, and it was not to have sex with him. I want to make that clear. I didn't go see him at his restaurant so that we could end up on the deep-fried couch in his office.

So tell me now what do I do? He said he would give me space, time to think. He promised to leave me alone for a while so I could sort some of this out. He swore on our baby. Any suggestions, dear Filofax? Any bright ideas? Anyone? One thing is sure: Whatever else you do, do not tell J. any of the details. . . .

* * *

Details are overrated. Here is just one example of a useless detail: last night Neil Topaz told Hope he would give her space. This morning the message he left on my answering machine said he had to talk to Hope and that he would call again. Now, as of this moment, he's outside my house, ringing my disconnected doorbell. No one keeps his word any more. No one can be trusted.

I nudge up one of the slats of the Venetian blinds in the master bedroom and I can see him standing on the front porch. He is holding a single long-stemmed white rose. According to Hope's description of him, he is wearing the same three-piece suit he wore last night. When he realizes my bell doesn't work, he knocks three times, each knock louder than the last. Then he climbs up on the railing and tries to look inside the bedroom window. Our eyes meet for a moment and I head immediately for the door. Neil Topaz doesn't

ANSWERED PRAYERS

look quite so prosperous or so 'forceful' this morning. Not quite so 'wham pow', if you know what I mean. There are dark circles under his eyes. His hair needs combing. His suit needs pressing. His vest is turned almost completely around. One Star-of-David cuff link is missing. He is not wearing socks, the laces on his shoes are untied and the rose is wilting.

'What, no box of chocolates?' I say, pointing to the flower. He ponders the question for a moment, wondering, I guess, where he can go on a Sunday morning in Court Séjour to buy quality chocolates. Then he starts laughing, a boisterous, fake laugh. Even after he stops, there is still a friendly smirk on his face.

'Pretty funny for a Sunday morning. I'm impressed. Hope always said you were a funny guy. She should have you on her show. You could be a regular. You know, her sidekick. You'd be perfect for that. Speaking of Hope –'

'I got your message.'

'Then you know why I'm here.'

'Not really.'

'I have to see her.'

'She's not here.'

'But that's her car in the driveway?'

'She's out. Shopping. She took my car. You know, Hope, she never can find her keys.'

'Shopping on Sunday morning?'

'Women, huh?'

'Right, women. Can I come in and wait?'

'Of course not.'

Ever since my parents died, I've felt abandoned in Court Séjour. Months, even years, would pass without anyone crossing the bridge from Montreal, invited or not. (Before he moved to Toronto, my brother made a point of telling me not to become a hermit. 'I have already decided never to clip my fingernails again,' I told him. He just frowned and shook his head.) But now the stream of visitors is steady. As if this place were some kind of depot where you could pick up what you were looking for and take it away with you.

'I have a right to see her,' Neil Topaz says.

'Why don't you leave her alone?'

'Have you fucked her yet?' he asks.

'She doesn't want to see you.'

'She was with me last night. With me. You understand what that means? Ask her yourself. Hope? HOPE? Tell him the truth. Tell him or I will.' I am leaning my arm against the vestibule wall and he slips underneath it and keeps shouting for Hope to answer.

'All right, let me put it another way: *I* don't want to see you.' I position myself in front of him, unwilling to give any more ground, guarding the hallway this time.

'Don't tell me: you hate everything I stand for.'

'That's right, I do.' It takes a moment, but I remember where I've heard that remark before. I said it myself. To Hope. This detail hurts as much as all the other painful details I know, but shouldn't, about their date last night; it means they talked about me and not just me but all manner of trivial details, the way, I assume, people who are truly in love do. The way my parents used to.

'Have you –'

I decide to punch him before he can repeat the question. I can feel the urge swelling and then pounding in my chest like a pulse. My right arm stiffens and my fist clenches, almost involuntarily. I am surprised and pleased: I don't feel light-headed at all, not at all. Who would have guessed: I am a fighter, not a lover.

'– fucked her yet?'

But then there it is again: my old problem. Protocol. I've never really punched anyone. Am I supposed to warn him first by putting up my fists? Or do I just hit him? And if I do, where do I hit him? The nose? The mouth? The belly? Right here in the vestibule? Or do we step outside? As Dr Howie would say, of all the things I lack, what I lack most is a sense of adventure.

Hesitation, it occurs to me, and not for the first time, is why I am where I am now. How I ended up here in the suburbs, in my deceased parents' bungalow, an aging orphan. A round peg in a square hole. A fish out of water. A thirty-five-year-old virgin, for God's sake.

How did I end up here? I hesitated – every step of the way. Which is why when I do finally throw my punch at Neil Topaz, it lands unimpressively on his shoulder.

Neil Topaz ended up where he is by never hesitating and so he doesn't. Before I can decide whether or not to hit him again, he is stepping into the hallway, crossing some imaginary threshold, forcing me back onto my heels, back into the house. He is moving towards me, raising both his arms. Without a cuff link, one shirt sleeve is waving like a flag. Now, I think. Do it now. Hit him in the nose. Or now. Or... But I flinch instead and then the next thing I know his arms are around my shoulders and his head is buried in my neck.

'What am I going to do, Glassman?' he says, hugging me. The stale trace of last evening's Obsession for Men still clings to the lapels of his suit. So does the smell of egg rolls. I pat the shoulder I punched, more to quiet him than to comfort him. And when I finally, reluctantly speak, I can only think to say, 'Don't worry. Everything will be all right.'

He is gasping for air and apologizing at the same time. 'I'm sorry. I can't go on without her. I love her too much. How can I make her change her mind? You know her better than anyone. Tell me, Glassman, how?'

I am still trying to calm him down when Hope sees us. She and Angie are standing in front of the screen door. Hope is holding the Snow White and the Seven Dwarfs mobile above her head. Angie still has Mr Rosenstein's rattle in her hand. It shakes as she says, 'Whoops.'

But Topaz is oblivious. He doesn't see or hear anyone else. I try to wrestle free of him, but he is clinging to me. So I shuffle my feet and pivot along with him as if he were a recalcitrant dance partner. When we are turned halfway he finally sees Hope and releases me.

Hope opens the screen door and drops the mobile, scattering Snow White, Prince Charming and several of the dwarfs across the hall floor. 'Get him away from me,' she says to Angie. 'I don't ever want to see that man again. I can't trust him.'

Both Neil Topaz and I stare at her. For a moment, neither of us seem sure who she is referring to. Then he moves towards her, his arms outstretched again. Angie steps in front of Hope.

'You said you'd give me space. This is not space. You swore. You said you'd give me time. This is not time,' Hope says over Angie's shoulder.

I am relieved until I remember what I was doing before everyone began to congregate in my hallway and I take off in the opposite direction to my parents' bedroom – Hope's room for the last three months – to return her Filofax to its hiding place.

* * *

Monday, September 21. My father died of a broken heart. The doctors said that it was cancer and that the cancer had spread more quickly than they expected and that there was never any way of predicting such things accurately. But I know that the real cause – the cause no one ever took into account – was a broken heart. I'm certain of this in a way that I'm certain of little else. Why shouldn't I be? It makes perfect sense: if your immune system can fail, just shut down, then why can't your emotional system. My father's started to fail the day my mother died.

I glance at Hope, asleep beside me, and I know what her reply to all this would be. She would say that I can't possibly know a thing like that – that I have been sentimentalizing my parents' marriage for so long now that any theories I have on their life together or their life alone are unreliable.

Unreliable?

I resist the temptation to wake her up and tell her that genuine love does exist. And then ask her who, at this particular moment, is in a better position to confirm this fact than yours truly? Instead, I let her sleep.

I am also more certain than ever about what made my father give up the way he did and relinquish his life. He had come to the end of the line. Even those things we usually rely on when we think we have come to the end of the line but really haven't – such as self-pity, denial, the generally unfounded belief that tomorrow will somehow be better – were no longer options. At the time of my mother's death, I thought we – my father, brother and I – were all suffering the same loss. I was wrong. There is a weight you feel when you are in love with someone and when they love you back that operates like a ballast, an anchor that holds you in place: confined and steady. My father was in love with my mother until the day she died; after she died he didn't know how to forgive her for setting him adrift. Now, for the first time in my life, I think I understand how upended he must have felt when that weight was lifted, that ballast gone.

Hope's breathing is steady. I watch her belly rise and fall under the bed sheet and gently place my hand above her waist, lowering it gradually until I am as close as I can come to touching her without touching her. It's five o'clock in the morning, late or early, depending on whether you're just getting in or just getting up. The answer in my case is neither. I haven't slept – not for more than a few minutes anyway – and I figure I will have to stare at the ceiling for at least two more hours before Hope is awake. But that's all right. In the meantime, there are plans to make.

Incidentally, I am naked under the bed sheet and so is Hope. Which raises a problem with keeping this journal that I don't think I considered before. What happens when you get exactly what you want? Do you still write it down? Do you risk jinxing it?

* * *

This is what happened yesterday: Neil Topaz sat at my kitchen table and refused to leave or even stand. Resting his head in his hands, he occasionally pushed his thick, unkempt hair back at the sides. Otherwise, he was motionless. 'More like catatonic,' Angie said. She filled me in on what was happening after I returned from hiding Hope's Filofax in its usual place on top of the armoire. I had been delayed. Standing on the stepladder to put the book away, I was distracted by a new entry. One I hadn't noticed. There was no date, but Hope must have written it yesterday morning before we left for the garage sale. It said: *Up early. I am tempted to tell J. about last night, only I can't. For his sake. And, yes, for mine too. Despite everything, I don't know what I would do without him...*

'Where were you anyway?' Angie asked.

'Nothing. I wasn't doing anything.' Who is 'him'?

'Hello? Jacob? I didn't ask you what you were doing. I asked you where you were.'

'Sorry. Nowhere.' Angie stared at me, her expression stern and suspicious.

In the kitchen, Hope was kneeling beside Neil Topaz, her hand on his knee, talking softly to him at first. 'You know you can't stay here,' she said. 'This is crazy.' But he wasn't answering. He was ignoring her and the more he ignored her the angrier she became until she was shouting at him to leave, slapping him on the back and the shoulder. He didn't react, except to take a comb out of his breast pocket and push it through his hair. Hope finally threw up her hands and walked out of the kitchen. She passed me on the way and said, 'Just get him out.'

'Or make him lunch,' Angie said.

I did neither. Neil Topaz's impromptu sit-in continued until well after noon. Hope came into the kitchen every ten minutes or so to see if he had left and when she saw that he hadn't she just looked at me and Angie and shook her head. He was as single-minded as Gandhi, if you can imagine Gandhi with a cellular phone. For a while, he even had the self-discipline to ignore the calls he kept getting, but eventually he picked up his messages and, reluctantly at first, then matter-of-factly, began to return them – as if he were in his car or office. Sunday is a busy day for a man who owns a kosher restaurant, who caters weddings, anniversary parties and bar mitzvahs. 'Other people's happiness is my business,' he said to no one in particular, after he'd soothed the nerves of an unhinged bridegroom concerned about his mother-in-law's allergic reaction to peanut butter sauce.

I confess I was intrigued by his behaviour, by his ability to deny his surroundings and his situation, and I was prepared to wait him out. Hope wasn't. 'This is ridiculous,' she said and agreed to have lunch with him just to get him out of my kitchen and my house. I didn't like the idea and said so, but Hope took me aside and told me they were only going to go over to the Happy Garden. 'Mr Ho will keep an eye on us for you. I'll be back in an hour and I'll be alone,' she said.

'Dim sum,' Neil Topaz added. He asked me for the number of the restaurant and called ahead on his cellular for a reservation. Then he took out an electronic personal organizer and punched in the appointment as if it were a last-minute business meeting. He was being so casual about everything all of a sudden, I was surprised he didn't invite Angie and me to come along – to double date.

'And what if you're not back in an hour?' I asked Hope as she was leaving. 'Do I come after you?'

'This is not a western, Jacob. But I'll take your car if that makes you feel better. And if you can loan me your keys. That way I have to come back, right? Besides,' she said, pointing to Neil Topaz, 'he's in no condition to drive.'

Angie stayed with me. It was the first time the two of us had been alone together in three months, though I can't honestly say if she was avoiding me since I'd been doing my best to avoid her.

'Geez,' she said, bending down to pick up the scattered pieces of the Snow White mobile Hope had dropped.

I leaned down to help her and I was close enough to smell the cherry gum she was chewing. She was wearing a T-shirt and shorts. I stared at the front of her T-shirt for a moment – a cow slumped over a crescent moon accompanied by the caption, 'Nothing is ever simple' – and then quickly averted my eyes. I had been trying not to think about what had transpired or, more to the point, what hadn't transpired between Angie and me, but I had lapses. I had wanted to see her alone, more than once. I had wanted to try to explain, to start over again, but her friendship with Hope had complicated every-thing. Especially my desire. Whenever I fantasized about Angie, Hope inevitably intruded. And vice versa.

'Do you think we should have let her go?' Angie asked.

'No. Not if anyone wants my opinion. But no one does. I don't get it. First she never wants to see the guy again, she's practically beating him up in the kitchen, and then they're going out for sweet and sour soup.'

'People are always doing things they shouldn't.'

'But what does she see in him? Never mind, I don't want to know.'

'Who knows what anyone sees in anyone? You can't know her private thoughts, Jacob.'

'Right, I can't … Let's change the subject. So what have you been doing that you shouldn't?'

'I wasn't necessarily talking about me.'

'Well, we both know you weren't talking about me.'

Angie blushed, this time on my behalf. This reference to our last date, to the details Angie knew about me that no one else knew, had been, of course, my main reason for avoiding her.

'Maybe I should go,' Angie said, handing me three of the seven dwarfs from the mobile. I was grateful for her reticence. So grateful I persisted in spite of it.

'I know this is embarrassing, Angie, but I want to try to explain –'

'There's nothing to explain,' she said, glancing down at the tops of her bare feet. She'd taken off her sandals and left them in the vestibule when she came in and now she was looking around for them as if removing them had been an unforgivably brazen thing to do.

'Then I want to apologize.'

'If anyone should apologize it should be me,' she said, raising her head, her face suddenly solemn.

'For what? You didn't do anything. It was my –'

'You don't understand,' she interrupted and walked slowly back into the kitchen, sitting in the seat Neil Topaz had vacated. I followed her, depositing the spare parts of the mobile on the table. I sat down across from her and realized immediately what she was about to say – that she'd made an enormous mistake that night three months ago, right here in this house, and that she has regretted it ever since.

I watched her mismatched eyes elude me as she patted my hand and tried to think of a way to explain her change of heart. Anything seemed possible. Or maybe nothing seemed impossible. After all, who knows who is meant to be with whom? If people did stand for things and if it was becoming more and more apparent, even to me, that Hope stood for everything I thought I wanted but would never have, then Angie stood for something else – something like the opposite of that. What I'd wished for and almost gotten. Something it suddenly seemed reasonable to wish for again.

'You don't understand,' she repeated, crossing her arms over her chest, over the upended cow on her T-shirt. 'I told Sandy about us.'

'Told him what? What was there to tell?'

'I told him about our ... well ... our date.'

'Our date? What about it?'

'I told him everything.' She lowered her head and closed her eyes when she said the word. As if she wanted to pretend I wasn't there to hear it. People don't stand for things. The mistake I keep making is believing that they do.

I knew that she and Sandy had started seeing each other again and, according to Sandy, they were working on a reconciliation, though in his present condition his version of events didn't seem particularly reliable. He was no longer capable of leaving his condominium for our weekly racquetball game, but I still called him regularly and occasionally had lunch at his place. We'd talk about the usual things – baseball or politics. The latest Expos collapse – we agreed they were on their way to being as traditionally jinxed as the Chicago Cubs. Or the upcoming Quebec referendum – we also agreed that the status quo wasn't so bad. Since he has become an agoraphobic I like Sandy better. I feel more comfortable calling him my best friend.

'By everything, Angie, you don't mean everything?'

'Yes.'

'Including the fact that we almost –'

'Yes.' Angie stared at me and I didn't know which eye – the green or the brown one – to meet. There was, it occurred to me, something profoundly untrustworthy about a person whose eyes refused to match.

'When?'

'You mean when did I tell him? About three months ago. After your accident.'

'But he's never said anything.'

'He blew up about it at first, his temper, you know, but then he forgave you. He'll be glad that you know he knows. He's been uncomfortable keeping this from you. Besides I told him nothing happened.'

'And he believed you?'

'Not at first. That's why I had to tell him the rest.'

'The rest?'

There are times when my inability to anticipate what is going to happen next is so extraordinary that sometimes I think of it as being a genuine knack – my one true talent. It's not just that I can't figure out what will happen next, it's that when it does happen, it is invariably the one thing I never would have dreamed would happen. Not in a million years.

'I had to convince him there was nothing going on between us, Jacob, and the only way I could think of to do it, the only way he would have believed me was if I told him about you. About how you'd, well, never, you know.... I'm sorry. I probably shouldn't have said anything, but Sandy wants me back and, well, I'm not sure that that's not what I want too. How's that for a double negative? Either way, I had to be honest with him.'

'Why didn't you just take out an ad?' I wasn't looking at her. Instead, I was trying unsuccessfully to find the seventh dwarf – Dopey, I guess it would be – among all the other spare parts of the mobile scattered on the kitchen table.

Angie handed me the missing plastic figurine, dropped her head a little lower and added, 'I told Hope too.'

* * *

The temptation to peek at Hope's body is irresistible and not for the first time this morning. I feel as if I've been fighting the urge for hours. It's like trying not to think about something you've been told not to think about. The feeling is an unsettling one, but, in this case, not without its curious pleasures and anticipations. Suddenly, anticipation is a word that holds more promise than it used to.

So I lie still, even though every part of me – from top to toe and other important stops in between – is itching, literally itching to move. Trying not to fidget, I fidget more: cracking my knuckles and toes, shifting my head on the pillow, then turning the pillow over, looking for the temporarily cool side. The morning light sidles in through a couple of turned-up slats in the Venetian blinds and falls on Hope, who is lying on her back. Her breathing is steady, though a slight hum is audible. Occasionally, she'll mutter a word or two and if I'm paying attention and listening hard I can hear what she is saying. The words are strange and familiar at the same time – 'Please, please me ...' or 'We can work it out' – and, with not much else to do but lie still and think, I eventually crack the code: she is mumbling the lyrics from Beatles songs. When she turns on her side and faces me, it still takes me a full five minutes to nudge the blanket and then the bed sheet up just enough so that I can track the freckles on her throat down to the top of her breasts. Another nudge and I can see that her breasts are small – smaller than I would have guessed last night in the dark. Another nudge and I can see her belly. It's also smaller than I imagined. The skin is pink and stretched tight. Another nudge and I can see... But Hope stirs and I let the sheet fall. Fortunately, I have plenty of time. I can start again.

This is the first time I've been this close to a woman's naked body and nothing could have prepared me for how odd it is. In some ways, more odd than stirring, the same way longing is more intriguing than the culmination of longing. Now, the urge to wake Hope is almost overwhelming. Almost. She needs her sleep.

In both *The Pregnancy Handbook for the Modern Woman* and *You & Your Baby: The Popular Guide to Pregnancy, Birth and Baby Care*, at least eight hours are recommended and Hope didn't come close last night. 'I said something wrong,' she mumbles, 'and so I long for...'

Yesterday took its toll. My goal is to make sure today and the day after that are easier. Of course, I have no idea how to accomplish that. Which is another reason I am careful not to wake Hope – so I'll have time to think.

'I need a place to hide away...'

Not careful enough, as it turns out. Her eyelids flutter and there is an instant where I think I should pull the bed sheets up over my head and hide. But her eyes are open and it's too late to do anything except study every single move she makes, study them for clues. She sees me and smiles a confused, uncertain smile. Then she puts her hand out, touches my beard and her smile is less confused.

'Hi there, fuzzy-face,' she says calmly and I know she is trying to be calm for both of us. 'Sleep all right?'

'Super,' I say. The lie is so transparent I begin to giggle.

'You didn't sleep at all, did you?' Hope asks, rubbing her eyes.

'I was thinking.'

'About?'

'What happens next.'

'You don't really want to know.'

'Shouldn't I – want to know?'

'Okay, I have to pee. Really bad. That's what happens next. Happy now? I warned you this wasn't going to be all candlelight and fireworks.' Hope slips out of her side of the bed and stands, naked, facing me. I am careful to hold her stare and not look down. I keep watching her face as she puts on the blue terry-cloth bathrobe – my bathrobe – lying by her side of the bed. 'Don't worry, I'll be back. We'll talk,' she says, leaning over to kiss me on the forehead, the silhouette of her body descending on me like shade.

'Then what?'

'Then breakfast.'

* * *

'She took your car for a reason, Jacob,' Angie said yesterday, reminding me of what Hope had already reminded me. 'Don't you see? That way she has to come back.' Angie was waiting with me on the front porch for Hope to return from her lunch with Neil Topaz. She was trying to be reassuring, but as the afternoon dragged on she was having less and less success. She also kept glancing at her watch.

Hope had been gone for three hours and the only thing I knew for sure was that she and Topaz were no longer at the Happy Garden. I'd already called there and spoken to Mr Ho, who told me they'd left more than an hour ago. 'But Mr Jacob, I give her and man one of your special fortune cookies. It says: *BE ALERT TO POSSIBILITIES*. Like always. Like joke. But they do not think so.'

'She's through with him, Jacob,' Angie said when I got off the phone with Mr Ho. 'She told me so.'

'That was before last night.'

'You have no way of knowing what happened last night.'

'I can make an educated guess.'

'Even if it is what you think, take it from me, sex doesn't change things,' Angie said, then she placed her hand on my knee, as if to pre-empt what she knew I was about to say. It worked. I kept my 'How-would-I-know?' to myself. Instead, I placed my hand over Angie's and said, 'What else did she tell you?'

'What do you mean?' She pulled her hand free.

'When you told her about me? About us? What did she say?'

'Nothing... I don't remember.'

'Was she surprised?'

'Not exactly.'

'Why did you tell her in the first place? How did a discussion of my experience or lack of it even come up in the conversation?'

'She wanted to know why we had stopped seeing each other after that first date. She kept asking me and so I finally told her. You know how good she is at asking questions. She's a pro.'

'And?'

'She was disappointed. She was hoping things would work out … better between us.'

'No kidding.'

'It's not what you think, not just what you think. She cares about you. So do I,' Angie said. 'I'm ashamed of what happened. Or I guess what didn't happen. But you scared me. Here I was thinking I was the one who didn't know what I was doing…. I'm sorry, but you know what I mean. I just didn't think I could handle that kind of responsibility at that particular stage in my life.'

This time the words were out of my mouth before I could stop them: 'Could you handle it now?' I leaned over to kiss her and she turned her face away from me. Her small, straight nose wrinkled. 'I guess not,' I said, more to myself than her.

If I know anything about women – and it's probably obvious by now I don't – I know this: they can smell desperation the way animals smell fear, miles away. It's intuitive. When Angie backed away from my kiss she didn't think: *No, I can't do this. Because he's really in love with Hope and he's really worried about her and frustrated and he's using me as a substitute.* She didn't have time for that. She just had time to think: *He needs this too much.*

'Everything is different now,' Angie said, trying to cover up her instinctive reaction with a reasonable explanation. 'Sandy and I are trying to work things out again. He has a lot of problems, but we're starting to make progress. Did he tell you that he's considering attending a meeting at the clinic for agoraphobics? It's an important first step.'

There are times when Sandy's agoraphobia isn't entirely convincing. Maybe I'd have to see one of his anxiety attacks to really believe it. Whenever he and I have had lunch at his condo, he has behaved in a remarkably self-assured manner. Occasionally, he'd become anxious when he walked me to the door. Once he even slammed the door in my face in the middle of a conversation, then apologized for losing control through the intercom in the lobby. 'Jacob? Good, I caught you before you left. I'm sorry, but I thought I heard someone coming,' he said, his voice cracking with what I assumed was static.

Maybe some men can make desperation work for them instead of against them. If he wants Angie back, as I'm convinced he does, then I don't doubt for an instant that he would be capable of embellishing a panic attack or two. I don't doubt that he would be capable, just like the rest of us, of doing anything to win her back.

'Have you and he –'

'Geez, Jacob, that's not exactly your business.'

'That sounds odd coming from you.'

'We have, okay. But we're not exactly in sync these days. Any days.' She laughed an awkward, feeling-sorry-for-yourself laugh and then she knocked her shoulder against mine. Whatever happened after that happened fast. I pulled her towards me and hugged her. What I'd intended as a companionable hug – a we're-all-in-the-same-boat embrace – quickly became something else. I held on to her desperately, like someone caught in turbulence. She didn't push me away, but she didn't reciprocate either. As if she were still making up her mind. I kissed her waist through her T-shirt – just where the caption read, 'Nothing is ever simple.' I was as confused about what should happen next as ever, but not unpleasantly confused, so when the telephone rang inside the house, I can't remember if I shouted, 'No, not again!' or just wanted to. This time we both knew it was Sandy. Angie was already a couple of hours late for their outing to the elevator.

'I have to go,' she said. 'He's waiting for me. We're going to the laundry room today. That's the plan. I better let him know I'm on my way.'

'You know this is all getting to be very hard for me to figure out,' I said, following her into the house, looking down at her sandaled feet.

'Welcome to my club.'

The answering machine picked up before I could. It wasn't Sandy after all. It was Neil Topaz. His voice was frantic. 'There's been an accident,' he said. 'At the mall. You'd better come quick.'

* * *

Dramatic events occur so infrequently in my life that I am not always the best judge of the appropriate way to react to them. In such circumstances, important decisions can and often do knock me off balance. Which is why the one thing I am always guarding against is being caught off guard.

What do I wear, for example, to breakfast this morning? While Hope is in the bathroom I try several different combinations: boxer shorts and a T-shirt, boxers without the shirt, a bathrobe. By the time I hear the toilet flush, I am dressed in jeans, a button-down shirt and sneakers – a cardigan sweater draped nonchalantly around my shoulders.

'What, no bowtie?' Hope asks as she catches me changing again, into a pair of sweat pants. 'Are you going somewhere, Jacob?'

'No. No, I'm just ... breakfast. I'm making breakfast.'

'Should I get dressed then?'

'Whatever ... whatever you want?'

'Okay.'

'How's scrambled eggs? Orange juice. English muffins. Marmalade or strawberry jam?'

'Marmalade. And black coffee.'

I leave the room and then duck my head back in. My bathrobe is lying on the floor beside the bed and Hope is liberating her underwear from the tangle of bed sheets. Once again, I am struck by how odd this all is. From this short distance, in daylight, I can clearly see the swell of her stomach, which is more prominent when she is standing than when she is lying down. Lifting one foot to slip into her panties, she loses her balance for a moment and then regains it. And I am surprised by a kind of intangible worry that is as startling as that twinge you feel when you accidentally bite down on a piece of aluminum foil. Am I worried for her safety? For the baby? The feeling is so unexpected, so overwhelming I don't even remember to take the stupid sweater off my stupid shoulders.

'Spying?' she says, patting her stomach with one hand, as if it were a habit, draping the other hand, more self-consciously, across her breasts.

'You shouldn't be having coffee, should you?'

'I can have a half cup. The doctor said so.'

'Really?'

Hope screams a mock scream and then picks up my bathrobe and throws it at me. 'You're not going to leave me alone for a moment, are you?' she says, a familiar exasperated expression on her face.

'That's the plan.'

* * *

Panic, not worry, was what I felt yesterday afternoon when Angie and I were in her Corolla on the way to the scene of the accident in the parking lot of the Court Séjour Mall. It wasn't a twinge so much as an ache. Not ordinary, run-of-the-mill concern either, the way you feel when you're late for a deadline or when your car is towed away. No, the kind of panic you feel when you think something irreversible is about to happen.

And, to be honest, yesterday it had less to do with Hope's safety or the safety of her baby than with Neil Topaz and a realization of what he was capable of. Not that he would harm her, but that he would change her mind. I'd read in Hope's Filofax about the time he showed up at her studio, an hour before taping, and begged her publicly, in front of her researcher, her cameraman, her producer, to talk to him for just a few minutes. He actually sank to his knees. When Hope walked away from him he crawled after her, into her office, over the thick cables and under the bulky lights and cameras. *Looking,* Hope wrote, *like Toulouse-Lautrec.* The station's security guard was summoned but he wasn't trained in the necessary techniques to apprehend a crawling man and, as a result, Neil Topaz made it all the way to Hope's desk.

Everybody is capable of everything. The possibilities are infinite. Dr Howie told me this and he's in a position to know. He sees Topaz every week at his True Life Companions workshop. I tried to get him to tell me what he thought, in his professional opinion, Topaz might be up to, but he said that kind of information was strictly confidential. However, he did offer to invite me to Sandy's – where their sessions are routinely held – to observe. 'Even participate, who knows? You could write about it in "Up Next!"'

The meetings have, according to Dr Howie, taken an unexpected turn. They have gone way past the stage of whining and complaining about women and the way we allow them to complicate and control our lives; they are now about self-empowerment. 'The parallel with the women's movement is striking. We are becoming our own best friends,' Dr Howie pointed out. 'This is the 1990s. Men have to stop behaving like damsels in distress, and the first step to doing that is to depend on each other. Then we conclude by singing 'My Way' and Sandy orders pizza.'

'Get out of here,' I said.

'Corny, but true. That new kind of pizza that has cheese in the crust. How about it?'

When I declined, Dr Howie, for the sake of our working relationship and perhaps because the whole point of TLC is that men should support each other, even if it means supporting each other against other men, volunteered this much information. 'Neil comes on self-confident, forceful, sure of himself. But, like most heterosexual guys nowadays, he is really just a scared little boy. More scared than most, as a matter of fact. So if your question is: should you be worried about him? The answer is yes, you better be.'

That's what was on my mind as Angie drove through the mall parking lot, past a half dozen teenage boys, who were rollerblading between stationary and moving cars. They were all dressed uniformly: in baggy jeans, hooded flannel vests and baseball caps with the peak turned around.

'Rally caps,' Angie said. 'See, I remember.' As she said that, one boy glided by her window and gave her the finger. Another one slapped his hand on the trunk of Angie's car.

'I think we're in their way,' Angie said.

'Don't kid yourself, we are.'

'Jacob, are you worried? About Hope? About –'

'I'm worried we're never going to find them. Where arc they?'

'Didn't Neil say? You should have picked up the phone and talked to him,' Angie said, weaving in and out of the parking lot which was crowded for a Sunday.

'I had other things on my mind, remember?'

'What happened between us before shouldn't have,' Angie said. 'There's Sandy to consider now.... And Hope, too.'

I resisted the urge to say what almost happened between us. Or the urge to ask why it almost happened again? But there was no point in that, especially since everyone is capable of everything. Since the possibilities are infinite. Besides, the explanation was obvious. It was right there in the two names Angie had mentioned. In the way we were both clinging to relationships that were either finished or had no chance of ever beginning.

And that's when I saw Joseph's converted yellow laundry truck. And behind it a familiar flash of red – my mother's Malibu. 'There,' I said, pointing to the Mitzvah Mobile. As Angie slowed down and we drove closer, I could no longer see my car or Hope or Neil Topaz. Just a bumper sticker which said, *I BRAKE FOR THE MOSHIACH.*

'There they are... Geez!'

Angie's 'they' referred to Hope who was sitting cross-legged on the asphalt, between the painted yellow lines of a parking space, holding one hand over the bridge of her nose. 'They' also referred to Neil Topaz, who was talking into his cellular phone, and Joseph, who seemed to be trying to attract my attention. Angie's 'geez' referred to my car.

The back end of the Malibu was nearly intact. The bumper was hanging loose on one side, but otherwise there was just a small scratch on the trunk. There was, in addition, a small dent on the roof.

The front end was another story. The hood had folded in on itself like an accordion. My confusion about how this had happened – it was clear the car had been hit from behind – must have shown on my face because Neil Topaz held his cellular to his chest for a moment to respond to my unasked question.

'The initial impact was from the rear,' he explained in a helpful, almost businesslike manner, 'but your car ended up sandwiched between our overzealous buddy boy there,' he pointed at Joseph, 'and a van that was stopped in front of us. The guy in the van refused to stick around. He didn't have any damage. Besides, I think buddy boy scared him off with some biblical quotation. We ... well, you got the worst of it.'

'I'm so sorry, Jacob,' Hope said. 'But it can be repaired. I'm sure of it. It can't be as bad as it looks.' She was standing now in her parking place and rubbing her eyebrow. I could make out a small purple bruise on the bridge of her nose.

'Forget about the car,' I said, though it was obvious to me and to everyone, except Hope, that it was beyond repair. In my experience, things are invariably worse than they look. 'I don't care about the car. Just tell me how you are.'

'I'm fine. I wasn't wearing my seat belt and I guess I bumped my head on the steering wheel, but otherwise I'm fine. Everyone is fine. The police are coming. Neil called them.'

'What happened?' Angie asked.

'I'm not sure. I must have stopped too fast,' Hope said. 'Neil was … we were … I'm sure the car will be okay, Jacob. I'll pay the deductible. It will be good as new.'

When I finally turned to Joseph, he looked more impatient than contrite. He looked as if none of this had anything to do with him, as if he were a disinterested bystander, waiting for me to show up for an appointment for which I was, as usual, tardy. 'She is all right, Jacob. Do not worry. I have been keeping an eye on her for you. But, tell me, why are you never where you are supposed to be?'

I assumed the question was rhetorical – one more Old-Testament quotation – so I didn't answer. Instead, I grabbed Joseph's black fedora from the top off his head and threw it as far as I could. The late afternoon breeze caught it and I watched it sail over the top of the Mitzvah Mobile and out of sight. With one hand clutching the top of his bare head, Joseph watched it too, watched as it reappeared in the grip of a teenage boy on rollerblades. The boy, in turn, tossed the hat to another friend on skates. They continued to glide and weave through the parking lot, passing it back and forth to each other as if it were a frisbee. Joseph had his work cut out for him. He glanced at Neil Topaz and Hope and me and said, 'Jacob, when will you learn who your true friends are?' Then he sighed, as if none of this was a new experience for him, and he ran off to pursue his latest persecutors.

* * *

'You really are scrambling eggs. You weren't joking,' Hope says, as she glances over my shoulder at the frying pan. She is still wearing my terry-cloth bathrobe and hasn't dressed for breakfast after all. The bruise on the bridge of her nose she sustained yesterday afternoon is still purple but fading. She yawns and runs a hand through her tangled brown hair and I shudder. She doesn't hear me the first time, so I do it again.

'You've seen me in the morning before, Jacob.'

'Have I? I don't think so. You look ... beautiful.'

'Usually, I'm throwing up about now. This is your lucky day.'

'Tell me about it.'

'Stop that, Jacob. Be serious. I want to talk about the car.'

'I'm going to call the insurance company this morning. But I told you, Hope: the car is not your problem. And not your fault.'

'It wasn't his fault, Jacob. Joseph's, I mean. He didn't have any warning. I stopped suddenly. I told you this already – last night. We were leaving the parking lot. I was coming back here, like I said I would, and Neil was threatening to call his wife. He started begging me to give him one more chance. He kept saying, "Are you testing me? Is this a test? Because I'll call my wife. Right now. I'll tell her everything. About you. About the baby. Are you testing me, Hope?" He was scaring me. Then he took out his cellular and pushed speed dial. He even held the phone up to my ear. I heard a woman say hello and I tried to grab it out of his hand and that's when I saw the van in front of me and I hit the brakes. Then Joseph hit me.'

'That sounds like his fault to me. He shouldn't have been following you in the first place. You could have been hurt. The baby ... could have been hurt.'

'He was doing it for you. He said so. He saw me with Neil and –'

'I don't need his help,' I say. Hope pats me on the back and turns to walk away and I reach out and grab the belt on my bathrobe. I pull her back to me and hug her from behind. 'I don't need anybody's help, do I?'

'No, you don't, big boy,' she says, trying, not entirely unsuccessfully, to imitate Mae West.

'Don't mock me.' I'm in my bare feet and Hope has flip-flops on so she is several inches taller than me. I stand on my tiptoes and bury my face in the nape of her neck and cup her breasts from behind – as if I'd been doing this all my life – and think how odd this is. How did I end up here? And more to the point, how do I stay right where I am? If I still prayed, this would be a good time to do it. What would I pray for? The status quo, what else?

'Who's mocking?' She turns and kisses me. It is a long kiss which I end up cutting short when the toaster oven rings. I let Hope go and reach for a spatula to flip the eggs, I push them over more than flip them over, then reach for a butter knife but end up holding a fork instead. It occurs to me that I may have bit off more than I can chew when I volunteered for this making-breakfast-for-the-woman-you-just-spent-the-night-with exercise. Particularly having as little experience spending the night with women as I do. And as little experience making breakfast as I do. I may be compulsive when it comes to housework, but the kitchen is the one place I've routinely avoided. Of all the rooms in the house it is the one where I still feel most like an intruder.

Maybe that's because it will always be the room in which we were most identifiably a family. Cups, glasses, saucers, kettles, all manner of vessels, retain some ghostly residue of the kind of unambiguous care and affection that ceased to exist in this house after my mother died. Wisely or not, I have left most of the rooms in the house more or less intact, including my parents' bedroom. But if I could have converted the kitchen to an office or a den or a walk-in closet, I would have. Instead, I have neglected it.

The kitchen table wobbles, the light fixture over the table flickers, none of the cabinet drawers close properly and the pantry is, for all intents and purposes, an empty shell. Whatever canned goods it contains probably predate my mother's death. I didn't buy them and I wouldn't dream of opening them. When my brother still lived here, he or my sister-in-law cooked sometimes, but usually I would just eat out or order in.

But I am committed to making breakfast this morning. Hope is seated at the kitchen table, waiting for a sectioned grapefruit, scrambled eggs, toasted English muffins, orange juice and a half a cup of black coffee. I was a little surprised to see all these things in the refrigerator, but then I remembered that Hope has been buying groceries since she started staying here.

I can see her now, out of the corner of my eye, holding her knife and fork, upright in her respective hands, and I feel as if I am being tested.

'Would you like some help?' she asks.

'No. Everything is under control.' I'm lying, of course. The eggs are mostly unscrambled, lumped together like a mountain range on a papier mâché map; the muffins are burnt; the coffee is… I had forgotten the coffee. So this is what a relationship is: one test after another.

* * *

If he had suspicions, Constable Roberge kept them to himself when he showed up at the Court Séjour Mall. Either that or he didn't remember Angie and me from the last time he'd filed an accident report for us because he just took down the information from Hope and Joseph and left. Neil Topaz then used his cellular to call a tow truck for me and a cab for himself. He tried to convince Hope to come with him, but his heart was no longer in it. If I could have been objective about his predicament, even for a moment, I would have acknowledged that there is nothing quite as disheartening as a disheartened salesman.

Angie had talked Hope into going to the hospital's emergency room to make sure she and the baby were all right and I agreed to accompany them. Just before Neil Topaz left he pulled Hope aside for a moment, lowered his head and whispered something to her. She didn't say anything; she just shrugged.

'What was that all about?' Angie asked after Hope rejoined us.

'Get this: he wanted me to know that it wasn't his wife on the phone. That he was bluffing. I'm sure it was her. I know her voice. So why would he make that up? It doesn't make sense.'

'Men and their pride,' Angie said, putting her arm around Hope's shoulder. I felt like I was eavesdropping on a private conversation. Which is why I didn't say what I was thinking. Pride? What pride? If the events of the last few months, even the last few hours, proved anything, it was that men have no pride. That there's no limit to which we will not go to be loved. To avoid being abandoned and left alone. No act too foolish. No ploy too obvious. Nothing wears out as fast as male pride.

When the tow truck finally came for my mother's Malibu, Hope and Angie's attention switched to me. I could feel them watching to see how I would react so I didn't react. No doubt, they would interpret that as pride, too, which is exactly what I wanted them to think. I signed the driver's release form and retrieved the registration, some cassettes and a flashlight from the glove compartment. Under all that, there was a yellowing photograph I didn't recognize. It was a picture of my brother and father and mother sitting on the hood of the Malibu. I couldn't remember the photo, but I must have taken it the day we bought the car. Hope and Angie were still watching me so I put the snapshot back in the glove compartment along with a couple of maps that belonged to my mother. Maps I had never used, never even unfolded.

'It can be repaired, can't it?' Hope asked the tow truck driver after he'd secured the hook to the back end of the Malibu.

'Not my job, madame,' he said and then he glanced briefly at me and frowned. An old-fashioned guy, he thought it was best to keep the unpleasant truth from women. A throwback, he still believed you could.

'They'll fix it,' Hope said to me as my crushed car wobbled away.

As the three of us left for the hospital in Angie's Corolla, I spotted Joseph at the far end of the mall parking lot, still chasing the two rollerblading teenagers. He had been pursuing them for nearly an hour by then. But I wasn't worried about him or his unretrieved hat. I knew he'd get it back. The two teenagers would eventually grow tired of their improvised game. Joseph would outlast them.

* * *

I have never believed in perseverance. It is a sentimental notion, as sentimental and impractical, I suppose, as love. I have persisted in some things and not in others and I never saw that it made much difference – at least not until last night. Now, sitting across from Hope at the kitchen table, watching her clasp her hands around a WHAT A GUY coffee mug she bought me for my birthday a couple of years ago but which I never had the self-esteem to take out of the cupboard until this morning, I know my perseverance has paid off. I know I've done something right. But I'm at a loss to know what it could possibly be.

After all, I should never have kept on loving Hope when I knew she would never be able to love me back. Everyone said so. I should never have let her stay here on weekends. Again, everyone said so: my brother, my sister-in-law, Angie, Trish Severs, Dr Howie. He called my compulsion to be close to the object of my unrequited love 'an emotional and romantic disaster of epic proportions.' He said that it was worthy of an entire month of 'Ask Your Therapist' columns on denial. Even Joseph, who, in his own way, has always expected more of me than anyone, and who assumed incorrectly that Hope and I were fornicating like there was no tomorrow, would shake his head every time he saw us. And, of course, if I had told anyone that I was secretly reading Hope's diary, they would have advised me to stop immediately. Even this morning, when everything seems possible again, I probably shouldn't keep asking Hope what happens next. But I do.

'I'd love to go back to bed,' she says. 'But it's Monday morning and I have to get to the studio. We're doing a special on the propensity of women to vote no in referendums.'

'No, I mean what happens next?'

'I can't really say, Jacob. But I thought we could go on pretty much the way we always have. Except we could be less strict. I mean I could be less strict.'

'Less strict?'

'Well, you know, about ... you know.'

'Right. I know.' If I were capable of seeing things objectively this morning, this would not be encouraging news. But then I don't know anyone who sees anything objectively, most notably me, and as news go, it is good enough.

'It was always my instinctive feeling that sex would be the end of our friendship. I'm willing to admit that my instincts might have been wrong. Again.'

'Told you so.'

'But, right now, I am seriously late for work. I have to get dressed.'

'Can I watch?' The question is out of my mouth before I realize what I've said. The tone is all wrong. It was supposed to be a joke, but it didn't come out that way. It came out sounding smarmy. The kind of question Neil Topaz would ask. The last thing she needs right now.

'Why not,' Hope says cheerfully. She rises from the table and undoes the belt around her bathrobe. She pulls me towards her and whispers in my ear, 'I'm not going anywhere. Except work. Get used to it.'

'Can you be a little late for work?' I ask, holding on tight.

She starts to raise her shoulders and then stops herself mid-shrug to say, 'I suppose so.' Which is lesson number two in my crash course on relationships: it seems you can say anything.

* * *

Last night in the hospital, waiting for Hope, I said nothing. I paced the hospital corridors instead, like a cliché, a stereotype of an expectant father, realizing how, up until that moment, I'd just been putting on a show of being supportive. I'd accompanied Hope to the clinic, to her doctor appointments, bought prenatal and postnatal books, dragged myself out of bed on Sunday mornings to make the rounds at garage sales all over Court Séjour, nagged her about drinking wine or coffee or sneaking a cigarette or not getting enough sleep, but it was an act. What I thought she wanted me to do. What I knew she wanted someone to do.

On some level, it was the kind of thing I was always doing to impress Hope, to make her see me in a different light. Circling the corridors, I passed Angie at a pay phone and eavesdropped as she explained to Sandy why she was late:

'No, it was Jacob's car ... No, nobody was hurt ... No, I wasn't there ... I was at Jacob's ... Sandy, don't be idiotic ... Geez, it's not like that ... I said I'd come and I will ... Maybe you should try going down to the laundry room without me ... it's late, nobody will be there ... Sandy ... Sandy, take some laundry, okay?'

I waited for Angie to hang up and we paced together until Hope came out of the examining room, a small bandage over the bridge of her nose and another over her eyebrow. 'I'm fine. Everything's all right. Don't make a fuss,' she said, looking directly at me.

Angie drove us home. We all noticed the Mitzvah Mobile parked in its usual place, but none of us commented on it. Angie was still expected at Sandy's and left us off. Hope yawned conspicuously and went straight to my parents' bedroom. I went into my office to watch a videotape of *The Apartment* as I'd intended to do all day, all weekend. More than an hour into the movie as Jack Lemmon was straining spaghetti through his tennis racquet, Hope knocked on the door.

'I couldn't sleep. I'm worried about your car,' she said. As she entered the room, I pressed the pause button on the VCR: the screen freezing on Shirley MacLaine kissing Jack Lemmon on the forehead. Hope was wearing a kimonolike robe, with big black oriental characters on it, the cord was tied beneath the swell in her belly. Instead of slippers she was wearing a pair of my flip-flops. She had her Filofax under her arm.

'For the last time, it wasn't your fault.' I was trying not to stare at the Filofax, but it wasn't like her to walk around with it. Unless she knew. Had I put it back in the right place? Had I left it open?

'That's the problem with keeping one of these things: it's a constant reminder, in black and white, of all your most humiliating mistakes.... Fred MacMurray still the bad guy?' she said, glancing at the television.

'Who else?'

'Clear cut and unambiguous, isn't it? Can I watch a little?'

'Sure,' I said, patting my hand on the empty space beside me on the couch. But Hope climbed onto the StairMaster instead.

'I probably should be working out regularly. Exercise in moderation is good for me. The doctor says I should walk an hour each day. What do *they* say?' She pointed to a pile of manuals and textbooks on the corner of my desk.

I picked up *You & Your Baby* and glanced at the index. 'Let's see. Here, it is: 'No matter how exciting they are, babies do not solve other problems. If you are having trouble at work or with your partner, try to work things out before you have the baby... Start to eat better and exercise more. Getting your life in order will make it easier to look after a baby; you will have more time and energy to enjoy being a parent."

'Too late for that,' Hope said, patting her belly and continuing to ascend an imaginary staircase, her flip-flops slapping loudly. 'You don't use this StairMaster much, do you?'

'I got tired of staying in the same place.'

'That doesn't sound like you.'

'Ha ha.'

'You know what else I could use now. A drink. There's some wine in the fridge.'

'The book says: "Alcohol is a drug. It passes from your bloodstream into your baby's.... No one knows how much alcohol is safe for a pregnant woman."'

'I know, I know. Another bad habit. Are there any things it's safe for a pregnant woman to do? Never mind, don't answer that.... Just a little bit of wine, Jacob. It will help me sleep. Oh, Jacob, bring the bottle, just in case.'

I frowned and waved the open baby book at her, but did as she asked. When I returned from the kitchen I handed her a quarter of a glass of wine and then put the bottle down on the floor beside the couch, closer to me than to her. But she immediately leaned down from the StairMaster for the bottle and filled her glass. I gave her another disapproving look, but she ignored me and put the bottle down, beside her, this time.

'Exercise and alcohol cancel each other out,' she said, then abruptly changed the subject. 'So do you know what's going on with Angie? With her and Sandy?'

'I don't know. They had a big date tonight. They were going to the laundry room ... I know – I shouldn't keep making jokes about it. Agoraphobia is no joking matter.'

'And, remember, he is your best friend,' she said, trying not to grin.

'Right. She's worried about him.'

'It's more than that, you know. I mean you do know that, don't you?'

'Yes. But I don't know why you're telling me that.'

'Because I want to make sure she's not leading you on.'

'I wish you two could stop discussing me and worry about the referendum like everyone else around here.'

'That's one thing: I've never led you on,' Hope said, breathing more heavily as she climbed higher.

'For which I am eternally grateful. We certainly wouldn't want anything like that, would we?' Out of the corner of my eye, I watched Shirley MacLaine running down the street to Jack Lemmon's apartment. I pressed the mute button on the remote control as the music swelled. I always get weepy at the end of the movie, but not this time, not this night. I wasn't going to be a sucker again for another silly, sentimental Hollywood ending. The ending where love triumphs, where the right people find each other and the music swells. Never again, I thought, will I allow myself to be misled so successfully. I planned to tape over *The Apartment* as soon as possible.

'Jacob, could we not do this again?' Hope said, refilling her glass. Her tone of voice was familiar, the usual incompatible mix of sympathy and frustration.

'You started it.'

'What do you want me to say, Jacob? For the thousandth time, what do you want? I can't change the way I feel, the way I am. I don't know what you want me to say.' She stopped climbing and the Stair-Master whirred to an abrupt halt. 'But I'll tell you something I shouldn't.'

'Not again.' I couldn't imagine what surprise Hope had in store for me this time, except that I had a hunch it would break my heart again.

'Okay, I'll tell you, but I don't want you to get the wrong idea. Lately, I have been thinking about you … about us, I suppose. How could I not? I love the fact that I can rely on you, trust you. That's more important to me than you can know. Lately, I've been thinking that I don't know what I would do without your support. But then, at the same time, I also know it would be wrong for us to become involved. More involved. You know what I mean. Something inside me keeps insisting it would be a mistake. I think, down deep, you know that too.'

'You're right. You shouldn't have told me.'

'I'm sorry.'

'So there is nothing else to say. Nothing, as you correctly point out, that we haven't said a thousand times before. Except –'

'Except what?'

'I don't think I can go on like this. I know I've said that before too and I know it was me who insisted you stay here, but now that Topaz is out of the picture –' I paused to see if she would react, but she just kept drinking, 'well, you'll probably be moving back into your apartment. So maybe we should stop seeing each other.'

'Altogether?'

'Altogether.' I had said this before, too, but I had never meant it. As much as I would have liked to, I still wasn't sure I meant it.

'Truly?'

'Yes … No … I don't know … Oh, fuck me.'

'I suppose we were overdue for one of these discussions, weren't we?'

And I knew how this one was going to go. Like all the others. I heard all I needed to in the 'here-we-go-again' way she said the word 'discussion.' I nodded and then buried my head in my hands. Pity, I thought. This is all about pity. About how I'm not above asking for it. And how she can't quite give it. Which is why I wasn't paying attention to what she said next. I knew what it would be anyway: more apologies, more excuses, more exasperation. Still, there was something about the tone of her voice – something like exasperation but different – that made me look at her, from behind my hands, and listen as she repeated the two words that were not an apology after all. She said them louder. More precisely. Enunciating the way she did on television. She said, 'Come here.'

But she still had to repeat herself several more times before I crawled, on my hands and knees, across the floor. My legs were wobbly when I did finally stand at the side of the StairMaster so it was lucky she came down off the machine, arms open wide, to hold me up. The pedals kept bobbing up and down for a while and Hope knocked over the bottle of wine, which was nearly empty and which spun in a circle on the floor. My first attempt to kiss her was met with a yelp as I bumped the bruise above her nose with my forehead.

After that, Hope held on to me for what seemed like an unreasonably long time. I finally pulled free and kissed her. Her mouth was closed, at first. I reached instinctively for the belt on her kimono. She reached for the belt on my bathrobe. But both were knotted. So I continued to kiss her, awkwardly on the mouth, then awkwardly and frantically on the neck and the shoulder and the wrist. At one point, I realized I was kissing the back of my own hand.

'Wait,' Hope said, 'wait. Don't go mental on me.' She pushed me away from her and then calmly undid her kimono, carefully draping it over the handlebars of the StairMaster. Then naked, she held out her hand and led me to the master bedroom.

'What's next?' I said, not sure where to look. 'You know ... I mean Angie told you ... I mean about me ... and ...'

'Forget about it. It won't be a problem if we don't want it to be,' she said as she lay down across the width of the bed. I still couldn't unknot my robe so I pulled it over my head. Just don't think, I kept thinking, as I wriggled unimpressively out of my pyjama bottoms and lay down beside her.

'Are you sure about this?' I said. Which I realized even then qualified as the stupidest question I've asked in a lifetime of asking stupid questions.

Hope kicked off her flip-flops – one toppled my parents' framed wedding picture on the armoire. She winced, then shrugged and I noticed that the difference between an encouraging shrug and a discouraging one was immeasurable. She pulled me on top of her and rocked me back and forth on her protruding belly. Everything was happening too fast one moment, too slow the next. My breathing was quick and shallow and I was scaring myself. But she just stroked the back of my head. 'Don't worry,' she said, matter-of-factly. 'Nothing has to happen right now.' An obvious reference to what didn't seem to be happening. I had always suspected there would be problems, but I had always assumed I'd be too fast, not too slow.

'We can just lie here like this,' she went on. Which only made me more anxious. More dizzy. I knew if I wasted this opportunity, I'd never forgive myself. Still, nothing was going as I'd spent far too much of my life imagining it would. This was a mess, a tangle of clumsiness and tenderness, impossible to determine where the one started and the other left off.

'Now, don't go mental on me,' she said again, as she spread her legs gradually, squeezing my hips between her thighs and continuing to rock me, now from side to side.

'Why do you keep saying that?'

'Because you can't see the look on your face.'

'Is it that bad?'

'No, no,' she said, smiling a foreign, seductive smile and pulling my head down until it was buried between her neck and her shoulder. I concentrated on not concentrating, which seemed to work for a while. Gradually, the blood began to rush out of my head and distribute itself more efficiently. Then Hope guided me inside her and since I wasn't sure if I should say the one thing I really wanted to say – which was thank you – I blurted out the next thing that came into my mind, 'Why are you doing this?'

'Why not?' she said.

* * *

According to *You & Your Baby*, 'many women feel differently about sex during pregnancy … perhaps you are not so interested in intercourse (though) you might find sex even more enjoyable.' Predictably, *The Father Book: Pregnancy and Beyond* tries harder to find a silver lining: 'The second trimester is often associated with a heightened desire for intercourse in many women.'

I've been lying in bed with my collection of pregnancy textbooks piled up on Hope's side ever since she showered, dressed, forgot where she put her key, borrowed mine, and, not-kidding-around-any-more late, left for the studio. 'You'll call me if you hear anything about the Malibu?' she said, patting my forehead.

Before she left, she also suggested I try to get some sleep. 'You deserve it and you're going to need it,' she said, winking. *The Father Book* adds, by way of explanation, that 'increased hormone levels may be contributing to (your partner's extraordinarily) increased sex drive.'

I appreciate her concern, but sleep remains out of the question. Instead, I go into my office to program the VCR for this afternoon's segment of 'Been There, Done That'. I expect to be able to read between the lines of Hope's script for any reference, any allusion she might make to how her life has changed since her audience saw her last. I want to see if she looks different.

Outside, Joseph is washing the Mitzvah Mobile. For the first time in a long time I am simply puzzled and not infuriated by his behaviour. After all, if it weren't for Joseph there is no telling how differently things might have turned out last night. I have a thought: maybe, I'll climb up to his window later and thank him.

The empty wine bottle is still lying on its side on the floor in my office and Hope's kimono is still folded over the StairMaster. I promise myself I'll start using the exercise machine regularly. Beginning tomorrow. I'll lose weight – it occurred to me last night as I lay awake that I could probably stand to be fifteen pounds or so lighter – I'll change my diet. I'll eat more fruits and vegetables, more roughage. I'll get more sleep. I'll work harder. I'll watch less television. I'll read more. I'll subscribe to more magazines and newspapers. I'll be better informed.

In the meantime, though, I also remember that I have to finish Dr Howie's 'Ask Your Therapist' column for this week. The deadline is today.

We'd agreed to start another series, this time on phobias, and I already have an outline and plenty of notes on the subject. (*Dear Dr Weiskopf: How do you know if you are really suffering from agoraphobia or if you just have no reason to leave the house? Signed, Home Alone.*) But this morning I can't bring myself to write, even this close to deadline, even on Dr Howie's behalf, about the ways in which we limit ourselves, the ways in which anxiety undermines our best intentions, our potential for happiness. Instead, I decide to write about love and commitment.

Dear Dr Weiskopf: How do you know when you are in love?
Signed, Still in the Dark.

Dear 'Still in the Dark': As a licensed psychotherapist (all his/our columns start this way) I am obliged to tell you that falling in love is never as simple as people like to think. Distinguishing between mere infatuation or sexual desire and genuine commitment is always a guessing game. However, again as a licensed psychotherapist, I do believe that there is one right, yes, even perfect person out there, for each of us, and that you will know when you have found yours. So if you haven't found the right person yet, don't give up. Persevere. Let hope be your guide ...

I go on like that for another 750 words. Unlike most of the columns and term papers I ghostwrite, this one seems to ghostwrite itself. I finish a draft in thirty minutes and fax it to Dr Howie's office for his okay.

Which leaves me time to contemplate what love and commitment really mean and what really happened last night. Whether something I said or did changed Hope's mind? Whether I just wore her down or she suddenly realized that she'd loved me all along? Hope's Filofax is in its usual place. I saw her scribble something in it this morning when she was supposed to be looking for her keys and I was supposed to be sleeping and for a moment I consider reading it – I even get the stepladder out of the kitchen pantry – but then I reconsider. Along with losing weight and subscribing to the *Utne Reader*, another promise I made myself this morning was never to compromise Hope's privacy or her trust again. It's a promise I am determined to keep, especially now that there is so much more to lose.

I am just beginning to feel proud of my resolve when I receive a fax from Dr Howie. It says: 'Jacob, I'm glad everything is peachy with you, but I'm not putting my name on that sentimental nonsense. I have a reputation to maintain, even if you don't. "Persevere. Let hope be your guide." What's next? If at first you don't succeed, try, try again? Please, pull the other one. I do hate to stifle your creativity – and, believe me, this thing is damned creative – but just do the piece we talked about. Okay? Give me 800 words on panic attacks. Signed, You Have to Be Kidding.'

I am no longer in a position to be fussy about the work I accept or turn down. I have already called Trish Severs to ask her to reinstate my 'Up Next!' column. 'Somebody's happy,' she said. 'How do I know? Female intuition.' There will also have to be more term papers. I won't be able to say no, as I have in the past, to writing about psychology or history or economics. Besides, they require more research, fewer opinions and therefore pay more than writing about John Cheever and Shady Hill.

So panic attacks it is. I work until late in the afternoon and then, exhausted, fall asleep like a kid in kindergarten, my head on my desk. The VCR clicking off at the conclusion of 'Been There, Done That' wakes me and it's only then that I realize I've inadvertently taped over the final few minutes of *The Apartment*.

Three

Mixed Blessings

Friday, December 22. My father became a stranger after my mother died. I used to think loneliness accounted for how different he'd become – or how different he seemed to my brother and me. But the truth is he didn't change so much as change back. What I couldn't understand at the time and am only now beginning to understand is that my father had become the person he was before he met my mother. A person I never knew.

Still, if I'd been paying attention, I would have noticed the transformation the day of my mother's funeral. Always so easy to console, even at the worst times, even the night my mother died, he became inconsolable. It was a blustery afternoon in late October and we had just returned home from the cemetery. My father took his seat in his mourner's chair – the chairs provided by the funeral home were so low and hard that for the next seven days either my brother or I would have to lift him out of it whenever he wanted to stand – and said the same thing to everyone who offered their condolences. 'What am I going to do now?' he muttered. 'I'd be better off dead.' After a while, I stopped hearing what he was saying and focused on the faint grass stain on the knees of his black pants where he had knelt beside my mother's grave. Helping him to his feet then had required all my strength. Each time I thought I had him upright, he would sink to the ground again, sorrow and resistance working in tandem like another, even more immutable law of gravity.

At home, he'd wanted to change his suit, but there wasn't time: the mourners started arriving as soon as we were back at the house. In some cases, they beat us home, hoping, I suppose, to get this uncomfortable obligation over with as soon as possible. Invariably, they all said the same things – how shocked they were, how sorry, how life goes on, how there was hardly any traffic crossing the Court Séjour Bridge.

Following Jewish tradition, people visiting a shiva house are not supposed to ring the doorbell or knock before entering, so when someone did knock, early that first evening, I ignored it. I assumed any visitors would see themselves in. But when they knocked again, I went to the door and was greeted by two small children. It was impossible to tell whether they were boys or girls because both were wearing pillow cases over their heads with holes cut out for their eyes. Even their shoes were concealed. One pillow case had the word BOO! written across it diagonally in black, indelible ink. The other pillow case was wearing a baseball cap and carrying a small plastic gun, which he or she pointed at me. Both ghosts had paper shopping bags held open in front of them and, not quite in unison, they shouted, 'Trick or treat?'

It was Halloween – a fact I'd probably noted some time earlier in the day but had forgotten about. For the rest of the evening my brother and I took turns standing guard on the front porch – to make sure no more children disturbed us. When a kid dressed in a pirate or a Power Ranger costume would arrive at the foot of the stairs I'd shake my head – shake it violently the closer they came. Some still didn't get the message or thought I was joking and persisted. I could think of nothing else to say to them but, 'Go away. Something bad happened here.'

'Your mother never liked Halloween. Do you remember?' my father said. He'd come outside to smoke. He'd given up the habit when he was a young man but had started again recently. My brother and I had argued with him about it. We told him it didn't make any sense to start smoking after so many years. But he just looked at us as if we were speaking a foreign language.

'I remember.' I said. 'She used to close the lights at eight o'clock and say, "That's enough." She'd always run out of candy, too, and have to scare up those little boxes of raisins that had been in the pantry for years. Decades maybe. For a fellow kid, it was very embarrassing.'

My father smiled and then took a short drag on his cigarette. He wasn't accustomed to smoking yet and he inhaled tentatively.

'Don't say that any more, Jacob.'

'Say what?'

'That something bad happened here.' He coughed abruptly and then looked away from me and stared out at the street absent-mindedly. I watched a bit of ash tumble from his cigarette onto the torn black mourner's tie the funeral home had provided and that the men in the family were compelled to wear throughout the week.

'Something did.'

'But don't say it any more, please.'

When he was a teenager my father spent nine months in an iron lung and almost didn't make it out. When he did, the doctors said that he would never walk again, and when he did walk they said he would never be able to lead a normal life. And though by then he had good reason not to believe them, he did. His expectations narrowed almost to the point of being invisible. He doubted himself, so much so that a day didn't go by when he didn't think he would have been better off dead.

My father grew up during the Depression: a shy, self-conscious man, more disabled by self-pity than by polio. That he met my mother at all must have seemed like a miracle to him; even her parents said he'd never be able to support her. They wondered, privately, if he was capable of having children. He wondered the same things and probably would never have married my mother if she hadn't been surer of him than he was of himself. He had never expected to have a wife, a family, and, eventually, a house in the suburbs and when he ended up with all those things he considered himself lucky. Blessed, really. It was not his natural inclination to feel that way about himself and his life. Optimism didn't come easily to him, but he could never quite dismiss the evidence all around him. My mother's death ended, once and for all, his run of good luck and facing that fact was even harder than facing the loneliness that was about to become an inevitable part of his new life.

* * *

I am panting into Hope's borrowed yellow scarf as I walk in circles around the block – my fingers crossed tight inside a matching pair of her mittens. Despite the colour, the scarf and mittens are conscientious choices: talismans. Crossing my fingers is a superstitious act, too, as involuntary as breathing. Except breathing – alternately slow and deliberate, then quicker and even quicker – requires concentration these days. Our Lamaze instructor Chantal Sansregret is teaching Hope and me to pant and encouraging us to practise whenever we can. So that's what I am doing – practising, preparing.

These daily walks – or forced marches, as Hope calls them – always take place at the same time: prime time, from eight to nine o'clock in the evening. The route never varies. I proceed down the street to the unfinished park at the corner (the park that was supposed to be completed a year after my parents moved to Court Séjour), past a couple of swings and a slide (which once fell on a child I knew and fractured his skull) then past the small slope where the few remaining small children in the neighbourhood cling to toboggans, shrieking with excitement, then around the block directly behind my house. Circling back, I end up across the street from my house where Joseph's yellow Mitzvah Mobile serves as a sort of neighbourhood landmark and finally a finishing line. I tap the back bumper for luck – the side with the sticker that says *Honk, If You Love the Messiah* – and then repeat the route. Seven times. Eight minutes each time. The route has been meticulously thought out and is meticulously followed so that there is never a moment when the dim halogen light burning in what was once my parents' master bedroom – where Hope is either reading or watching television or napping – is out of my sight.

Hope initiated these walks – the doctors as well as the books recommended exercise – and she used to take them with me once she realized I could go for weeks, even longer as the days become shorter and colder, without ever leaving the house. When she stopped joining me on the walks a few weeks ago because her blood pressure was up and because she was advised to spend more time in bed, she encouraged me to keep going out on my own. I tried to convince her I was getting all the exercise I required on the StairMaster, but she insisted I needed fresh air.

'But what happens if –'

'I'll be fine,' she said.

'But what about –'

'You'll be fine,' she said.

For Hope, one of the side effects of being pregnant is an

enhanced and eerie ability to read my mind. While there was a time when this would have worried me, it doesn't any more. I know now that there is not much more on my mind than how deeply, how foolishly I'm in love with her. And how she hasn't yet said, in so many words, that she loves me back.

For me, one of the side effects of Hope's being pregnant is that in the last three months my vertigo has become steadily worse. Before, when I was home, alone, it was never a problem, but now I sometimes feel faint just washing the dishes or answering the telephone. Sometimes my head spins so badly I have to lean it against the refrigerator door to make it stop.

The books I've been consulting maintain that sympathetic pregnancy is a practically unheard-of, practically apocryphal phenomenon. Which is what Hope's obstetrician told her when she asked on my behalf. Except dizziness isn't my only symptom. I'm having trouble sleeping, too. I'm nauseated most mornings. I pee constantly. I have lower back spasms and unprecedented heartburn. My nipples hurt. Explain how that's apocryphal.

Also, once a week for the last three months Mr Ho personally delivers a special order from the Happy Garden: one imperial roll, sweet and sour spareribs, moo goo guy pan, cherry Jell-O and, of course, a fortune cookie. It always says the same thing: HAPPY EVENTS WILL TAKE PLACE SHORTLY IN YOUR HOME. 'For the lady,' Mr Ho will say, grinning and handing me a brown paper bag with a grease spot the size of a softball in the centre. I will nod and hand him a ten-dollar bill and tell him to keep the change, but he refuses to accept a tip from me.

'What happened to the regular delivery boy?' I always ask because he enjoys being teased.

'Special order, special customer. Lady must keep strength. Additional plum sauce.' The lady – Hope, that is – wouldn't eat this stuff if her life depended on it. The MSG alone, she insists, is enough to ensure that her child will be a high-school drop-out. No, the craving is all mine and it's genuine. I have watched so many television sitcoms and old movies in which pregnant women devour ice cream and sardines or some other preposterous, unpalatable combination that I feel obliged to uphold the tradition.

The other reason Hope insisted I continue the walks without her is because when I'm around her for too long, I tend to stare at her in a way, she says, that goes way beyond ordinary staring. The other night, for example, we were watching a documentary about the aftermath of last October's referendum. Expert after expert stated unequivocally that even the 'No' vote was, in actuality, a vote for change and, according to Hope, I didn't take my eyes off her once for the entire sixty minutes, commercials included. Not even to make a joke about Camille Laurin, the cabinet minister who, despite being in his seventies and a psychiatrist, continues to dye his hair so black it is nearly blue. In my own defence, staring has become as involuntary as crossing my fingers. I don't even realize I am doing it until Hope warns me to stop.

'Cut it out,' she said to me this evening, as I waffled on whether or not to take my walk.

'Cut what out?'

'You know perfectly well what. All this love and concern. It's creepy. It makes me want to drink or smoke or do drugs or something.'

'I was just thinking maybe I should skip tonight. It's snowing and you, in case you haven't noticed, are unusually crabby.'

'Don't be such a baby, Jacob. Besides, it's lovely – the first real snowfall of the winter. I wish I could go out. Go somewhere. Go anywhere. So go, will you? For me? Put on a hat. Take a scarf. And a key. I think I'll lie down for a while.'

'Lie down?'

'Don't go mental on me – I'm tired, that's all. This is not 'The Dick Van Dyke Show'.' Hope is reading my mind again – referring to the episode in which Dick Van Dyke recalls the anxious days leading up to his son's birth. It's a caricature of the overwrought expectant father, which culminates with Dick Van Dyke sleeping in his suit, the telephone resting on his chest, his index finger poised in the dialling position.

'You said you liked that episode?'

'Yes, Jacob, I liked it. It was funny. The first time.'

The snow has started to turn to ice so I am walking more cautiously than usual. My ankle is still not one hundred percent. It continues to ache whenever the weather is damp. Otherwise, my luck is holding and has held for three months. But being lucky, as I am discovering, is neither as easy nor as random as I once believed. What I've begun to realize is that the luckier I am the more important and the more difficult it is to remain vigilant. Sometimes, I even miss my old hapless self, because now I have to be on guard against anything – no matter how minor or trivial – that threatens to disrupt the status quo.

* * *

Take the Stanley 2001, for example – the spare automatic garage door opener, which has been missing for at least a week, though probably a lot longer. I trace its disappearance back three months, to the afternoon Joseph's Mitzvah Mobile collided with my Malibu at the parking lot of the Court Séjour Mall. Hope thinks she remembers me removing it from the glove compartment at the time or maybe removing it a few days later when I signed over the Malibu to the scrap yard. (That's funny coming from her; she's the one who's always misplacing things.)

I remember nothing of the kind. Still, I've only started wondering where it is lately because at least once a day for the last week, the garage door has opened on its own. True, this is not unprecedented – sometimes a passing car phone or even a low-flying airplane will set off the Stanley 2001 – but now it's especially unnerving. What if the device has fallen into the wrong hands? What if someone out there – maybe a stranger, though more likely not – is just biding his time before he intrudes on our happy home?

That's the thing about being lucky: you can never believe in coincidence again. Take, for example, Angie's recent decision to have a child, with or without Sandy's help, and through whatever means necessary, including artificial insemination. I confess, next to that, the disappearance of the spare automatic garage door opener is what Dr Howie would call 'small potatoes.' I learned of Angie's plan last week when we bumped into each other in the lobby of the Court Séjour Medical Centre.

'What brings you here?' Angie said, startling me. I was leaving the elevator and she was entering it when we noticed each other. We both hesitated for a moment looking for a way to reverse our field – I even took a step back into the elevator. Both of us, as it turned out, had a reason for being there that we preferred the other not know about.

I made up a story about doing research for my column. In fact, I had come to the clinic to see Hope's doctor. Hope had dropped me off on her way to the studio and it was at her urging that I had agreed to discuss my sympathetic pregnancy symptoms with a professional. I had wanted to talk to Dr Howie about my symptoms, but, as Hope correctly pointed out, that wasn't such a good idea. ('Do you really want to write about, let alone read about your symptoms in the *Snooze*?' she pointed out. 'Think about it, Jacob, "*Dear Sore Nipples*"?') Even so, I only agreed to see Hope's ob-gyn because she had already discussed my problems with him. Hope was particularly concerned that what she calls my chronic insomnia was affecting her own ability to get her rest.

To be honest, I never had trouble sleeping until Hope and I began sleeping together. I suppose I had romantic notions about that, too, about how two people in love would naturally drift off in each other's arms. But we've both had to make adjustments. She to my snoring, my knuckle-cracking, my habit of falling asleep with the television or VCR on. Me to her sprawling. Sometimes I'll wake up and find her, arms and legs spread out, pushing me nearer and nearer the edge of our queen-sized bed. I've tumbled off twice in the last three months. I have also had to get used to Hope singing in her sleep. Though it's never loud enough to wake me, it's loud enough to keep me from falling asleep. She doesn't know she does this and I haven't figured out yet whether or not I should tell her. Still, I find myself listening too intently for some clue, in the Beatles lyrics she regularly murmurs, as to why she is here with me. 'Strawberry Fields', a few weeks ago, then last week 'Penny Lane', and then just a few nights ago after we'd made love and she had fallen asleep not so much in my arms as on my arm, I believe I heard her mutter: 'She loves you, yeah, yeah, yeah.'

'Why don't we just humour her,' the doctor had said, referring to Hope and refusing to accept my medicare card. 'I wouldn't want to have to explain this appointment.' He also told me to be patient with her and to call him when my contractions were five minutes apart. 'Otherwise, just try to relax,' he said. 'Drink some warm milk or sleep on the couch for a while. It will be good practice. For the future.'

Angie's story was that she was at the Medical Centre to attend Sandy's third agoraphobia meeting on his behalf. She went into more detail than was probably necessary about the two previous meetings: how, for example, she was the only person there, aside from the therapist and a few other concerned spouses. But when I volunteered to attend the meeting with her – when I lied and said that it might even make an interesting column – she reluctantly told me the truth.

'Artificial insemination? And Sandy doesn't know?' I asked.

'He knows I still want a baby, he knows that all right.' I remember noticing that Angie was dressed oddly – not untidily, but not at all like herself. She was wearing a navy blue business suit and high heels. Her hair was up again and she had a little too much make-up on. And while everything matched, except her eyes, nothing seemed appropriate. It was as if she couldn't quite figure out what to wear to an appointment to discuss her suitability as a candidate for artificial insemination so she had decided to be as businesslike as possible. Like she was showing up for a job interview.

'Sandy is in denial,' she went on. She stared at me for a moment and then closed her brown and green eyes and took a deep breath. 'But then who isn't?'

I recognized the look. It was the same one I saw in Joseph's expression when he leaned over me in his backyard last summer. Or on Neil Topaz's face when he refused to leave my kitchen. To tell the truth, I've probably seen it on my own face a time or two when I glimpsed my reflection in the mirror as I was reading Hope's diary entries. It is the look of someone who's about to go off the deep end. Or who's already gone.

'We seem to be incapable of keeping secrets from each other,' I said.

'Which reminds me, I have a sperm sample in my purse.'

'Congratulations.'

'Correction: a stolen sperm sample.'

* * *

The snow is turning to sleet and my breathing is uneven. In Lamaze class, sleet was not factored into the equation. The visibility is bad enough to make it almost impossible to see the light from my master bedroom. It's almost nine and I'm behind schedule. I'm thinking Hope will be waiting for me, maybe even worrying, when up ahead of me a station wagon's reverse lights blink on and the vehicle swerves backwards on the icy road. Even from behind, particularly from behind, I recognize the driver: the oval shape of her head, the rounded slope of her shoulder. The car skids to a stop as the electric door locks pop up like fingers snapping and the electric window on the passenger side slides down.

'Hi, stranger,' Angie says, leaning across the passenger seat.

'Hello ... yourself.' I push Hope's scarf away from my mouth to greet her. My moustache freezes instantly.

'We have to stop meeting like this.' Angie's car radio is playing at a whisper – a nightly on-air personals column called 'Radio Rendez-Vous'. I can hear a woman, with a French accent, being urged to make a list of her most appealing qualities. She is struggling to come up with some other way to present herself than, 'I am good fun to be with.'

'What brings you out on a night like this?' I ask. The question makes me sound suspicious and I'm afraid that's what I am. Why *do* Angie and I keep meeting like this?

'I could ask you the same thing.'

'This is the famous forced march.'

'Want to take a break?'

'I shouldn't. I should get home.'

'To the little woman.'

'Not so little at the moment.'

'You're soaking wet,' she says, glancing down at the cuff of my sweat pants.

'All right, just for a minute.' I open the passenger door and slip in beside Angie. She turns up the heater. The car still smells new. The dome light stays on for a moment and, once again, I see in Angie's expression something to worry about.

'You men are such fragile creatures, aren't you? Much more fragile than us.'

'You won't get an argument from me.'

* * *

Learning last week that Angie was carrying a stolen sample of Sandy's sperm in her purse fit easily into the category of more information than I needed. So did trying to figure out how she might have obtained that sample without Sandy's knowledge. Or what she intended to do with it. Which is why I should have passed on her offer in the elevator to go to her appointment with her. I should have taken a bus home.

'It won't take long,' Angie said, 'and I can give you a lift after. You, take a bus? Anyway, there's something I want to show you. And something I want to talk to you about.'

So I waited for her. Maybe it was just the fact that she had to ask that made saying no impossible. That the man who should have been here carrying his own sperm sample, a voluntary one, wasn't. I also needed a lift. When you live your whole life in the suburbs you develop elaborate strategies to avoid public transportation. Given a choice between staying home and taking a bus, I have invariably stayed home.

The receptionist at the offices of the Court Séjour Institute of Reproductive Technology (CSIRT), which took up an entire floor of the Court Séjour Medical Centre and was in the process of expanding, greeted Angie and me warmly. As if she thought she knew more about us, about our secret desires and the lengths we were willing to go to fulfil them, than she should have. The doctor who greeted us was also friendly, too friendly. He shook Angie's hand and then vigorously shook mine. There was in this nonchalant act, which should have been routine but seemed rehearsed, a recognition that this whole procedure was a curious one. More curious, as it turns out, than he knew.

'This is not my husband,' Angie said, trying to explain. 'He's a friend.'

'Fine, that's fine.'

'No, just a friend. He's here for moral support.'

The CSIRT waiting room was, unlike Hope's obstetrician's waiting room, high-tech – laid out with space-age chrome chairs and

Plexiglas tables. The message was clear: this was serious science. Nothing even remotely natural was going on here. At first glance, a squat three-story clinic in a strip mall in Court Séjour seemed like an odd place to set up a fertility clinic. Compared, let's say, to a high-rise office building downtown. Then again, if you thought about it: what place could be more appropriate? After all, the suburbs were built on the assumption that you could manufacture or, at the very least, simulate happiness.

The waiting room was humming with all the energy we invest in our wildest dreams. A receptionist wearing a headset spoke into an intercom and announced the names of patients, informing them where to report. Nurses wearing latex gloves and white lab coats rushed from one examining room to another. Men, reluctant partners, tagged along behind their wives and significant others to witness blood tests, ultrasounds and pelvic exams. Everyone was preoccupied. Everyone had a purpose. A conspicuous effort was being made not to remind people why they were here or what they were here for. As if the room had been sealed off from disappointment. Even the magazines – *Car and Driver, Business Week* – seemed to have been chosen specifically for their lack of lifestyle content, for the likely absence of pictures of gurgling babies and doting parents. Behind a partition, tucked into the corner of the waiting room, there was a bulletin board with charts and graphs on the small odds of in-vitro fertilization and flyers announcing self-help seminars for couples taking the procedure. But everyone avoided that corner of the waiting room, veering away from it like a pothole in the road. No one had time for charts, for the laws of probability.

Angie's appointment didn't last long enough for me to finish a three-page article on mutual funds. She nodded her head towards the door when she saw me and I stood and followed her. Dr Beliveau, a name inspiring enough to be an alias, was also trailing behind and he caught up to her just as I did. He shook my hand again and then slipped a pamphlet on sperm microinjection into my coat pocket.

'Don't be upset. This is not the end of what we can do. We have many options,' he told Angie and me. Dr Beliveau looked as gallant as the former hockey star whose name I suspected him of borrowing: he was taller than he needed to be, with salt-and-pepper hair and old-fashioned sideburns. His stethoscope was tossed over his shoulder like an aviator's scarf. He followed Angie to the elevator, talking softly to her all the while. She nodded but didn't turn around. I don't think either of us would have been surprised to see him blow her a kiss as the elevator door closed. Angie didn't say anything all the way to the parking lot. No hint of what she wanted to talk to me about. The first sound I heard coming from her direction was the squeak deactivating the alarm on her new wintergreen Subaru.

'Yours?' I said. 'Your station wagon?'

She nodded.

'Congratulations. You got what you wanted.'

'I wanted a Volvo.'

'Well, this is pretty close.'

'Pretty close, as Dr Beliveau just reminded me, is only good in horseshoes.'

* * *

Angie's new wipers are on intermittent and can't keep pace with the ice forming on her windshield. The interior of the station wagon is warm and the freezing rain makes a clicking noise when it hits the glass sun roof. On the radio, a man calling himself Reggie says that he is looking for a woman with a friendly smile who believes in an afterlife and reads Tarot cards. Then he goes on to list his most appealing qualities: 'I am sensuous and caring and patient and ...'

'Fat,' I say.

'Really, really fat,' Angie adds. She is laughing so hard at our shared joke that she begins to cough. I pat her on the back and then accidentally run my mittened hand across the nape of her neck. She is startled and jolts forward so quickly her seat belt locks.

'Geez, that's cold,' she says, glaring at me and then laughing some more. I pull off Hope's mitten with my teeth and place my warm hand on her cold skin apologetically. Angie stares at me, unfastening her seat belt and I take my hand away.

'Déjà vu all over again,' she says. Lit by the glow from her brand new dash, Angie's green eye is even greener. She is wearing a black duffel coat and ankle boots and nothing else that I can be sure of. She shifts in her bucket seat as her coat falls open, revealing a bare, dimpled knee. Her hair is down and wet, as if it has been freshly shampooed. She is chewing gum and blowing bubbles.

On 'Radio Rendezvous', a man who refuses to give his name replaces Reggie. The host of the program is trying unsuccessfully to convince the new caller to reveal his identity, pointing out that that's the whole purpose of the show. But he says that he doesn't care and that he is past the point of no return. 'I am a successful businessman,' he says, 'a prominent member of my community and I need someone to share my life with me. I thought I found that person, but she will have nothing to do with me. I can't give my name because my wife is in the other room, listening.'

'Do you think there is such a thing? A point of no return?' Angie asks.

'I think so. Or I'd like to think so,' I say. Although Hope and I have been together only three months, it's true that I can no longer see us breaking up. (In much the same way I could never see us becoming a couple before we became one.) This does, I realize, point to a failure of imagination on my part, but it is a failing I am grateful for every day.

What I can't imagine is how Hope could extricate herself from our situation. Because I know that I couldn't and because everything I've done in the last three months has been done to make what initially seemed like a likelihood an impossibility. This is, I know, an absurd way to think. Even worse, it's dangerous. I am just asking for trouble.

'I don't know if I do,' Angie says. 'Believe in a point of no return.' And then she hits a button on the dashboard that activates the lock on my door. 'Childproof,' she adds, leaning across my seat and putting her arms around me. I wriggle a bit, trying to judge whether this is an awkward hug or something more, but Angie won't let go. I can't move much more than that because I have my seat belt on. I'm not sure why I put it on if I knew I wasn't going anywhere. I'm not sure why I got in the car at all. Unless Angie decides to open the sun roof and I stand on her new bucket seats, I have no way of seeing my house from here.

'Angie, what's this all about?' But she doesn't answer, perhaps because my words are muffled. I am speaking directly into her woollen shoulder and I feel an irrepressible urge to sneeze. I remember someone telling me once that if you said the word grapefruit out loud you could hold off a sneeze and so I do, which startles Angie more than my inevitable sneezing does. Each sneeze propels my head a little further down Angie's body until my ears are resting perfectly between her breasts. I've come full circle. Angie pats my perspiring bald spot.

'Remember I said there was something I wanted to talk to you about? Well, what if I said I came looking for you tonight?' she explains to the top of my head. 'That I knew you would be out walking and that I knew where to find you because I've been following you all week. Ever since that day at the infertility clinic. I'm not saying that's what happened, I'm just asking what if it was?'

'I'd say you were making a mistake. That you ... GRAPEFRUIT.'

'Bless you.'

'That you'd gone off the deep end.' The fact that some men become more attractive to some women once they're married or engaged or otherwise spoken for has never been a problem I've had to deal with. So I can talk a good game when it comes to fidelity because I've never had to do anything about it. Temptation, I realize, with one of Angie's toggle buttons jammed into my ear, is the one temptation I've never had to think about.

'Isn't it ironic, Jacob? All those years, Sandy and I couldn't have had a baby even if we wanted to. His sperm is clumpy. That's the technical term. Clumpy. There's no margin for error. That sample I brought in – it was the second one. The second one to flunk "the semen survival test." That's what they call it.'

'I'm sorry Angie, so sorry, but –'

'I bet you're wondering how I got it without him knowing?'

'No, Angie, I'm not ... GRAPEFRUIT.'

'Bless you. Used condoms, that's how. After he fell asleep, I fished them out of the garbage, put them in vials and stored them in the freezer behind the burgundy cherry ice cream. What a waste of time. You told me once that every decision is the wrong one, Jacob. You were right,' she says, her hand on the waistband of my sweats.

'I didn't say that. I was just quoting.'

'How can you build a relationship without trust? I was prepared to trick him. I'm still prepared to…. All I want you to do is think about it? This doesn't have anything to do with anything else. No one else has to know.' Her hand is inside my waistband.

'I don't know what you're talking about, Angie.' I have managed to raise my head so that it doesn't sink any lower, into a more embarrassing place.

'Just think about it,' she says with a sigh I can feel more than hear and she lets go of me. My waistband snaps back against my belly. The childproof door locks spring up. I unfasten my seat belt and back out of the car. As I am leaving I hear Mr Point-of-No-Return say: 'Advice. Sure I need advice. From you and from anyone listening. What do you think I called for? A date? How desperate do you think I am anyway? What do you mean I have the wrong program? Sorry, can you hold, I have another call…. Sorry, are you still there? It's her. She needs me. I have to go.' I close the passenger door as Angie blows a pink bubble, it bursts, and she drives off. I watch her for a moment skidding along the icy street and when I look up again it is to see the light flickering on and off in the master bedroom in my house.

* * *

In our first Lamaze class a month ago, Chantal Sansregret told us that panic is good. Panic is your friend. Chantal is an obstetric nurse and has been for twenty-seven years. She is a fifty-two-year-old woman with three children of her own, a head full of dyed blond hair and the absolute minimum requirement when it comes to a sense of humour. She follows every statement of fact by saying, 'Any questions?' She's worn the same maroon track-suit with fluorescent stripes down the side to every class; she also wears a whistle around her neck which she uses to great effect whenever a prospective father tries to sneak out during a discussion of episiotomies.

What Chantal actually told us in that first class is not that panic is good, but that it is unavoidable and that there is no practical reason for making a distinction between the two, between what is good and what is unavoidable. 'Remember, we can channel our panic,' she said. 'Use it to stay alert to potential problems, small things we take for granted otherwise.'

Chantal's job is to teach us to relax, but what she has told us every week for the last eight weeks is that we can forget about relaxing. 'Jamais, jamais, jamais. Never happen.' All you can do is control your anxiety, she said, not let it get ahead of you, ahead of what is going to happen next. 'Any questions?'

As I get closer to the house I notice that the light in the bedroom has stopped flickering. It is just on. As are all the other lights in all the other rooms. When I am opposite the house, at my usual finishing line, Joseph's Mitzvah Mobile, I also notice that the garage door is open and Hope's car is still there. I am hyperventilating now, but because of my training at least I'm aware I'm hyperventilating. I stand motionless at the top of the driveway and calm myself by panting and by repeating Chantal's advice: 'Good air in, bad air out.' I wish I had a brown paper bag. I wish I had my stopwatch with me.

I decide not to enter the house through the open garage and enter through the front door instead. I call Hope's name. Almost whispering at first and then speaking more loudly. No reply. Stalling, I remove my wet boots, then Hope's scarf and mittens and lay them out by the heating vent in the vestibule. I shout Hope's name again and there's still no answer. I want to pretend that nothing is wrong, that nothing has happened. That nothing is about to happen. But I realize that would be the kind of mistake Chantal warned us about. Good air in, bad air out. In a birthing situation, she said, do not trust reason. Trust panic. Panic knows.

While I volunteered to take the prenatal course with Hope, I tried my best to back out when the time finally came to show up for the first class. Garage sales I could handle, but, in the end, Hope was right: I am squeamish. So I hinted about how fainting runs in my family and hemmed and hawed about going until Hope finally said, 'Jacob, if you don't think you can do it, then don't.' At which point I agreed to attend the classes. What else could I do?

Now, with only a couple of weeks left in the course, I wish they could go on and on. I have turned out to be Chantal's star student. Because of all the extra research I had done, I was able to answer most of her questions when they came up for review at the end of the evening. Questions that left the other prospective fathers in the class and most of the mothers bewildered with worry.

In the first class, for example, when Chantal explained to us that the Lamaze method is psychoprophylactic and then asked if anyone knew what that meant, I raised my hand. 'It is the prevention of physical pain through psychological means,' I said.

Chantal blew her whistle, pointed at me, like a basketball referee awarding a free throw, and nodded. Everyone else looked at me the way you look at the teacher's pet in third grade. Since then, things have deteriorated with my classmates. I seem to have my hand up all the time, giving complex answers to everything from why you should squeeze your partner's ankles to the use of a breast pump. There are nights even Hope refuses to talk to me after class.

* * *

Panic is good, panic is your friend, I keep repeating to myself as I search for Hope. I can't find her anywhere. This is a bungalow, a small domicile by definition, and there are only so many places she could be and she is in none of them. Unless she is hiding. But why would she be? Unless she has been taken away. But who ...

All the closet doors in the house are open, so is the refrigerator door. In the bedroom, several dresser drawers have been upended. Clothes are scattered on the floor. My first thought is the Stanley 2001. Whoever has it must have used it to get into the house and to either take Hope away or convince her to leave. But just as I'm about to dial 911, I notice Hope's plaid canvas overnight bag open on the bed. Some underwear and a flannel nightgown have been folded into it. Beside the overnight bag, there is a three-subject notebook: spiral, navy blue, the word SEPTEMBER written in large bold indelible ink on the cover. The handwriting is, of course, mine.

What Chantal never got around to telling us is that there is a difference between panic and dread and that it is the difference between expectation and reality. Panic anticipates that the worst will happen. Dread takes over after it has. Dread is what you feel when you've reached the point of no return, the end of the line.

One of Hope's business cards is sticking out of the middle of my notebook. I open it to a line at the top of a dog-eared page: *Until I started reading Hope's diary ...*

'Out loud,' Hope says, 'read it out loud. No secrets here.' She is standing behind me in the doorway. I turn around just in time to see her wince and lower herself to the floor. She lands on her behind with a small thud.

'A contraction,' she explains. 'They're coming closer together.' She is holding my stopwatch in her hand. 'I called the hospital. They said it wasn't anything to worry about but that maybe I should come in. I was going to pick you up on the way ...' She stops abruptly, closes her eyes and breathes in through her nose and out through her mouth. Good air in, bad air out. Between breaths she pants lightly and exhales rapidly. 'Only I couldn't find my damn keys again,' she continues, 'I don't know where I put them. I flashed the lights. I thought you would see.'

'I'm sorry, I didn't. Did you look in the car?'

'I looked in the car. I looked in all my coat pockets and yours. I looked everywhere, Jacob. Everywhere. I didn't find the keys, but I did find –'

'I can explain. Let me explain.'

'Don't bother,' Hope says. 'Just make yourself useful: squeeze my ankles. Hard. Harder.'

* * *

You can never be too prepared, Chantal told us over and over again. Expect the unexpected. Because something unexpected will always happen. Any questions?

Two days ago, I packed Hope's overnight bag – not the one on the bed, a backup bag – without her knowledge. I didn't tell her because I knew if I had she would have just given me one of those shrugs of hers. (Yes, I still get them.) *You & Your Baby* suggests packing a month before your due date. In the spare bag, there's an extra stopwatch in case the first one doesn't work, also an extra nightgown, an extra bathrobe, an extra toothbrush, magazines, several paperback novels, two decks of cards, two rolls of quarters, a package of blank looseleaf pages to be inserted in her Filofax, and a dozen pair of panties, assorted colours, which I bought myself from a suspicious saleswoman. Everything – I realize as I am emptying the overnight bag, blue, white, pink panties floating to the floor like oversized confetti – except a spare set of car keys.

I look for the keys everywhere, including all the unlikely places Hope has already looked: the medicine chest, the microwave, the refrigerator, and the underwear drawer in what used to be my bedroom, which is, incidentally, where I have been hiding my journal for the last three months.

Trust is overrated.

My mother routinely kept secrets from my father about all sorts of things – from the price of a new dress to her first doctor's appointment to have a small lump on her breast examined. She did it for his sake. She did it because she didn't want him to worry. You could call that dishonest. You could even call it a betrayal. You could call it love, too.

If Hope were still talking to me, I know what she'd say: There, you're doing it again, idealizing your parents' marriage, making it into some kind of shining example that the rest of us here, in the real world, in this real house, where you did this real, awful, inexcusable thing, have to live up to.

I said I could explain but, of course, I can't. All I can think of saying is that some things are more important than trust. Gratitude, for example. Companionship. Concern. I could say loyalty is more important, but I don't.

If I hadn't gotten into the car with Angie and taken my eye off the light in the master bedroom it's likely none of this would have happened. My secret would have been safe. Maybe forever. The possibility that all of this could have been avoided by just remaining vigilant, by not taking my good luck for granted, makes me light-headed in an unfamiliar way and I have to lie down and catch my breath. I have to remember how to breathe normally. Panic is no friend of mine. Hope passes by the room, sees me and mutters loud enough for me to hear, 'Typical'.

Even lying down, trying to do nothing more than remain conscious, I realize I should have a plan. So I call a taxi. When I give my address to the dispatcher on the other end of the line he clicks his tongue. He can't guarantee when a cab will arrive or even if it will. The roads are that bad. The Court Séjour Bridge, the only practical connection between Court Séjour and Montreal North where our hospital is located, is worse. The snow and sleet have changed to freezing rain. The dispatcher advises me to call an ambulance, but Hope, who is now lying beside me on the bed, overhears and shakes her head. Her contractions are closer together, getting stronger. She is timing them herself, with my stopwatch, and clutching a pillow between her thighs. In between contractions, she lies calmly on her side of the bed, her legs stretched out and her arms folded over the pillow.

This is supposed to be my job. I'm supposed to be timing contractions. And supporting Hope and regulating her breathing. I'm the coach. But Hope refuses to respond to any of my questions – basic ones about the type of contractions she is experiencing. Are they Braxton-Hicks? She also refuses to respond to my more complicated questions like can she ever forgive me? I tell the taxi dispatcher to hurry. He says he can't make any promises.

'I'm calling an ambulance,' I say, after I've hung up.

'MY ANKLES!' Hope shouts suddenly, scrunching into an enormous ball. 'How can I ever trust you again? SQUEEZE.'

I am squeezing Hope's ankles so fiercely my head spins. If Chantal were here right now, saying, 'Any questions?' I know what I would ask her. I'd ask how I was supposed to plan for this?

'Again,' Hope shouts. 'HARDER!'

* * *

Three months ago, I told Hope she could count on me, that there was nothing too big or small I wouldn't take care of. But I didn't mean it. How could I? I wanted to take it back the moment I said it. We were in an examining room at the hospital at the time, waiting for a technician to arrive and administer an ultrasound. Hope was lying on her back on a narrow medical table, prepped, a lime green sheet covering her up to her waist and a hospital gown pulled up above her belly so that just that and nothing else was exposed. I sat in an office chair beside the table, holding Hope's hand. The chair had wheels and I rolled back and forth a few feet and then side to side as if we were a couple dancing. I had been telling her jokes to make her relax, but she had asked me to stop because her bladder was full for the exam and laughing made the already pressing need to pee unbearable.

'Jacob, say something serious, okay?'

'You look lovely,' I said staring at her stomach.

'I look like a speed bump. Serious. Really.'

'I won't let you down, Hope. You can count on me.'

'All right,' she said and nodded as if she believed me.

I let go of Hope's hand once the technician arrived and began to apply a viscous, yellowy oil to her abdomen. The technician dimmed the lights in the room and pushed a wandlike instrument over the slope of Hope's stomach. A moment later, no more, a high-pitched electronic beep startled me. Hope reached over and patted my hand. Then a flash of white light appeared on the monitor next to the examining table, followed by a blurred image, which was followed, in turn, by a clearer image, moving in a slow, pulsating motion.

'C'est ça,' the technician said. He was a bald, baby-faced man and he smiled broadly at Hope and then at me as he lifted the wand over his head. In the meantime, I had, without even knowing I was doing it, wheeled myself back into the corner of the small, dark room, as far from Hope and from the monitor as possible. The technician explained to us what we were seeing, but I wasn't paying attention. Instead, I stared at the black-and-white tiled floor and wondered how I'd ended up here, in this examining room, with this pregnant woman, looking at the electronic image of someone else's child. Barely enough time to sneeze and I was breaking my promise. I was already letting her down.

'My God, look at that,' Hope said, her voice full of unconditional wonder and I knew I had been kidding myself all along. She couldn't count on me. It was foolish, I thought, just foolish to expect that there would be some kind of connection with this random collection of dots and dashes. This was not my baby. This was nothing to do with me. As Hope had said to me so many times in the past, in different circumstances, you can't force yourself to feel something you don't feel.

'I can tell you whether it's a boy or girl,' the technician announced. 'Some people like to know.'

'Not us,' Hope said and she stretched out her hand to me. The gesture caught me off guard and I hesitated before rolling myself back to her side. But by the time I had wheeled myself across the room, I was doubting my doubts. I don't know what I thought – originally, I suppose, that it would be easy, that despite these unusual circumstances, I could act as if the baby was mine, as if loving it would be the most natural thing in the world. Then I thought I would never be able to feel that way, that the distance between Hope's child and me would grow wider, that I would always feel distant, finally resentful. What I wasn't prepared for was feeling both ways at the same time. I took Hope's cool hand in mine again and the lump in my throat was as big at that instant as our big, complicated love.

'Are you crying?' Hope asked.

'Yes, I'm having a poignant moment, if that's all right with you.'

'That's fine with me.'

* * *

Hope and I are searching for the car keys at opposite ends of the bed when there is a loud knock on the door. We glance at each other and, despite everything, share a moment of relief. We panicked for nothing – the taxi is here. But when I open the door to tell the driver we'll be right with him, the relief vanishes and the worry returns – more acutely than before.

'Do you know that your garage door is open?' Joseph Alter says.

'Where's the taxi?' I look frantically over his left shoulder, then his right, but the street is empty. The sleet is bouncing off the piece of plastic covering Joseph's black fedora; there is more plastic covering the shoulders of his shiny black suit and the wind is whipping it back and forth like a cape. But other than that, Joseph has made few accommodations to the weather. He is not wearing an overcoat or gloves. Instead of boots he is wearing slippers. Fake leather, I hope, since they are soaked. He has dressed hastily, the fringes from the ritual prayer shawl he wears around his waist – the fringes usually concealed beneath his suit – are exposed.

'Is something wrong, Glassman?' Joseph is staring at the spare stopwatch around my neck which I am using to time contractions. I can't be as accurate as I'd like since Hope will not reply when I ask her if she just had one. In other words, I'm guesstimating. When I hear a gasp from the bedroom, I press the button down, look at the watch – fifteen minutes – and start timing her again.

'I can't talk to you now, Joseph.'

'I was concerned,' he says, his tone changing, becoming hurt and huffy. 'I apologize for being concerned.'

'Jacob… Something's happened.' Suddenly, Hope is standing behind me, clutching her overnight bag to her belly. She is talking to me again and so my first reaction is relief, but when she hands me her bag I notice a dark wet stain soaking through the plaid canvas. 'My water.'

'Are you sure? This shouldn't be happening yet. Chantal said –'

Hope frowns at me and leans against the nearest wall. 'No taxi?' she asks, wincing.

'No, I'm sorry. Is the pain bad?'

'No, it's good, Jacob, it's good pain.'

'Well, actually, Chantal told us –'

'Jacob!'

'Find a focal point,' I say. She is staring at my sternum, concentrating all her anxiety there. I fidget and she shakes her head. 'Now, take a deep, cleansing breath.'

'I know how to breathe.'

'I'm calling 911.'

'No. No ambulances. Ambulances aren't safe. Don't you know that. We did a show on it last month. Besides, I already called the doctor. He said there's still time. He said he'll meet me at the hospital, but that I shouldn't rush. As long as the contractions don't get any worse or closer together. He also wanted me to ask you why we don't have an extra set of car keys.'

'Wise guy.'

'I will go now. I only wanted to help,' Joseph says, clearing his throat. He's been standing back, watching us argue, probably annoyed that we'd forgotten about him. Which we had. As he turns, grabs onto the railing and cautiously approaches the first icy step, I come up with a back-up plan.

I shout at Joseph to wait, but he ignores me. I turn to Hope to tell her to hold on, that everything is going to be fine, and then I lunge at Joseph, clutch the flapping plastic around his shoulders and pull him back to me. His pigeon-toed feet slide out from under him. He falls and I leap on top of him. We struggle and roll across the length of the porch landing until we've reversed positions and he's on top of me.

'This must stop, Glassman. Your persecution of me must stop,' he shouts into my ear, pinning me in place with a headlock. I don't know why I never realized it before, never realized that Joseph is much bigger and stronger than I am.

'I have only ever tried to help you,' he goes on. 'As tonight I have tried. But you do not want my help, do you? You only want to make me look foolish. That is all you have ever done. From the start. What did I ever know of football? In Job, it says, "Let me alone, that I may take comfort a little."'

'Let him alone, Jacob,' Hope says. Through the crook in Joseph's elbow, I can see her clutching her belly. In the meantime, he tightens his grip.

'Your truck,' I mutter into Joseph's armpit. 'You can drive us to the hospital.'

Joseph lets me go. He looks surprised, then worried. 'I am sorry,' he says, 'but I will not drive on the Sabbath. I cannot drive on the Sabbath.'

'Fine, I'll drive.'

'You do not understand. No one may use the Mitzvah Mobile on the Sabbath.'

'Is it an automatic transmission?'

* * *

There are sins and sins, I am thinking as I adjust the rear-view mirror, then pull the bench seat in Joseph's truck forward. Gradations of sin, I argued persuasively. Or so I thought. But it wasn't me who convinced Joseph to hand over his keys. There are degrees of responsibility. The actions you take cannot be completely detached from the reasons you take them. Sometimes, I explained to Joseph and Hope, too, the end does justify the means.

'You would say that,' Hope interrupted.

I smiled a 'not now' smile at her and she stuck her tongue out at me. I have seen the gesture before, but this time it wasn't playful. So I ignored it. I was trying to locate my own focal point – concentrate on what mattered and deny, for the moment anyway, that it was beginning to look as if Hope would never be able to forgive me for what I had done.

'Rules are made to be broken, Joseph,' I continued.

'Where is such a thing said?'

'The Talmud … it must be in there somewhere. Everything else is. Look I'm not an expert on Talmudic law the way you are, but isn't there a clause, you know, a loophole that states that if a person's health is somehow in jeopardy the usual laws are suspended.'

'I do not know what you are referring to,' he said, giving every indication that he knew exactly what I was referring to.

'I remember my grandfather used to fast on Yom Kippur and a couple of times he fainted in the synagogue. His rabbi, who was as old school as they come, insisted that he eat a sandwich. My grandfather was given a sort of – what's the word? – dispensation. He didn't listen to the rabbi, of course, and kept right on fasting and fainting, but that's not the point. The point is you have to let us borrow your truck.'

'And I am telling you it is the Sabbath and it is not permitted,' Joseph said, stubbornly crossing his arms over his muscular chest. There was a smug look on his face that made me think how much I wanted to get him in a headlock, hold him still, while Hope searched his pockets for his keys.

Instead, Hope invited Joseph in out of the freezing rain. She placed her hand on his elbow and whispered something to him. He stooped to make it easier for her. Every now and then he would raise his head, look at me and nod, not exactly with contempt, but with an obstinate, unrelenting frown. Finally, Hope released his elbow and just said, 'Please reconsider. For my sake.' Joseph reached into the pocket of his jacket for his gold-plated *chai* key chain and handed it to me. He followed us out to the truck, opened the passenger door for Hope and then got in beside her.

The drive to the hospital is only twenty minutes in normal conditions. I know because I did a dry run with Hope three weeks ago, timing the trip with both stopwatches. I've also done a couple more dry runs since then, without Hope's knowledge, to calculate the traffic on the bridge at various times of the day. If Hope had read further in my journal she would have seen a chart of the results.

Conditions tonight are not normal. Along with the ice on the roads and the gathering fog, I've never driven any vehicle as large as the Mitzvah Mobile. A van, when I had a summer job installing air conditioners, is as close as I've come. It's also been a while since I've driven a standard transmission. Alongside me, Hope is alternately stone-faced and screaming with pain. Beside her, Joseph's also divided: spending half his energy comforting Hope, the other half lecturing me.

'Too close, too close!' he shouts whenever Hope has a contraction and I take my eyes off the road momentarily. The truck, as he points out every time my foot rests on the clutch too long or the gears grind, is his responsibility.

'Look, why don't you drive if I'm making you so nervous?' I say, lifting my hands from the steering wheel.

'This is bad enough,' he says, turning to whisper something to Hope. She whispers back and then he adds, 'Glassman, be prudent, please. This one time.'

'What's that supposed to mean?' Is it possible that he saw me in the station wagon with Angie? Or did Hope tell him about her Filofax? Can a man's reputation, his character change as suddenly as the weather does? When did I go from being hopelessly passive-aggressive to a reckless gambler? When – I'd like to know – did people start seeing me as impulsive and foolhardy, a man who is capable of doing anything to get what he wants? And why am I not pleased with this turn of events?

'Pump the brakes!' Joseph shouts as I ignore another stop sign.

Hope has been my responsibility for the last three months, whether she is aware of it or not. I've spent hour after hour watching her sleep, watching what she eats, driving her to work, fending off nuisance calls from Neil Topaz, picking her up after work, debating with her about not smoking, rubbing her neck, her shoulders, her back, squeezing her ankles, going to Lamaze classes. I know that her life is about to change dramatically and forever, but my life is changing too. I am, after all, the one being imprudent, sailing through stop signs – shifting and grinding gears.

* * *

Prudent? What else have I ever been? It should be my middle name. Jacob Prudent Glassman. All my life I have been cautious, remained in the same place, stayed the course. I have made no big mistakes, taken no big chances, at least no mistakes, no chances, that would seem big to anyone else.

I have always trusted the status quo; more than that, I've believed in it. Believed in it as unwaveringly as my father did. Just the other day I reread John Cheever's journals for a term paper I was reselling and noticed a quote I had once highlighted. 'A man can be given nearly everything the world has to offer,' he wrote to himself, 'and go on yearning.' I closed the book angrily, but not before I wrote, in ink, in the margins: BULLSHIT!

Dr Howie once said my motto should be: Maybe it won't happen. So, naturally, if there was a way to stop this truck right now, right here in the middle of the Court Séjour Bridge, still far enough from the hospital's emergency room that the hospital seems like a mirage, I would do it. I would hold on to the status quo for dear life. Because I know what I know: once Hope has this baby everything will be different. How could it not be?

'Glassman, be careful. The light is red!' Joseph shouts and then he drapes his body over Hope's to protect her and her about-to-be-born child from the impending collision. He is swaying slightly – even at the wheel I can feel him moving – and muttering something from the Bible. I begin to pump the brakes but I'm convinced they won't hold on the icy road. Since making it over the bridge – which was slick as a rink – maybe I have become overconfident, maybe I have picked up speed. Maybe it was a mistake … maybe … I consider downshifting, trying the brakes again, but then reconsider. There's no point in slowing down now, no point in stopping for the red light since there's no one else on the road for me to collide with. No one else as imprudent as me.

'Naked came I out of my mother's womb and naked shall I return thither,' Joseph says, reciting the words softly to Hope.

'Thither?'

'The Lord gave and the Lord hath taken away; blessed be the name of the Lord,' he goes on, ignoring me. I slip my arm around Hope and smack Joseph on the back of the head. His fedora falls over his eyes. He fixes his hat and fixes me with a dirty look. I return it, wondering if his prayer is a comment on my driving, wondering, too, why he couldn't come up with a more innocuous passage for a woman on her way to the hospital to have a baby. But Hope's eyes are closed, her breathing relaxed for the moment and Joseph keeps talking:

'And the Lord said unto Satan, Hast thou considered my servant Job, that there is none like him in the earth, a perfect and upright man, one that feareth and escheweth evil? and still he holdeth fast his integrity, although thou movedst me against him, to destroy him without cause.'

'You memorize that stuff?' I'm ignoring traffic lights and stop signs now and making much better time. When I finally skid the Mitzvah Mobile to a stop in front of the emergency entrance of the hospital, I am only twenty minutes off schedule. Both Hope and Joseph look up at me, astonished that we've actually made it. I try not to gloat, but I can't resist saying to Joseph, 'You might want to look into this new thing they have nowadays; they're called winter tires.'

As I'm shifting gears into neutral and lifting the hand brake, I hear a tap on my window. I roll it down and an elderly security guard tells me that I'm going to have to move and move now. Even after he sees Hope struggling out of the other side of the truck, leaning on Joseph, holding her belly, the guard remains adamant. 'Hey, buddy boy, you can't block the entrance with this jalopy. Parking lot's around the corner,' he says.

But I pretend not to understand his instructions and slip past him into the hospital. Hope is already in a wheelchair, being pushed by a nurse toward the elevators. Her head is leaning against Joseph's hip and he is walking alongside her, rubbing her shoulders. He continues to totter and sway. I notice, for the first time, that he is wearing pyjama pants, the cuffs are rolled up and still dripping from our wrestling match on my front porch. His slippers, meanwhile, flap on the tile floor, leaving an arrowlike trail behind him as he walks his pigeon-toed walk toward the elevators and farther away from me.

Turn around, I think, trying to send Hope a message through the antiseptic halls. In the weeks and months and, yes, the years before we became a couple, when we were just friends, after we'd been out to dinner or a movie, I would do this all the time – send her messages. I'd drive her home, stop in front of her apartment building, wait for her to kiss me good-night, on the cheek, and then I would sit in my car and watch her walk into the lobby. She'd retrieve her keys from her purse, open the security door, and disappear from my sight. That was my cue to leave. Except I never did. I'd stay, knowing that if just one time she turned around and looked back at me everything would be different. Everything would change. Magical thinking, that's what Angie called it. Now, I'm doing it again, thinking if Hope would just look back once before the elevator comes to take her up to the delivery room, then everything will go back to the way it was. 'Turn around,' I say aloud to myself again and again, as if I am singing a popular song. But a bell rings, a green light flickers above the elevator, and Hope doesn't look back. I'm about to follow her anyway, impose myself on her the way I used to, the way I always have, when I feel a hand on my shoulder.

'Move it or lose it. Toot sweet. Move that rabbi-mobile or I'll have the thing towed,' the security guard says.

'But she needs me. I'm the coach,' I say, pointing to the elevator doors. Panic, my old friend, is evident in my voice. The nurse has handed over control of the wheelchair to Joseph and the last thing I see before the elevator doors close is Joseph removing his plastic covered fedora to reveal his head of bushy auburn hair.

'Looks like you've been replaced, buddy boy.'

* * *

Saturday, December 23. In the last year of his life, my father's world became narrower and narrower. It was as if what he had suspected when my mother first convinced him to move to Court Séjour was finally happening: everything was changing for the worse. Maybe that explains why he became satisfied with less and less: a productive day's work, a customer who stayed an extra half-hour to keep him company, a visit from a neighbour, though visits were rare. The small circle of friends and neighbours he relied on to keep in touch after my mother died seldom did. At the time, I was angry at them for abandoning him. I wanted to believe they did it maliciously. Now, I'm not so sure. Perhaps, they just realized that they had always been more comfortable in my mother's company. Now, I'm not so sure I didn't feel the same way.

With my mother gone, there was no buffer between my father and me and for the first time in my life I was face to face with a man who was too scared to even admit how scared he was. Whatever emotional loss he was feeling he kept to himself and converted into physical symptoms. He never said that he was lonely, for example, instead he complained constantly about some roaming stiffness – in his shoulder one day, his back the day after that. My brother and I weren't much comfort. After my mother died, we became accustomed to his complaining, accustomed enough to resent it and to resent his weakness. Now, I'd like to be able to say I was wrong – that he wasn't weak. But I haven't changed my mind; if anything I'm more certain than ever that I was right. He was weak, all right. Under similar circumstances, I know that I would be too.

Whatever the reason, my brother and I didn't take him or his physical complaints as seriously as we should have. Actually, we didn't take him seriously at all until one morning he decided that he couldn't go down to the basement to work any more, that the trip down a single flight of stairs and then up again in the evening – the trip he'd been making every single day, Saturdays, Sundays and holidays included, since we moved to Court Séjour more than fifteen years earlier – was too taxing. I suppose I should have made him see a doctor then, but I didn't. I just never thought there was anything really wrong with him. One more failure of imagination on my part.

Three years before my mother died, my father was diagnosed with colon cancer. The doctors removed the tumour and informed us that they had gotten it all. My father had radiation treatment and some follow-up appointments and was told that everything was fine, that he was in the clear. But when he became sick again just ten months after my mother died and when my brother and I convinced ourselves and finally convinced him to go to the hospital, we genuinely believed he could be helped. And when we found out it was cancer again and the cancer had spread, we believed it could be treated. We believed he could live another year as my mother had after her diagnosis and that there could still be some good moments as there had been with my mother. And when my father died, we believed that, at least, he was out of his suffering. What else could we believe?

The doctors were only surprised that we were surprised. Almost fifteen years later, I still am. What I couldn't comprehend, what I still can't comprehend, was that this was all happening again. It was as if some immunity I assumed I'd be granted after my mother's death had been revoked.

Just as it's impossible to imagine the best things happening, it's also impossible to imagine the worst. The only day I cried for my father was the day I realized, a couple of months before the fact, that he was going to die. I became dizzy and sat down on our front porch and wept the way a child weeps – more for myself than anyone else. And with no immediate plan to stop.

* * *

'I'm not the kind of guy who likes to say I told you so, but I did – tell you so,' Rusty Mintz says. 'This day had to come, Jakie. Can I call you Jakie? I don't want to rub it in, but this was in the cards.' When Mintz telephoned this morning, his regular weekend call, I told him I was, indeed, thinking about selling my house. He said that he would be right over. He is, needless to say, early.

Rusty is smaller than I remember – not just short because he's not that much shorter than me – but reduced, like a photocopy that has been reproduced at seventy-five percent of its original size. In person, his voice is also more high-pitched than it is on the telephone. He is carrying an expensive leather briefcase and wearing an equally expensive beige cashmere overcoat, but when he takes off his shoulder-padded coat, his boots and sunglasses, he becomes even more reduced. 'Jumped in the car and here I am,' he says. He is a man who takes pride in stating the obvious.

'I'm glad you're still interested, but there was no hurry.'

'No hurry? I wanted to get here before you changed your mind. That was a joke, Jakie. I know you're not the kind of guy who changes his mind easily, not once it's made up. I know you've given this a lot of thought.'

Rusty extends his small, delicate hand and keeps it extended until I shake it. He has his business card in his palm which he passes to me invisibly as if I were participating in a magic act. Maybe I am. Rusty is going to make my house, make me – if everything goes according to plan – disappear.

'To be honest, I haven't. Given it much thought, I mean.'

'Great. By the way, if you're making coffee I wouldn't say no. Get on the ball, fella? Jakie? I'm joking. Where's your sense of humour? Who died around here anyway?' Rusty says, wandering through the house with me tagging along after him.

'I'm sorry. Do you want coffee?'

'No, never mind, I can see you mean business so let's crunch some numbers. I can get you ninety-five grand tomorrow. All I need is your signature,' he says, pulling a contract out of his briefcase.

'That's all. Ninety-five? You said a lot more.'

'You probably could have gotten a lot more just a few months ago. But the referendum last October turned this place into shit. The market likes stability and, in case you've been in a coma for the last fifteen years, we don't have that here. I suppose you could wait until the next referendum and hope it goes your way, but that would be taking a big chance. No, ninety is the best you're going to do.

'Want to know the truth – selling now is your only choice. It's a buyer's market and that, my friend, is the understatement of the year. Statistics don't lie: one buyer for every twenty-one sellers. You know that some people are actually giving away stereo systems, microwaves, brand new cars to whoever buys their place.'

'I don't have a car any more.'

'As it is, Jake, you may have waited too long.'

When it comes to important issues I'm easily distracted. I have always adopted the Scarlett O'Hara approach to referenda and elections and real estate values. I prefer to think about them tomorrow. Except tomorrow is today and while the political landscape was collapsing around me, what was I busy doing?

Spying on Hope. Reading her Filofax.

'But I remember you telling me once that I could get as much as one hundred and fifty thousand. You said that was the minimum.'

'Once is the key word,' Rusty says. By the exasperated look on his face – a look with which I am far too familiar – I know what he is about to say next before he says it: 'You're living in the past, Jakie. We're talking eighty-seven, tops.'

* * *

Hope didn't ban me from the delivery room, after all. I left the Mitzvah Mobile in the hospital parking lot, glared at the security guard at the Emergency entrance and took the stairs up to the maternity ward. Joseph was waiting for me by the elevator. The moment he spotted me, he grabbed my arm and led me to a small alcove crowded with vending machines. There, he pushed me up against a microwave oven and shook his long index finger in my face. He didn't say anything. He just sighed and tottered back and forth.

'Where is she?' I asked once it became obvious that he wasn't about to volunteer the information.

'She is being prepared. In the delivery room.'

'How is she?'

'How should she be? How would you be? I have been disappointed in you before, Glassman, as you well know. But never like this. Never so profoundly. She told me everything,' Joseph said, sounding philosophical, sounding like the rabbi he would surely never be. Why, I wondered, does everybody feel the necessity to tell everybody everything?

'Look, Joseph, I appreciate the use of the truck. I appreciate that you're breaking your own sacred rules just by being here tonight. I even appreciate you being some kind of support to Hope, but this is really none of your business. I know I've told you that before and I know it hasn't exactly deterred you, but this time I mean it. Look in my eyes. I mean it. You can't go on intruding in my life for no reason.' I waved my hand at him dismissively and then noticed what I should have noticed right away – he was wearing a green surgical gown over his clothes and a shower cap on his head.

'No reason?' he said, lifting and holding a surgical mask over his mouth with his hand and mumbling something in Hebrew. 'Is that what you think? I have no reason. That I am just an accidental presence in your life. That there is no hand guiding our actions. That the truck was just there tonight waiting for you. Or that time in the parking lot. Or that I …' He turned away from me and began to knock his head gently against a change-making machine.

'What are you talking about now?'

'You know the way you are, Glassman, well, you can no longer be that way. You cannot pretend that everything that happens happens only to you. Can you not see that? She trusted you,' Joseph said and walked away from me.

'What did she tell you?' I asked, following him.

'Everything…. She loved you.'

'She said that?'

'She said that she did not know if she would ever be able to forgive you for what you did, but –'

'But what?'

'But she wants to see you – in the delivery room.'

'For God's sake, why didn't you say so.'

'Because, Glassman, I am not sure you should be in the delivery room. I am not sure you are ready.'

'What do you mean? Who's ready? You, I suppose?'

'More than you.' Joseph reached behind him to tie the strings of his mask. I put my finger up to the side of my head to twirl it, but Joseph grabbed my wrist. The mask drooped over his chin.

'Do not,' he said, but he looked more desperate than angry.

'You're nuts, you know that. Just nuts.'

* * *

Rusty Mintz instructs me to place the stepladder in the corner of the closet in my parents' bedroom, directly under the door to the attic. He insists this will be his final stop. He's already been all over the house, inside and out, making notes, talking endlessly about commissions and visiting hours, about who will be most interested in the house and why, and who we can immediately cross off the list of potential buyers: men in their thirties. Unattached. Single. Me, for example.

'First things first. You have to have an open house. The sooner the better. How does this afternoon sound? You've already wasted enough time. I took the liberty of calling a few of my more enthusiastic clients and a couple of them should be here any time now.'

'Today?'

'Yes sir. Real estate is about striking while the iron is hot.'

'What iron?'

'Figuratively speaking, Jakie. I can call you Jakie, can't I? Did you say?'

'But I wasn't prepared for anyone today. The house is a mess —'

'It looks fine to me,' he interrupts. 'A little too tidy, if anything. You want to give people the chance to feel superior, to feel like there's room for improvement.'

'But I'm not ready —'

'He who hesitates. You can guess the rest. Real estate is about opportunity. You learn to take advantage of every opportunity. Accentuate the positive. I respect you as a writer and an artist, you know that, but as a writer and an artist you have a tendency to look at things too negatively. Remember that article you did about the community centre? About my Jewish Instructional Program? A perfect example of what I mean.'

'What do you mean?'

'I'm talking about accentuating the positive. Take the unfinished park at the end of your street. How long has it been like that? Ten, fifteen years. But when your parents first bought this place, what, thirty, forty years ago, they were a young couple, with young kids, and I'll bet you that one of the first things their real estate agent told them then was, "Mr and Mrs Glassman, there is going to be a park at the end of your street. Not too close, but close enough so your kids will have somewhere to go after school and on weekends."

'Am I right? Sure, I'm right. Do I know what I'm talking about? Course, I do. Now, we have a young couple, Greek or Armenian or something like that, coming over here any minute and they're probably thinking about starting a family. and so we tell them, "Folks, the community's going to be building a park at the end of your street for your kids. With a swimming pool and tennis courts and a soccer field." We don't mention it was supposed to be finished thirty years ago. We don't mention that this unfinished park has become a hang-out for a bad crowd. That a car blew up just around the corner last summer. We just say, "There's going to be a park. Are you guys ever lucky?" See what I mean? Nod, Jakie, if you're with me.'

I do. I nod, more out of astonishment than agreement. The man is speaking so fast he is practically whirling. Something occurs to me: real estate statistics and buyer's market notwithstanding, Rusty Mintz is going to sell my house this afternoon.

'Now, we better get busy. Can you hold this thing? I'm a little scared of heights,' Rusty says as he approaches the top of the stepladder. There's a problem though: even when he extends his tiny arms he can't reach the entrance to the attic. Like part of an acrobatic act, I climb up on the ladder with him, clasp my hands together while he places his tiny foot between my interlocked fingers. 'On three,' he says and on three I boost him up.

As I stare at Rusty Mintz's backside, I'm beginning to wonder whether I should be giving this decision more thought. To be honest, the real reason I allowed him to come over this morning and stick his nose into my attic is so I could tell Hope, if she ever talks to me again, that I am selling the house. I want to see how she'll react. Or if she'll react. Even now that everything has changed between us, perhaps irrevocably, nothing has changed. I am playing the same old games. Deciding whether or not to tell her things that aren't, strictly speaking, true. Things I've dreamed up to make her pay attention to me and my latest plan. Except this time, precariously balanced on a stepladder in the closet, propping up a real estate agent as single-minded as Rusty Mintz, I recognize that, in the long term anyway, there are flaws in all my plans.

* * *

'We never fight. Have you noticed?' Hope announced as we lay in bed on Halloween morning two months ago. 'Or even argue.'

Our situation, as Hope sometimes called our relationship, was exactly forty days old and I was too happy to worry about anything other than the fact that I was happy all the time. I confess I was in a rut – oblivious to the events taking place around me. For example, Hope and I had stayed up late the night before watching the referendum results on television and, for the first time, I had fallen asleep before her. She tried to wake me to hear the province's premier blame 'the ethnic vote' for standing in the way of his dream to create a sovereign nation, but I was snoring, she said, happily snoring away.

'Situation? Is that what you call what we have?' I asked as I stroked her face.

'I meant to say relationship.'

'You meant to say love affair.' I bit her ear.

'Yes, right. But you don't have to always feel that you have to be on your best behaviour around me. I sometimes think you're walking on eggshells. Just tell me something, something about us, about me that annoys you.'

'This is really about what annoys you about me, isn't it? Tell me what you want me to stop doing and I'll stop doing it,' I said boastfully. 'Was it the snoring? Would you rather I didn't bite your ear?'

'There,' she said, struggling out of my reach and out of her side of the bed, 'that's exactly what I'm talking about –'

The telephone interrupted her, as it had been interrupting us all morning. We had been taking calls, practically since dawn, from distraught relatives and friends in the rest of the country who were concerned about our future. This time the call was local, but no less anxious. It was from Trish Severs, who wanted me to contact Dr Howie about doing a special 'Ask Your Therapist' column on stress – specifically the kind that might result from the recent political events.

'Find out if there have been more visits to shrinks, more people on medication or higher doses of medication. I know my estrogen treatments have gone through the roof,' she said.

'Yes, boss. I'll get right on it,' I said, changing the subject the way I always do when Trish begins to fill me in on her latest female problem. New as she is to being a woman, she's not missing out on any of the available fun. Nothing matches a new convert for enthusiasm.

'You sound cheerful this morning, unlike everyone else I've been talking to. There is panic, there is hysteria in the streets,' Trish said, sounding close to hysterical herself.

'Hope and I are about to have our first fight. I'm looking forward to it.' I glanced at Hope who smiled, despite herself.

'You shouldn't make a joke of this,' Hope said as soon as I hung up the phone. 'Everything is about to change, whether you like it or not, and you can't just go along with things because you're trying to make me happy. What if I said I don't think we should be living in this house, in this place any more? What then?'

'Then we pack our bags,' I said, humouring her.

'How can you say that? You've lived here all your life, Jacob. This is your home. I would never ask you to sell it for me.'

'I know that.'

'Especially not today.'

'Halloween?'

'The anniversary of your mother's funeral.'

'You know I forgot.' I hadn't really. A memorial candle had been burning in the kitchen all day yesterday.

'Well, okay then, but we still have to start thinking about our options – like everyone else.'

'All right.'

'There, you did it again. You don't believe in options. You're happy with everything just the way it is. Why don't you say so? Stop trying to please me.'

'I don't believe in options,' I announced. 'I am happy, no, I am thrilled with everything the way it is.' As Hope threw up her hands and left the room, I started figuring out how, next time, I would have to pick a real fight with her.

* * *

'You definitely need better isolation,' Rusty says. Or is that 'insulation'? I am having a hard time understanding most of what he says because his head is extended above the entrance to the attic and out of view. He can't weigh more than one hundred and twenty pounds, even so my grip is beginning to slip. But just before it does, he lifts the remainder of his body into the attic until he is completely out of sight. He's silent for a moment, which worries me, but then he begins to jump up and down, gently at first, then with a kind of escalating enthusiasm.

When I ask him what he is doing, his reply is muffled, though it sounds like he is saying, 'rejoice and shake'. So I decide, reluctantly, to extend my own arms and pull myself up into the attic before he crashes through the ceiling. Rusty is bouncing up and down, doing jumping jacks, a big smile on his small face.

Which is when something else occurs to me that probably should have occurred to me long ago: everyone I know is crazy. Absolutely nuts. It's almost as if they were organized, as if they attended secret meetings in which, one after another, they outlined what their future erratic behaviour would be. At one meeting, Ted Severs announces he is going to change his sex. At another, Sandy decides he won't leave his apartment ever again. Angie carries around sperm samples. Joseph insists on assisting in the birth of Hope's baby. Rusty Mintz starts doing calisthenics in my attic.

I could go on, but I know how this makes me sound. I know you can't claim that everyone around you is crazy without sounding crazy yourself. But this is not paranoia talking. I don't believe anyone is out to get me any more. I just believe they are out to confuse me.

'Your joists are shaky,' Rusty explains. 'You may have problems you didn't know about.' He is still talking, going into detail, when I step back off the ladder and pull it away from the opening to the attic.

'Hey, what are you doing? Jakie? This is no time to be kidding around. There are people coming over,' Rusty says as I lean the stepladder up against the wall outside the closet. It collapses with a satisfying snap, like a brief burst of applause. Is this what closure feels like?

'Have you gone crazy?' Rusty shouts at me.

* * *

At the hospital last night, the nurse provided me with a shower cap of my own, a gown, paper slippers and a surgical mask. Joseph's mask was already secure, though a few stray tufts of his auburn sidelocks jutted out. The nurse then led me to a row of stainless steel basins just outside the delivery room. Joseph tagged along, shadowing me as closely as a cornerback in bump-and-run coverage. I glanced at the nurse, shifting my eyes above my mask in Joseph's direction, trying to alert her to the fact that only one of us should be allowed into the delivery room and that the other one of us was insane. But she didn't get the hint. It could be that she'd seen stranger things than the two of us in her time, though, right then, I couldn't imagine what they might be.

We washed our four hands, clumsily squeezed them into latex gloves and then the nurse pointed to a pair of swinging doors, lowered her own mask and said, 'Go in when you're ready. But make sure you're ready.'

I hesitated for a moment and Joseph was through the doors. He ended up holding them open for me with his elbows. I don't know what I expected to see, but I didn't expect to see Hope walking around the room, chatting with the doctor, the hem of her hospital gown smeared with blood, a Styrofoam cup full of ice chips in her hand. The doctor, a young woman filling in until Hope's own doctor arrived, turned out to be a fan of 'Been There, Done That' and Hope was signing the sleeve of her gown.

'I know what I'll write, too,' Hope said, 'I'll write: thanks for the epidural. That beautiful, beautiful needle. God bless you.'

I placed my hand tentatively on Hope's shoulder to let her know I had arrived. She turned and swallowed an ice chip before she said, 'There you are. I sent Joseph out to find you. Joseph's been here forever. The more the merrier. He's been like a guardian angel to me. You know for a religious nutcase, he's not so bad. No offence,' she said to Joseph, 'the needle is talking.'

'Her contractions were extremely severe so we administered a local,' the doctor explained. 'But it's not supposed to have this kind of effect. She obviously has a very low tolerance. Are you the father?'

'Guess again,' Hope interrupted, giggling.

'It's a long story,' I said.

'That's right. Jacob, here, is ... what are you anyway, Jacob? I know, he's my editor. He reads everything I write,' Hope said, leaning over the hospital bed and panting while I rubbed her shoulders. Joseph was standing by the doors to the delivery room, staring at me, challenging me to make everything right.

'Then he decides how he can fix things. How he can make them better. Do I have that right?' Hope continued. 'For my own good, naturally. It's all for my own good. If you ask him, just ask him, that's what he'll tell you. The good news is that my taste in men is showing a marked improvement. From a cheat to a snoop. That must be a step up, relatively speaking.'

'Forgive me,' I whispered in her ear.

'Then what?' she whispered back.

* * *

Every chance is a new chance, according to my real estate agent. Which is something he insists on believing even though he is, at this moment, trapped in my attic with prospective buyers about to arrive. 'This is an opportunity that will not come again,' he shouts down at me. 'Do you know that last year it took an average of one hundred and eleven days to sell a house? This year that's up to one hundred and twenty-five days. I don't make this shit up, Jakie. These are the statistics.'

There are only two kinds of men – salesmen and everyone else and it's salesmen who make the world go round. It doesn't matter what they're pushing either – a product or an idea or, in Neil Topaz's case, themselves – they are able to believe what the rest of us can't: that you make your own luck. The rest of us might as well be sitting on the sidelines.

If I have learned anything about myself it is that it takes a certain kind of personality, a personality fundamentally different than mine, to seize the moment. I used to think this was because I just didn't have enough practice or incentive. Now, I'm almost convinced it's genetic. I only say 'almost convinced' because I could probably make the case that holding my real estate agent hostage in the attic is, at least, a step in the right direction.

My mother first noticed my father the evening she broke her engagement to another man. Her fiancé had slapped her in public for showing up late for a dinner party and my mother walked away from the restaurant table and a promising future and never looked back. (Her ex-fiancé eventually inherited his father's lucrative textile business and then sold it to Japanese buyers for millions.) When she returned home she found her father, her brother, a few neighbours and my father playing pinochle in the kitchen. Her brother teased her about getting home so early and about not giving her husband-to-be a proper good-night kiss. My father, who had been fond of my mother for some time but was usually too demoralized by bad luck and self-pity to tell her so, interrupted the conversation to say in front of everyone at the kitchen table, 'If I kiss you, you'll stay kissed.' That's all he said, but it attracted my mother's attention

It was one of the few times he spoke up on his own behalf. In the end, it was my mother who had to ask my father out on their first date and my mother who eventually had to ask my father to marry her. Or, more accurately, she asked him to ask her. Her parents were against them seeing each other from the start, mainly because my father was what people unselfconsciously called a cripple then. And even though he was hurt by their doubts, he had the same doubts himself. My mother convinced him that her parents would come around and, in time, they did. She also made it clear to him that if he asked her to marry him, she'd say yes. According to the story, that's when my father fainted. Hit the floor.

Of course, now, every story I remember about my parents' life together – from their first kiss to their last breath – sounds apocryphal. Preposterous as a fairy tale. Sentimental as an old movie.

And now every chance seems like a last one. 'All right, you're having second thoughts, Jakie,' Rusty Mintz shouts down at me. 'That's only normal. Everyone has second thoughts when they enter into something like this, but you have to get me down from here.' Rusty is more insistent than he's ever been, which is saying something. 'Do you understand? This is no longer funny, you bastard. I told you I'm afraid of heights.'

It occurs to me that anyone who thinks my problems can be explained by saying I am having second thoughts is not the person who should be selling my house. Second thoughts don't even begin to cover it.

'Okay, forget about me. That couple has an appointment, Jakie … Jake? Glassman? Just let them in and show them around. If you don't, they'll leave. They'll leave mad. Every chance is a last chance …'

'So go ahead and jump.'

'Jump?'

'Yes, Rusty – I can call you Rusty, can't I? – seize the moment.'

* * *

The author of *You & Your Baby: The Popular Guide to Pregnancy, Birth and Baby Care*, highlights three stages in the birth of a child. The first stage starts 'when the contractions follow a regular pattern and get stronger and longer and closer together.' This stage was relatively uneventful for Hope. She worked the delivery room, the bottom half of her body pleasantly numb, like she was Phil Donahue. She talked about diets with the nurses, politics with the doctors, religion with Joseph. In between, she hummed the tune from *Ticket to Ride*. She was on. There was no other word for it. If there had been a television producer in the room, observing her impromptu performance, he would have signed her to a long-term contract on the spot. No audition necessary. I had a stopwatch around my neck and I timed her: she kept the patter up for seventy-seven minutes. Forget Oprah; she made Oprah look like a wallflower. For all the reasons I've loved Hope in the past, some clear, some not, it wasn't until then that I knew exactly what it was I loved most about her. Her good nature, her irrepressible good nature.

Inevitably, the second stage of birth, which begins, according to *You & Your Baby*, 'when the head is in the vagina and will soon appear,' was a test of Hope's good nature and of my own. This wasn't a surprise. I assumed, even back when I was the star student in Chantal Sansregret's Lamaze classes, that the second stage would separate the men from the boys. I assumed that if I was going to faint, always a distinct possibility, that it would be during the second stage.

Hope pushed and argued and begged, mainly for another epidural. Her own doctor, who had finally arrived, told her that he didn't think she needed it at which point she literally growled. I might not have believed what I heard except that I saw the doctor and several nurses surrounding her, saw Joseph too, take a step back from the bed where she was now upended. I moved closer. I was still her coach, after all, and in addition to holding her hand, squeezing her ankles and regulating her breathing it was my job to get her to focus on something other than the pain, something beyond the pain. In this, I was more successful than I could have hoped.

'You want me to focus on something else? Fine.' She spit out a mouthful of ice chips at my chest. 'How about on a person who is supposed to love another person, respect another person and still invades that other person's privacy. Reads that other person's private thoughts. And doesn't just do it once. But goes right on doing it. Sneaks away to do it. How about that? This is not a rhetorical question, Jacob, go ahead and answer.'

All I could do was apologize and keep on apologizing for what seemed like – for what was hours. Even when Hope was making her final pushes, she would stop in between to scold me all over again. I admit that I was no longer worried about blacking out. I was worried about walking out.

'Enough already. I can't take this any more,' I announced to Hope, who was grunting and swearing now, her knees raised, her legs apart. I was holding her hand and her knuckles were red with strain. Her face was covered with sweat.

'You're not the only one suffering here,' I said and I felt a roomful of eyes shift to me. Everyone, except Hope, was wearing a surgical mask, but I did see Joseph put his hand up to his head. The doctor said that maybe I was carrying this sympathetic pregnancy thing too far. But I ignored him and went on:

'All those years I loved you and you just wanted to be friends. Do you have any idea what that was like? What that did to me? Do you know what it took to pretend we were friends? Just friends? I was never your friend. Do you know why? Because I knew we were meant for each other. I knew I could make you see it and I finally did. Finally, we have something real and wonderful and you want to throw it away over one little mistake.'

'ONE FUCKING LITTLE MISTAKE?' Hope said, incorporating the words into a command from the doctor to push. 'You deceived me, you manipulated me. You're a fucking peeping Tom. No better than a stalker.'

'Men!' a nurse muttered.

'Shut up,' Hope said, 'I'm talking here. MEANT FOR EACH OTHER?' she went on, still pushing. 'You needed me to fucking rescue you. You never saw me as a person but as some kind of fucking salvation from your self-imposed exile from fucking adulthood. Why do you think I kept calling our relationship, a situation. SHIT.

FUCK. Because I had no part in it, not really. I could have been any-one.'

I felt her grip on my hand tighten and I heard Joseph mutter, *'Mensch tracht und Gott lacht.'* I glared at him as if to say: What the hell does that mean? One of the nurses started to laugh or cry, I couldn't tell through the mask.

'If you think that,' I said, 'then I don't even know what I am doing here.'

'Excuse me, I hate to interrupt,' the doctor interrupted, 'but I can see the baby's head now and I need you, Hope, to give me one big push. Let's try concentrating, all right?'

Hope looked straight ahead, but she kept shouting until she was practically out of breath. 'Maybe I did fucking love you. Did you ever think of that? Only you are impossible. SHIT. PRICK. ASS. Maybe, I do love you. How would I know? With you the way you are and me the way I am. You won't give me a chance to decide for myself. You won't let me breathe. BASTARD. CUNT. PRICK.'

'Breathe,' I whispered as I stroked Hope's forehead, thinking, *finally, our first fight.*

I don't remember much about the third stage of Hope's delivery except that, once it was over, once the baby, a boy, had been born and placed on Hope's breast and Joseph had shouted, 'Mazel tov!' and slapped me on the back, my knees began to tremble unexpectedly and I felt a familiar cold sweat on the top of my head. Then Hope looked up at me and smiled broadly, as if nothing else mattered. When she said, 'I forgive you,' I fainted. The last thing I remember seeing was Hope and her new son shrugging.

* * *

Another missed opportunity, I am thinking, as I raise a slat of the Venetian blinds in my parents' bedroom and peek out at the young couple at the front door. According to my stopwatch, which I have yet to remove from around my neck, they have been knocking for exactly three minutes and twenty-six seconds. They will give up soon, I think, as Rusty screams from the attic to me to let him down. Or let them in. He is also shouting at the young couple to help him. They can't hear him. I can barely make out what he's saying or the frantic tone of his voice. Solid doors. Soundproof walls. Another selling point.

The man in the couple is the one who wants to leave first, but the woman holds on to the sleeve of his new leather jacket and looks up at him, pleading for a little more time. She points to the car parked in front of the house, Rusty's car, with its Mintz Real Estate logo on the passenger door. The man shakes his head and keeps knocking.

The woman can't be much more than twenty-one. From what I can make out between the blinds, she is stocky and pretty. Her hair is cut short and stylish and doesn't quite suit the sturdiness of her face. She doesn't look anything like my mother at a similar age, but she reminds me of her just the same. Something about her single-mindedness. She keeps her husband, who is growing more and more frustrated and knocking louder and louder, from giving up on this opportunity through the sheer force of her hopefulness. It is something to see: the way she strokes his black leather sleeve, leans closer to him, rises on her toes to whisper in his ear.

* * *

When the taxi dropped me off at home last night it was closer to morning. I already knew there was no point in trying to sleep. So I tidied up. This time the house really was a mess. It looked as if it had been ransacked, far worse, in fact, than that time we'd been broken into. House plants were turned over. Every drawer and cabinet door was ajar. Magazines and books were scattered on the floor. My last task was making the bed in the master bedroom. I straightened sheets, fluffed pillows and floated the comforter over the queen-sized mattress again and again until it looked like it belonged. I have never learned to make a bed properly. My mother never taught me and, of course, never will. So symmetry was out of the question. Fake symmetry was the best I could hope for. Like revising someone else's term paper, there was no end to the small adjustments you could make so I made one final one, held my thumb up in front of my eyes, squinted and thought: Not quite.

There was a pink spot round as a dollar on Hope's pillowcase. An early sign of labour, 'the bloody show', that's what they called it in *You & Your Baby*. Suddenly, all that information seemed wasted on me.

'Why wasted?' I asked Dr Howie. 'Because I subconsciously thought that one day Hope and I, together, would have a baby of our own? Could that be what I mean?'

'Do you know what time it is?' he said, breathing heavily into the telephone.

'Did I wake you?'

'What's with you? You are hopeless, you know. Yes, you woke me. It's seven o'clock, Saturday morning, of course, you woke me.' Perhaps, calling Dr Howie was not the most reasonable thing to do, but I needed to talk to someone.

'I'm sorry,' I said, 'but I've never bothered you with my problems before –'

'You never what? What do you think we've been talking and writing about for the last two years? Your problems. Nothing but. *Dear Living in the Past … Dear Still in the Dark … Dear Home Alone … Dear Mama's Boy … Dear Unrequited …* Jacob, believe me, everybody reads everybody's diary. It's small potatoes.'

'Do you even know how to spell unrequited?' I said and hung up. Dr Howard Weiskopf was just an overweight young man with a bachelor's degree in psychology. I stripped all the linen from the bed and started over again. When Dr Howie called back ten minutes later I was in the laundry room and I let the answering machine pick up. His message began with an apology, but then quickly became a lecture about how we have to stop being dependent on women for our sense of well-being and self-esteem. 'You are a grown man, remember that, Jacob, I know you are there, so pick up, talk to me. I am a licensed therapist.'

* * *

I intended to wait as long as I had to for the young couple on my front porch to leave, but I'm not so sure I want them to any more. I find myself pulling for them like a hometown fan, pulling, in particular, for the young woman. So much so that when she finally accepts the fact that no one is home and turns to leave, I bang on the window and hold up a single, encouraging finger. That's all it takes. The young man is angry. But his wife's quick smile transforms into a loud, relieved laugh that I can almost hear from my side of the windowpane.

I grab my wallet, keys and coat and make my way to the door. When I let them in I apologize for taking so long. 'I was unconscious,' I hear myself say.

The young woman is still smiling, but her husband – or maybe her fiancé – looks impatient and confused. 'Unconscious?'

'Not literally.'

'Where's Mr Mintz?' the young man asks.

'In the attic. Look around all you want. This place was meant for you. I wish I could stay, but I can't. I have another appointment.'

'You're going?' the young woman says.

I take a quick look around the house, my eye pausing at the forest-green sofa in the living room which still looks as new and as out of date as it did when my mother bought it thirty years ago, and I nod my head. It takes less time to answer than it probably should. The answer turns out to be a simple one. A nod. I am going. I don't belong here any more. I haven't for a long time.

* * *

When my family moved into Court Séjour thirty years ago, we did it tentatively, almost secretively. There was no fanfare, no housewarming party, no neighbourhood welcome wagon. No one carried anyone over the threshold. We were all subdued for different reasons. My brother and I because we would have to make new friends. My father because he thought he was in over his head and would be out of business in a year. My mother because moving was her idea to begin with. But we all did the only thing there was to do: we settled in. Settled in and stayed put.

I know: this is becoming an old, old story, by now – how I remained here, in the suburbs, after my mother died and then my father, and how, eventually, it seemed as if nothing had changed. How for a while I was ashamed of feeling that way – embarrassed, too. How I was afraid, probably without knowing it, that if I left Court Séjour it would be too easy to forget my parents. So I stayed and it was still too easy.

Or was it? That I am asking myself this question now is the best proof I can think of that I've been wrong all along. I could have gone anywhere, done anything and I still wouldn't have been able to forget. Instead, I went nowhere – did nothing.

I suppose this qualifies as an epiphany; I suppose I should just underline it in this journal and be grateful. Except when it comes to epiphanies I've never understood what all the fuss is about. Self-revelation only matters in fiction; in real life, it never makes a difference, not a lasting one.

Take, for example, the three words Hope said to me last night after her baby was born. *I forgive you.* You'd think that would be enough to transform a person's life, my life, forever. But I know that her forgiveness will remain, like so many things about Hope, open to interpretation.

Anyway, I'm doing something now, even if it's only waiting around the corner from my house for a bus that will take me out of Court Séjour. As usual, the weather has changed drastically from one day to the next: everything that was about to freeze last night is frozen solid this morning – frozen beyond any immediate possibility of thawing. The suburbs were designed for cars, so the wait for the bus is a long one. When it finally arrives my fingers are numb and I fumble through my pockets for more change. I have underestimated the exact fare. The last time I took a bus it cost one quarter of what it does now.

Even on a Saturday afternoon, I have to search for a seat: most of them are taken by middle-aged women, holding Christmas packages and staring unhappily out the window. At the back of the bus boisterous teenagers wrestle, throwing gloves and winter hats at each other. I decide to stand and cling to a strap from the ceiling. I feel like a snob for missing my car, any car, but I miss it anyway. I am reminded of how narrow my world has been and, even so, how hard it will be to leave it behind.

But I no longer want the responsibility for defending the suburbs. John Cheever took it on and look what happened to him. In his stories, he promised hope; in his journals, he just complained. He drank too much, yearned for new lovers. He was even arrested in the suburbs once for vagrancy, for being sloppily dressed in public. I didn't choose to live in Court Séjour and, in the end, I didn't choose to stay. I was left behind like some kind of foundling.

This is what's happened so far: I am as carsick as a five-year-old as the bus stops and starts, making halting progress through an unrecognizable part of Court Séjour. I've never driven through this neighbourhood before. Gaudy duplexes, fast food joints and squat office buildings line the streets. Young boys play hockey in their driveways. Posters left behind after the referendum still cling to telephone poles, store windows and porch railings: one block resolutely 'Non,' the next confidently 'Oui'.

This doesn't count as much of an epiphany either, but, as the bus crosses the bridge leading into the city, I realize that I have no idea what is going to happen next. So what else is new? I don't know my stop either, though I know where I'm headed – to the hospital to see Hope and her baby. This is, it also occurs to me, more use than I've gotten out of the public transit system in my entire adult life.

Born in Montréal, Joel Yanofsky has worked as a freelance writer, and as a literary journalist for the last fifteen years. He is currently a book columnist for the *Montréal Gazette*. His reviews and articles have appeared in the *Village Voice, Canadian Geographic, Chatelaine, The Globe & Mail,* and *The Toronto Star* among other publications. He has profiled and interviewed dozens of authors including Martin Amis, Margaret Atwood, Saul Bellow, John Updike, John Irving, and E. Annie Proulx, and has the dubious honour of having once been kicked out of the Ritz Carlton bar in Montréal in the company of John Updike.

Joel Yanofsky is also the author of a collection of humorous essays, *Homo Erectus ... And Other Popular Tales of True Romance* (Nuage Editions).